CICAI

Ed Goodall

John,
Hope you enjoy.
Ed Goodall

BLUEBERRY

First published in Great Britain in 2004 by
Blueberry Publishing,
4 Parkmount Road,
Belfast BT15 4EQ
www.blueberrypub.com

A catalogue record from this book is available at the British Library.

ISBN 0-9548705-0-6

Printed and bound in Great Britain by Shanway Press, Belfast.

'Stars, I have seen them fall,
But when they drop and die
No star is lost at all
From all the star-sown sky.
The toil of all that be
Helps not the primal fault;
It rains into the sea,
And still the sea is salt.'

(VII, A.E. Housman, More Poems)

For James

CHAPTER 1

SLEET melted on the headstone of the Statue of Liberty as they passed on the Staten Island ferry to Manhattan. The sea spray lashed the windows behind them. Tina Turner's voice soared high on a passenger's radio. News of a space orbit crackled through the air.

His mother grasped his hand. 'Don't worry, Gus, your Dad and I hope that the doctors will be able to cure this problem with your kidneys.' He noticed the dark rings beneath her eyes. The ship's heating had failed but his forehead was covered in sweat. Apart from summer camp, he had never been separated from his parents. He knew that he had to have treatment but dreaded the confinement.

The boat docked. 'There's Dad,' she cried. 'I was worried that he might be delayed because of the bad weather.'

'How are you feeling, son?' His Dad put his arm around his shoulder. Gus shivered. He got into the back of the black Ford and clutched his side.

'OK,' he winced. His mother sat beside him and stared from the window at the snowflakes settling on the route to the hospital. He looked up at the skyscrapers and felt faint. The freeze had thinned shoppers from the busy sidewalks.

'Very appropriate,' said John McWilliams as he switched off the car radio. 'That guy Dylan is some wailer. I don't want him to turn my battery flat. Here we are at last.' The car entered the hospital grounds through an archway that led to a red four-storey entrance area. Gus and his mother got out and John McWilliams went to park the car.

The three were directed along a corridor to the wards. The Receptionist at Admissions checked her notes and smiled sympathetically. Despite the early hour, the lights had been switched on. He felt his stomach muscles tighten.

'I think we have all your details,' she said. 'Just let me check that date of birth again. Tenth of June 1953?'

'That's correct,' said Liz McWilliams. He was given a bed at the end of the children's ward.

'The doctor will see you in the morning,' said his Dad. He shifted the brown fedora on his knees. Gus looked down at the polished black shoes beneath the grey suit. 'Well, I guess I'll have to get back to work.' John McWilliams worked for a firm which arranged insurance for

1

commercial property. Gus's parents had emigrated to the US from Ireland after the end of the Second World War. His mother had stopped working to raise a family. It hadn't worked out as planned for he was their only child. His mother kissed him on the forehead and said that they would be back tomorrow.

The adjacent bed was empty. Other boys dozed and looked unwell compared with him. Supper came early and the lights were switched off, apart from a lamp over a central desk where a nurse worked on reports.

He tried to stay awake. His kidneys had become worse in recent weeks. It would be embarrassing to wet the bed. You woke in the middle of the night. There was a feeling of warmth and then the cold. He heard the nurse approach and closed his eyes tightly. She made some notes on a clipboard and turned to the other side of the ward. Gus drifted into sleep. A radiator rumbled far away and, at six, the lights were turned up. There had been no accidents. He drank lukewarm coffee and ate toast from a tray.

After breakfast, Gus visited the bathroom and splashed what he could into the small container provided for him. Later in the morning, a nephrologist felt the tender area and examined his scrotum and penis.

'How's his blood?'

'Seems satisfactory,' said the nurse. 'Everything else appears to be normal. We won't have the full test results until later in the week. The laboratory is short of staff. Two have called in sick with colds and a third has been caught upstate in a snowdrift.'

'I'll see him again when I've had a chance to look at the diagnostics.' They smiled at Gus and crossed the ward.

Gus's parents visited every day and brought candy. When he had been there for four days, a nurse interrupted their conversation. 'Dr Kennedy would like a word with you.' His parents glanced at each other and followed her to a side-office.

'There is a kidney infection which we can treat with drugs. The problem should clear up but may recur in later life. We'll cross that bridge when we come to it. There is an additional concern in the scrotal area which has probably been exacerbating his bed problems. For that, I recommend a minor surgical operation. Don't worry, it's a simple procedure which I hope you can agree to. If so, maybe you'd like to break the news to him before you leave today.'

They told Gus about the doctor's plans for Monday morning and that he would have to fast on Sunday. As they left the ward, he saw them stop to speak to a woman with black hair. Later that day, the screens were placed around the bed beside his own. They remained in place throughout the weekend.

When his parents visited again, they consoled him about the lack of candy. 'Cheer up, Gus,' said his Dad. 'You're going to have some company for the rest of your stay. The boy behind the screens is my cousin's son. You wouldn't remember Mike. He visited us once when you were a young child. After emigrating, he found a job in Washington and commuted from Maryland. We ran into his wife yesterday.' He hesitated and looked behind him. 'The boy's name is Bill Connor. He was rushed in with appendicitis yesterday and is recovering from the operation. I'm sure you'll become firm friends.'

On Sunday evening, he was given tea at five o'clock and told that there would be nothing else until after the operation. There was no noise from the next bed apart from the occasional rustling of starched sheets. Gus counted the seconds, closed his eyes and thought of sheep jumping over fences. At nine in the evening, he was asked by the nurse to swallow a pill with a sip of water.

Two staff came for Gus early in the morning and brought him to the operating room. He lay terrified as the big mask was placed over his nose and mouth. The anaesthetic took hold and he felt himself rise. Wild dreams tormented him and when he woke up he was back in bed. His mouth was caked dry and he longed for a glass of cold water.

'You can't have anything just yet,' said the nurse. 'It will only make you nauseous.' She replaced the screen as he tossed and turned.

By Wednesday morning, he felt better apart from one problem. He had been given a urine receptacle as he was not allowed to go to the bathroom. The urge to piss was tremendous but, instead of the usual flow, it came out trickle by trickle. Each drop passed with a waspish pain that made him want to stop just as the jet stung its way to the tip.

In the afternoon, the screens were taken away. The boy in the next bed introduced himself. 'My Dad's from Ireland – just like yours. Your parents were very nice to me yesterday when you were out cold. They told me how we were related. Your grandfather on your father's side –

Thomas McWilliams – had a sister called Jane who married a man called William Connor.' Bill paused and went on. 'Mom and Dad separated late last year. He has a job in Washington. She'd just come back home to be near her parents – they're Italian – when I got my appendix problem.'

They found time to talk in the lengthening evenings after the visitors had departed. 'I haven't had a proper piss for a week,' said Gus. 'It takes me about a half hour each time.'

'You're lucky,' said Bill. 'I haven't had a crap for over a week. She'll be around shortly to shove something up my ass. Says if it doesn't work, it'll have to be the soapy bubble treatment. Know anything about that?'

'Yes. They get a long plastic tube and pour washing-up liquid down it. They attach one end to the bathroom tap and the other to you. Then they turn the water on. I hear it's very effective.'

On the following evening, the screens were placed around Bill's bed and Gus heard him grunt. Gus held the base of his nose tightly as a powerful stench pervaded the ward. A boy at the opposite end cried out in disgust as the nurse passed with the steel bedpan.

In the evenings afterwards they passed the time by telling stories. 'Do you know any real scary ones?' asked Gus.

'Well, as a matter of fact, there's a true one my father told me last Halloween – before they split up. It happened fifty years ago to a relative of his in the North of Ireland.'

'Shoot.'

'Has your Dad told you much about where he came from…the history, what it's like over there? I don't want to stop and explain everything, if you already know.'

'He's told me some things. I don't want to spoil your story. Go ahead. I can fill in the gaps.' Bill told his tale.

In the late summer of 1914, three boys – two in their early teens and one younger – set off by steam train from Belfast for the seaside town of Warrenpoint, forty miles south. Although the carriages and aisles were packed, more passengers were picked up at each station.

'Be careful with those windows,' shouted a guard. 'Or you'll get your head carried off.'

George, the youngest boy, slumped back.

4

'We should be there by one o' clock,' said John McManus, the oldest boy. 'We'll get something to eat first before doing anything else.' He commanded the obedience of the other two, Eugene and his brother George. They took off their jackets and wandered around the little port.

'Let's find the beach,' said John. 'And cool off for a while.' They had no swimwear but took off their shoes and socks to edge across the pebbles to the crowded water. A conversation was struck up with some farm boys.

'Those country boys can talk,' said George as they walked back from the beach to get ice-cream. The brothers laughed as John imitated a rural accent.

The noise of a fairground attracted them and the remains of their money was spent on a ghost train. John became friendly with a girl. As they chatted, George and Eugene poked at the ground.

'Can we go home now?' asked Eugene. 'Time's getting on.' John had forgotten the time and they rushed to the station but it was too late. The last train had gone. A porter ignored them when they asked for help. Their tickets were useless.

'What are we going to do?' asked Eugene, beads of sweat clinging to his face.

'We'll find the road for Belfast,' John assured him. 'The train would only take half an hour if it didn't stop all the time. We'll walk and maybe someone will help us.'

As they approached a junction at the end of town, they met an old farmer who exuded a smell of tobacco and whiskey. Not understanding them, he directed them towards the town of Rostrevor.

In the gloaming, they saw a large obelisk. They stopped to peer at the worn inscription which commemorated a Major General Robert Ross who had conquered in America and fallen victorious at Baltimore.

Rostrevor was still - apart from the muffled sound of a church bell. The road turned away from the sea and they were surrounded by fields.

In the darkness, fear descended on Eugene and George but they trusted John to lead them out of trouble. A flash of white sparkled in the distance and they heard the neighing of a horse.

'We will have to ask for help at a farmhouse,' said John. The air was chilly and they knew that they were lost. George held on to his brother's coat.

About a mile later, they saw the lights of a house gleaming faintly in a valley across a field.

'This may be our last chance,' shouted John. 'Let's go for it.'

A barbed wire fence obstructed their passage and they took turns to lift the wire. The house was further away than it had appeared. Suddenly, its lights faded. They kept going and found a deserted stone house with no roof.

'It must have been the moonlight shining through the gaps in the walls,' said John. 'But we'll have to make the best of it. We'll camp down here until morning.' He pushed open the front door.

The interior of the house was ruined. There was a smell of cow dung and something else. Despite their fear, they were so tired that they lay down sheltered by an inside wall. As they drifted off to sleep, they heard the rusty screws in the door turn in their sockets in the night breezes.

In the hours before dawn, the brothers were shaken awake by a frantic John. They saw, glinting through a windowless wall, two yellow lights in the shape of lanterns on their sides. They scrambled through the door and sprinted across the fields.

Eugene and George, leaner than John, opened up a lead. They heard his scream as he cursed and fell. Looking back, they saw the yellow eyes hovering above him. John lay silent.

Sick with terror, the boys raced on towards the barbed wire fence. Eugene caught his foot in a rabbit hole and lost balance. George looked back to find the yellow eyes on top of Eugene and to hear his brother's last cry.

Dawn was coming up – hoarfrost on the grass – as George got through the fence. Blood dripped from his forehead as he looked back and saw that the yellow eyes had disappeared.

In the early morning light, he reached a farm where milking had begun. The farmer caught George in his arms.

The police were contacted. They listened to George's story. The bodies of John and Eugene were recovered. Autopsies revealed that their hearts had stopped. Eugene showed evidence of concussion. The parents were identified. George was admitted to hospital and later removed to a mental institution.

Bill finished his story and revealed that George was his father's older brother and - as far as they knew - was still alive.

Bill's mother came to see him in the evenings, sometimes with his grandparents, their faces creased and lined. Gus's parents visited in the early afternoon. He saw his opportunity two days later when Bill left for the bathroom.

'Dad, you never told me about your cousin who was killed back in Ireland.'

'I suppose Bill told you all about it. We didn't know the family well – your grandfather's sister Jane was a strange woman – so I never found out all the details. I'd have probably told you when you were older. Don't let it give you nightmares.'

'Is your other cousin still alive?'

'I don't know. Could be. We've lost all touch. It's tragic but I don't want it to bother you. Just get well. The past is history.'

However, the story preyed on his mind and he did not forget it. Bill's father never came to visit. He's a very busy man, he thought. Works in the Pentagon, Bill had boasted.

The urine flow became easier for Gus. The boys now sat in armchairs and looked out through glass doors at the hospital lawn. Snowdrops mingled with daffodils.

'I hope we can meet up when we get out of here,' said Gus.

'Sure. I'd like that,' replied Bill. 'We're living in the Village. It's not too far from where your ferry docks.'

'Now that the weather's better, you could come over and visit us on the Island. Maybe during the Easter vacation?'

'I'll ask Mom.'

The boys were released from hospital. They did not keep in contact. Two months later, his father told Gus that Bill's mother had taken up with someone else. He had heard that the guy was originally from a place called Yugoslavia.

He thought about his hospital time as the years passed. His father said that the family had moved to Canada. Then, about five years later, a letter arrived to say that Bill's father had gone missing in Vietnam. He called Gus at College.

'Before he left, he provided the authorities with the addresses of two close relatives,' said Mr McWilliams. 'They've heard nothing from his ex-wife. The last Canadian address yielded nothing.'

'What about her parents?'

'They're long gone, just like your own grandparents.'

As for Bill, the millennium had passed before Gus saw him again.

CHAPTER 2

RAIN drizzled across the windscreen of the silver Mercedes as the airport cab sped along the road towards Belfast.

'Have you been here before?'

'About fourteen years ago – in 1987' replied Gus.

'Back on business?' The cab driver noted the dark suit and tie.

'My late parents came from Ireland. My last remaining relative here – my mother's younger sister – died last month. A few things require settling.'

The tall oaks in the Avenue were in full foliage. A neighbour who kept the keys said that she'd stocked the fridge for him. 'She kept her spirits high almost until the end. Always talked about you. I remember you from your last visit.'

'I should have kept in touch with her more often.'

'She was a good neighbour to me…and her parents before her. It's a pity you couldn't have got over for the funeral.' She looked up at him. He felt that she was examining the authenticity of the mercury fillings in his upper teeth. 'The music at the service was magnificent. It's a pity she wasn't there to hear it. There was a huge procession afterwards. Now…I must go. I'll leave you to it.'

Tired after the overnight flight from New York to London, he found a bed and slept until the late afternoon.

After a shower, he walked around the neighbourhood to find his bearings again. The house lay in the shadow of Cavehill with a view of Belfast Lough from the back windows. A forest covered the lower slopes of the mountain. Above it lay a long plateau leading to a brooding black cliff face called Napoleon's Nose. In the middle of the forest sat Belfast Castle. The area had not changed much from his previous visit. The rain had stopped and the air was fresh.

The phone was still working and he got through to his son Ed in Columbus, Ohio. 'Is your Mom back yet?' His wife Lucia taught in a local High School but usually came home for lunch.

'No sign of her yet.'

'Tell her I got here safely and I'll call her tomorrow. Everything fine with you?'

'Sure. Don't worry.'

Duty done, he found a bottle of Bushmills, poured a double measure into a glass and added water. There was a collection of classical records.

He remembered how pleased Celia had been when he had arranged her trip to the New York Met. He chose a recording of *Lucia* with Joan Sutherland and Pavarotti in the lead.

Finding some fresh banty eggs in the fridge, he cracked three into a cup. Their pale green shells produced bright orange yolks which he whisked for an omelette. Wild cloves of garlic and herbs from the garden completed the meal. Celia had kept a fine winecellar and Gus selected a wine from Puglia which he had not experienced before.

He felt the earthy glow of the dark wine as he explored the house. Some modernisation was needed but it was in good shape. It belonged to him and he had no intention of selling it. The sabbatical was for a year and he liked the idea of living there.

'I know you feel you've been getting stale,' Professor Carroll, the Head of Research, had said. 'The break will do you good.'

'Progress in Bioinformatics has been slower than I thought. We're going round the boundaries of knowledge with computers and microscopes.'

'There are many big problems still to be solved. You're too pessimistic. I feel *you* haven't recovered from the serious illness that your son had before Christmas. We were worried about you. How is Ed?'

'The loss of his kidney hit him hard. He may have inherited his problem from me. He's had it from birth. The major worry for us is what happens if the other one fails.'

'You mean the lack of a suitable donor?'

'Yes. My own medical history doesn't make it viable and his mother's blood type is also incompatible. Even less common than mine. Also she was raised by foster parents and never knew her real parents so no possibility on that front.'

'What about your relative in Ireland…the one who died recently?'

'We checked that out on my last trip there. Total incompatibility.'

'Maybe you'll trace someone in Ireland.'

'There's one long shot which I've never been able to do anything about.'

'Well, I'm glad to be able to help.' They shook hands.

'I appreciate that and I'm glad that you've accepted my application for a year's leave.'

The wine took hold and he chose a room in which to sleep. He switched off the light and looked out at the Lough. A full moon sprayed a yellow fanlight across the dark blue surface. The lights on the far shore stretched out to the lighthouse at the Copeland Islands. He lay down and sleep came quickly. The boys appeared to him again in his dreams.

In the morning, he did light exercises before having tea and toast. The MX-5 fired at once and he drove through light summer traffic to Queen's University. The road glistened from overnight rain. The mathematicians had their rooms in the original Lanyon building. Gus approached the main entrance by a pathway surrounded by manicured lawns. Their borders were filled with roses.

'Good to see you again,' grinned Tony Hamilton. Although in regular touch by e-mail, they had not met since a friendship had developed at an International Conference many years before. 'I see you've kept your hair – unlike myself. And you've lost weight since I last saw you.'

'I'm looking forward to working with you.'

'We've got a desk for you. No computer yet, but we have excellent facilities in the library and I've arranged a special identity pass.'

'I have a laptop. However, the house is not properly connected yet so I'm grateful. Have you had a good year?'

'I've had a heavy teaching program this year,' replied Tony. 'And so my research has suffered. I will probably struggle to keep up with you.'

'I don't think so. I have to give a lecture in Holland in July on the Genome Project but I'm not well-prepared. I e-mailed you about the family problems I've had this year – especially my son's illness. It wrecked my concentration for months.'

'Yes. I was sorry to hear about that and I'm glad that he's recovered.'

'Not quite. I'll fill you in on that later. Let's refresh our minds.'

'You followed the major Conference last year. June, wasn't it?'

'I did my best. Your Prime Minister Blair and Bill Clinton held a joint Press Conference, linked via satellite, to announce the completion of the draft of the Human Genome. *The New York Times* ran a banner headline about it: 'Genetic Code of Human Life is Cracked by Scientists.' It was the culmination of over a decade of work. The biggest landmark since Crick and Watson published the structure of DNA just before I was born.'

'I hear there was a lot of politics involved.'

'There was certainly intense competition between the commercial sector – represented by Celera Genomics Corporation – and the publicly funded scientists from the US. It was exciting to see them all square up to each other.'

'Certainly the sciences of biology and medicine have changed forever. OK. Maybe we could make a start on the computational problem we explored last year.'

Later over coffee, they discussed mutual friends.

'What's happened to Burgess?' enquired Gus.

'Burgess has fled to Italy,' laughed Tony. 'After his mother died, his research assistant moved in with him. They say she has him by the balls. She's still here – a very bright woman called Arna Breen – and well respected for her advances in molecular biology.'

'I mentioned the trip to Amsterdam earlier. I also intend visiting an old colleague of mine from Ohio State University...Primo Conti who lives with his wife Gina in Naples. Maybe I'll have an opportunity to see Burgess again.'

'Only Arna Breen knows exactly where he is.'

They did some work in the afternoon but, by five o' clock, jet-lag hit Gus with a vengeance.

'That's enough, I think, for today,' said Tony. 'Emma and I would love to have you for dinner – if you feel up to it.'

'I'll look forward to it.'

'Grab a nap and I'll have my son pick you up at eight.'

Gus brought a bottle of Chardonnay and a Cabernet Sauvignon from Washington State. They had organic smoked salmon from Glenarm for starters followed by a venison steak. 'Emma – that was absolutely delicious. I would pay a king's ransom for a meal like that in New York.'

'Think nothing of it. I'm going to leave you to it. I'm sure you've plenty to talk about. All that science drives me crazy.'

Tony poured some old brandy. They talked again about Burgess and his work on DNA.

'As you know, Burgess was originally a pure mathematician who thought himself to be in the top rank. However, his eccentricity did not go down well with the bureaucrats of this world and he never got the rewards he deserved.'

'Crossing to DNA analysis was a strange move.'

'His kind of mind could tackle anything. He hinted at important new discoveries but never published anything on the subject.'

11

'I'd like to meet the research assistant.'

'I'll see what I can do. You're not going to spend all your time working?'

'There's something else that's been on my mind for a long time. I'd like to do something about it, especially now after Ed's illness.' Gus told Tony the story that had troubled him from youth.

'And so you see where I'm coming from. The only hope I have is that there are living descendants of the Connors here in Ireland. That would only be the beginning of the battle. There might be no tissue/blood matches and, even if there were, I would be looking for an older relative who might be prepared to donate a kidney when they died.'

'What about this guy Bill?' asked Tony.

'Disappeared without trace. His father is dead. There was a rumour one time that his mother had gone home to Europe.'

Tony placed his hand to his head and rubbed hard. 'Your only connection is with the guy who was detained in the mental institution all those years ago. I know someone in the Department of Health who may be able to help you. He will have all kinds of government contacts.'

Tony's friend called Gus on the following evening.

'Tony filled me in about the background. If the story is correct, the boy would have been removed to an institution outside Belfast – about twenty miles to the north. I'll make inquiries if you like.'

'That's very kind of you.'

A week later, he called again. 'I've not been able to do very much, I'm afraid. We can only go on my original hunch. The consultant – Dr Canavan – has agreed to speak to you. He will need to have proof of your identity before revealing anything about a patient. However, he realises your dilemma and has given me the phone number of his personal assistant.'

Ten days later, Gus went to keep his appointment with Canavan. The building reminded him of his old hospital – the same low storey redbrick edifice. Two young men stood outside Reception. He noticed that they wore no shoes. The doors of the geriatric ward could only be entered with a security pass. A male nurse asked him would he like some coffee. Dr Canavan had been delayed by a sectioning.

About thirty minutes later, he was welcomed into the consultant's office. Gus showed him his ID papers. The man removed his spectacles and sat back in his chair.

'I have some good news for you. The old boy's still here,' said the doctor, a lean man of his own age.

'Do you mean he was never released?' Gus asked.

'He was allowed to leave one time in the nineteen-thirties. Held down a job on a farm. Married for a short time and had a child. Didn't last. Couldn't cope with all that. Back in here ever since.'

Gus felt as if an electric cable had been connected to his heart.

'Does anyone ever come to see him?' he asked.

'Many years ago, according to our files, a brother used to inquire, but I believe he emigrated to America. A priest called Father Murphy visits. One of the older nurses told me that a man appeared once, claiming to be his son. She said that there was a resemblance. However, he was tough looking, in his early forties, with darkish hair and a hard menacing accent. She thought that she recognised his photograph in the news a year or so later. It was in connection with an atrocity committed by terrorists along the border. Around the late 1970s - near Carlingford Lough.'

The doctor brought Gus to see the old man. Bald and clean-shaven, his vacant eyes stared out of the window as he sat in his wheelchair. He nodded his head when introduced. There was no other reaction. They paused for a few minutes and then went back to the doctor's office.

'Does he ever speak?' asked Gus.

'Not much.'

'Are there many records for him?'

'There is a hard copy of what had allegedly happened to him and the other boys. Their original clothes are still here. Medical staff, police, social workers have all interviewed him but never got anywhere.'

'What does he say when he speaks?'

'In the middle of the night, he sometimes gets the sweats and mumbles feverishly in his sleep – 'No, Ross! Ross! No!'

'Has anyone ever attempted to elucidate a strange cry like that?' asked Gus.

'I don't think so,' replied Canavan. 'I've told you already that interviews with him don't lead to anything useful. As far as the police are concerned, the case is a complete dead duck. I really can't tell you too much.'

'You realise the problem that I have,' said Gus.

'I know about your son and I'll do anything I can to help you.

However, you must know that I'm bound by the rules of confidentiality.'

'Mr Connor is a reasonably close relative to the family.'

'I know and there may be no problem. But I must keep myself right.'

'I appreciate that.' Gus gave him all his contact numbers. They shook hands and he left.

He discussed the visit with Tony that afternoon over a drink. 'Hardly much you can do,' said Tony. 'Think of the time he's been there. It can't go anywhere. Let's stick to our research work. Our collaboration is going well.'

Gus phoned his wife in Ohio as soon as he returned. 'How's everything going over there?' she asked. 'You haven't called for some time. I was getting a little concerned.'

'I'm fine, honey. I've settled into the house and the work is going well.' He paused and took a deep breath. 'I've got some exciting news. I didn't want to say anything before in case it turned out to be a dead end. Remember why I came here. Well, this morning I visited the hospital where George Connor had been committed all those years ago. I made a good contact through Tony. Imagine how I felt when I found out the guy's still alive. I saw him!'

'I need to take this in. You mean to say there's some hope. I can't believe it. What else did you learn?'

'The consultant – a guy called Canavan – can't tell me too much. Not yet anyway. Confidentiality. All that. I'm determined to find out. There's some other stuff which I'll mail you about. My head's still not clear.'

'I hope you're not drinking too much.'

'I told you before leaving that I won't be drinking anymore.'

'I know what that means. You won't be drinking any less either.'

'Everything's under control on that front. Look, I'll call you immediately if I get any more medical data on George Connor.' He rang off.

In the following weeks he alternated his time with Tony by settling the remainder of the estate issues. One evening, his life changed forever.

A phone call came from Canavan. There was a catch of excitement in his voice. 'I'm still waiting for permission to release George's detailed records to you. I'll contact you if it comes through. There is one more important matter which will interest you. I took you up on your idea of having some modern forensic tests done on the clothes.'

'The DNA report came through this morning. His brother's clothes showed specks of blood attached to a thread which seems to have come from a button off a military uniform. The odd thing is that the thread belongs to a different time altogether – my lab friend thinks early nineteenth century. Additionally, what you will want to hear is that the DNA structure of the blood is unique, of a kind never seen before, not in this world.'

CHAPTER 3

'ROSTREVOR is admirably situated as a residence, for persons in delicate health. An eminent physician in Dublin has been heard to remark that it was the best situation for invalids he had ever seen. While completely sheltered from the cold easterly and northerly winds, it enjoys the refreshing influence of the southern breeze, and the genial warmth of the mid-day and evening sun. The grounds, too, are free from unwholesome damp, and the roads are so well formed, and of such good materials, as to dry up very quickly after rain. Those who reside here may therefore expect to enjoy all the benefits which warmth, dry air, regular exercise, and enchanting scenery can impart' (From *Newry Magazine*, 1815)

HE CLEARED the rush hour traffic in the city and joined the M1 motorway for Newry. The sun broke through the clouds and he stopped at Hillsborough to open up the roof of the car. Lush green fields on either side of the road were heavily sprinkled with black and white Friesian cows. The pungent smell of slurry was everywhere as he approached the Border.

The signs directed him through Newry and he got caught in heavy traffic. He thought of his conversation with Canavan as the cars and lorries crawled through the town. The doctor had not released the records for him to see nor had he indicated what they contained. However, Gus's spirits had soared. He felt that he had grabbed the man's imagination. There might be a chance for Ed if problems arose with the remaining kidney.

Then there was the advantage and disadvantage of the alleged son. If the latter existed, could he be found? Perhaps he was in prison. If so, for the crime described to Gus, he was likely to prove to be a tough prospect. Why would he help? There was a clear blood link with Gus and his family. That was the only positive angle. Maybe money could do the talking.

A left sign showed the road to Warrenpoint. The name came back to Gus down through the years. A faded spa town, a backwater, Tony Hamilton had said. Faded or not, the road to it was magnificent. The route to it was almost empty as he drove the six miles along Carlingford

Lough. The sun danced on the summer waters. Across the bay was the Republic of Ireland.

All he saw was a thick forest encompassing the hillside. In the middle stood a lonely white mansion. One small rowing boat rose faintly in the sea. It reminded him of Puget Sound in Seattle. He could not understand why there was only one house on the hill. Planning was tight, he supposed.

Tony had said that the area had been a boom spot many years ago – before the Troubles. When you could not get an alcoholic drink on Sunday in the North of Ireland, visitors travelled from Belfast to Warrenpoint and boarded a boat to take them across the bay to Omeath in the South – where licensing laws were more relaxed.

The open MX-5 attracted stares from shoppers when he entered Warrenpoint. There was a small carpark in the middle of town. He fixed the hood of the car upright and secured it. His attention focused on a busy central square. Many of the shops were freshly painted as if the town had been reinvigorated. On the drive here, he had noticed the red, white and blue of Union Jack flags fluttering on farms. Also what he knew to be the special Ulster flag in white and red. Although still in the North of Ireland, a green, white and gold flag flew here in the summer breeze.

He had rung ahead to check for the existence of a tourist office. 'Can you help me?' Gus asked an assistant who introduced herself as Theresa. 'I'm particularly interested in a monument to a soldier called Ross.'

'It's famous round here,' said the girl warily. 'There's plenty of other things to see here and in Rostrevor. Let me see. Here are a number of brochures for you to look at.' She gave directions for the monument.

As Gus drove along the winding sea road from Warrenpoint, he saw the obelisk to his left. He parked the car and walked across the road. A gate opened onto a path leading up through thick grass to the monument. He waved away the insects buzzing around his head as he studied the defaced inscription on the base.

MAJOR GENERAL
ROBERT ROSS
SERVED WITH DISTINCTION
HOLLAND EGYPT
ITALY SPAIN AND FRANCE
CONQUERED IN AMERICA AND
FELL VICTORIOUS AT
BALTIMORE

The letters **P I R A,** in faded brown, had been painted over the engraving.

He photographed everything and went back to the car. The brochures, provided by Theresa, highlighted a similar dedication to Ross in Kilbroney Parish Church – located in the central Square of the town.

Gus found it at the bottom of a steep hill. A store opposite advertised sea angling in the Lough. The town had an air of prosperity. It reminded him of Nantucket.

'Do you mind if I take some photographs?' he said to a sharp-faced man entering the church with hymn books under his arm.

'No problem. We welcome visitors,' he answered. The right side of his lower lip drooped and gave him an appearance of surliness. 'American?'

'Yes,' said Gus. 'I'm doing historical research on the region. Do you mind if I ask where does the name Kilbroney originate?'

'Ask me anything you like,' replied the man. He did not introduce himself but gave his information in a soft burr. 'It was a woman who founded Rostrevor in the valley of Kilbroney. She was called the Virgin of Glen Seichis – Bronach ogh o Ghliend Seichis – Saint Bronach. We don't know where she came from with any degree of certainty. That she and her fellow virgins existed is beyond dispute. They founded a religious settlement here in the sixth century and carried the message of the Christian gospel far and wide. Half a mile up the road is the site of the Ceill Bronach from which the valley gets its name. The bell which helped to carry that message still exists in the town – just up the hill from here in St Mary's Star of the Sea Church.'

'Ah yes. I'm with you. I've seen it in my brochure.'

'Our choir practice is starting. I'll have to leave you. But if I can be of any further help, we'll be finished in an hour. Go in. Photograph what you like.'

Gus entered the small church and walked to the top of the aisle. The inscription to the left of the altar caught his eye.

SACRED in the MEMORY
Of MAJOR GENERAL ROBERT ROSS
Late LIEUT COLONEL and COMMANDING OFFICER
of the XX REGIMENT of FOOT
who fell on the 12th of September 1814
in the attack on BALTIMORE
This MONUMENT is erected
By the OFFICERS, NONCOMMISSIONED OFFICERS
and PRIVATES of that CORPS
To perpetuate his WORTH
and remain in testimony of their
ESTEEM and SORROW.

He found additional leaflets at the base. A similar dedication existed in St Paul's Cathedral, London. Kilbroney Church had been built in 1822 to replace one called St Paul's in Crag Graveyard which lay nearby.

Gus found a bar in the Square and ordered a pint of beer with prawn sandwiches. He studied the brochures again. There was much to see in such a small place. Crag Graveyard was dominated by a large Celtic cross. It had been erected at the behest of an Elizabeth Ross – a daughter-in-law of Major Ross. The cemetery also contained the remains of the original St Paul's built in 1733.

He left the graveyard and saw the choirmaster approaching, clearly intent on opening up a conversation again.

'You've been looking at our original site I take it,' he started up. 'There's no shortage of sights to see in Rostrevor. I couldn't help noticing your interest in our inscription. Is there anything specific I can help you with?'

'Where did the Ross family live?'

The small man sniffed his breath with disapproval. 'I don't know about the General. His descendants used to live in Greenpark Road.' He pointed his middle finger firmly in the opposite direction. 'They call it TopsyTurvy House because of the mix of architectural styles. It belongs now to the nuns of the Order of Our Lady of the Apostles. They call it Mission Convent. I hear that they're thinking of putting it up for sale.

It's noted for its beautiful shrubs and trees. Anyway, I have business to attend to. I must go.'

Gus remembered his original intention in visiting the town. He needed to spend more time on a second visit. Dr Canavan had said that the boys must have taken the road towards the town of Kilkeel – the slower route back to Belfast. As Gus drove along the country roads, he could not tell from his current knowledge where the tragedy had happened.

During the drive back, he passed a number of towns and eventually stopped at the seaside town of Newcastle dominated by the Mountains of Mourne. Gus hummed to himself the song which his father used to sing after a night of drinking with Irish friends.

A Victorian pile called the *Slieve Donard* Hotel caught his interest. Even on this fine summer day, a peat fire glowed in a large fireplace. He ordered a pint of Harp and thought about his strategy.

The work with Tony Hamilton was only intermittent. He could not take up all of the man's time. From his own point of view, the research had only been a mask for his more pressing priority. His son could die. There had to be an option for him – whatever the human or financial cost. The key to opening up the lock had to be the solution of the mystery. If he could find the answer, maybe some kind of dialogue could force open George's mind. The man could speak and had his original nightmares. He must remember something.

Gus finished his beer and walked along the strand in front of the hotel. Fresh knowledge about the reasons for George's traumatic early life could also lead to tracking down the man claiming to be his son. The risks would have to be taken. There was no choice. Hungry now, he walked back to the Slieve Donard and had a seafood salad. No oysters but plenty of other shellfish were washed down with a glass of Chardonnay. Ross had to be the key. It was too much of a coincidence. He must have more information about the Major-General who should have died at Baltimore.

He reached the University by the early evening, identified himself at the Seamus Heaney library and surfed the Internet for data on Ross.

Major General Robert Ross was born in 1766, in Ross-Trevor (now Rostrevor), County Down, Northern Ireland. He graduated from Trinity

College in Dublin, Ireland and, at the age of 19, joined the British Army's 25th Foot, an Infantry Regiment. He rose steadily through the ranks, being promoted to Captain in the 7th Regiment. Later, as a Major in 1799, he joined the 20th Regiment and assumed command of it in 1803. As a brevet Lieutenant Colonel commanding the 20th, Ross saw significant action in Spain, Egypt, Italy, and the Netherlands. He was wounded 3 times, two of which were severe. For his conspicuous gallantry, leadership, and heroism, he was awarded three Gold Medals, the Peninsula Gold Medal, a Sword of Honour, and he received the thanks of Parliament.

Robert Ross was a seasoned veteran of the Duke of Wellington's campaigns and a strict disciplinarian who drilled his men relentlessly. Nevertheless, he was very popular with his men. He was always ready to share in his soldiers' hardships and fight alongside them in the thick of battle – as attested to by his three wounds. In 1812, Ross was promoted to Major General.

When the Napoleonic War ended, Wellington sent Ross to North America to unite with Royal Navy units under the command of Rear Admiral George Cockburn and Vice Admiral Sir Alexander Cochrane. He commanded a 4500-man army, comprised of the 4th (King's Own) Light, 21st, 44th and 85th Regiments of Foot. The mission of their combined forces was to divert the attention of United States forces from other theaters of the war by raiding the coast of North America.

The military action Major General Ross is most widely known for is the capture and burning of the nation's capital, on 24 August. That act followed the Battle of Bladensburg, where American militia forces broke and ran before the attacking Regular British Infantry, sadly remembered in history with the shameful title of the 'Bladensburg Races'. The only real defence offered by American forces were 500 flotillamen and 120 Marines, manning 3 heavy Navy cannons and 3 lighter field artillery pieces, commanded by Commodore Joshua Barney. Ross, again leading from the front, had his horse shot out from under him while directing his regiments in the eventual capture of the cannons and a badly wounded Barney. Later the same day, Ross had a second horse shot from under him when he entered the town of Washington. On 26 August 1814, Ross and his men embarked their ships and sailed North in the Chesapeake for Baltimore.

On a moonless night from 3 to 7 o'clock in the morning of 11 September, Ross and his men began landing on the North Point

Beachhead. Still in high spirits and morale from their capture of Washington less than three weeks earlier, they formed into march columns for the assault on Baltimore. The column stretched from the beachhead to Todd's Inheritance. Patrols were dispatched throughout the lower North Point Peninsula to reconnoitre for the defending Americans. Several British soldiers happily ate, drank, or carried-off everything they could find in Doctor Trotten's House on Sparrows Point.

While Major General Ross and his staff occupied the Shaw House to coordinate their attack, Eleanor Shaw, daughter of the house's owner, was forced to climb out of a second story window, screaming, to avoid the unwanted advances of a British lieutenant. Ever the disciplinarian, Ross ordered the officer back to the ships for later punishment. As history does not record the name of this officer, it seems clear that his career was ended that day.

The 4th Regiment was placed at the head of the British column to lead the main body and serve as a skirmishing line. It was a hot morning and the British soldiers were severely fatigued by the march. While Ross halted his men beyond the Gorsuch Farm (somewhere near the present intersection of Wise Avenue & North Point Road), he, Rear Admiral Cockburn and their staff imposed themselves upon Mr Robert Gorsuch to cook them breakfast. While having their meal, British flank security elements captured and brought in three American Light Cavalrymen. When questioned by Ross about the American defences, the three prisoners told him Baltimore was defended by 20,000 soldiers and 200 cannons. Ross reportedly laughed and said, 'But they are mainly militia, I presume.' Having almost effortlessly scattered what he believed to be similar militia at Bladensburg, Ross said he'd take Baltimore, 'If it rains militia!' Afterward, when Ross, Cockburn and their staffs prepared to leave, Mr Gorsuch asked sarcastically if they would be returning for supper. Reportedly, Ross replied, 'I'll sup tonight in Baltimore – or Hell.'

The American field commander, Brigadier General John Sticker, had camped the previous night less than 4 miles from where Ross had breakfast. Stricker and his brigade of just over 3,100 men had been ordered down the North Point Peninsula by Major General Samuel Smith, the Commander in Chief during the Battle of Baltimore. Smith was convinced that the British would attack Baltimore via the North Point Peninsula and had prepared his defence accordingly. When he learned conclusively that the British fleet had assembled in the Patapsco River at the mouth of Old Roads Bay, Stricker's brigade was ordered to meet them and fight a delaying action.

Stricker, upon learning the British had halted to eat breakfast, was insulted at their arrogance. Several American officers volunteered to move forward and dislodge the British from the Gorsuch Farm. Major Richard Heath, with two companies of the 5th Maryland Regiment, and Captain Edward Aisquith's rifle company, with one cannon, about 230 men in all, moved forward.

Soon after midday, as Major General Ross and his staff were riding through an area locally known as Godly Wood, the British 4th Light Infantry Regiment made contact with the men commanded by Major Heath. Riding to the sound of musketry to be at the front with his men, Ross had mingled with the skirmishers and was shot through his right arm and breast by a musket ball. He fell into the arms of his aide-de-camp, Captain Duncan McDougall, and was moved to the rear and laid beneath a tree on Robert Gorsuch's farm. He lived long enough to name his wife and commend the protection of his family to his country. He was 48 years old.

Credit for the killing of Ross is given to Privates Daniel Wells, 19, and Henry G. McComas, 18. Both were members of Aisquith's Rifle Company and died at the same time that Ross was shot.

Robert Ross's body was taken to Vice Admiral Sir Alexander Cochrane's 80-gun flagship, H.M.S. Tonnant, and placed in a barrel of rum to preserve it for the return to his home in Ireland. However, due to impending operations at New Orleans, he was buried on 29 September 1814, with full military honours at St. Paul's Church in Halifax, Nova Scotia.

Gus surfed for information on the area around Rostrevor. He focused on events which had occurred in the late nineteenth and early twentieth century.

As he logged off the computer, he noted the two remaining students in the PC centre. They had been watching him with concealed interest for some time. No attempt at conversation was made. Gus picked up hard copies of his material from the printer and returned home.

CHAPTER 4

THE SUN shone on the quadrangle as Tony and Gus walked back from lunch in the Great Hall. 'I could see your mind was elsewhere,' said Tony. 'You seemed in a daze when you arrived this morning.'

'You can see why,' said Gus. 'The boys are killed outside Rostrevor in 1914 in the early hours of the morning. On the previous night, they see a giant obelisk dedicated to a guy called Ross who died in the States in 1814. The survivor still cries out in his sleep – as if defending himself – No, Ross! Ross, No! The two events are never followed up by anyone.'

'It's a coincidence. The most traumatic happening in his life occurs hours after seeing the monument to Ross.'

'You are probably right but I can't help thinking about a link. We've discovered many strange things in our work which would have seemed impossible a hundred years ago.'

'I agree that the appearance of the son is intriguing. There was an atrocity in Warrenpoint in 1979. Twelve British Army soldiers were killed by an IRA bomb. It was on the same day that Lord Mountbatten and his family were blown up at Mullaghmore Bay in Donegal – that of course made all the news and the other bombing was relegated in people's memories.'

'I'd like to dig a little deeper.' They worked until mid-afternoon and then Gus left to collect his photographic prints.

That evening, after heating up some carbonara, he drank the remains of last night's wine and studied the photographs. Although Tony had never seen the monument, he had remembered reading about the defacement by republican supporters. The phone shattered his concentration. It was Lucia.

'I have no more news for you about the medical data. Dr Canavan hasn't received the necessary clearance yet.'

'You've not been able to do anything else?'

He hesitated and then finally decided that she would have to know.

'Well, Dr Canavan had some other interesting information and I don't know what to make of it.' He told her about Ross and the visit to Rostrevor.

'What does PIRA mean?' she asked.

'Provisional Irish Republican Army.'

'Don't get involved in anything.'

'I won't. Maybe you could find some more information for me concerning Ross's attack on Washington. It's an interesting sideline if nothing else.'

'If I get the time. Kay is coming back soon. We're planning to travel over in late August.' His daughter was at College in Boston. Lucia rang off.

In the morning he contacted the hospital again and obtained an appointment for the following Monday. He had to maintain the doctor's interest.

The doorbell rang. A plump unshaven man said that he had come to update the telephone connections in the house. 'These old houses can be a bollocks for new lines but we will sort you out.' After an hour, Gus was told that the new system was on-stream. He attached the laptop, switched on and tried the Internet. On Sunday evening, he re-ran the searches on Ross and Rostrevor. He rose early next morning, arrived at the hospital before nine o'clock and was admitted to see the doctor immediately.

'I still can't provide you with confidential information on George,' said Dr Canavan. 'However I've been doing some digging and I see no harm in letting you have a look at basic historical data on him and his dead friends.'

The three boys had all been born in the early part of the twentieth century in a townland to the north of Belfast called Ballypalady. The death certificate for John McManus recorded death from a heart attack. Eugene Connor had died from concussion. This had all been reported in the press at the time.

The details were sketchy in the clippings held by Canavan. The First World War was on the horizon. Political news dominated the front pages of the newspapers. The doctor's information came from a faded copy of an initial report in the Northern Whig. The heading on a second page paragraph read:

MYSTERY DEATHS NEAR KILKEEL

Gus glanced over it quickly. There were only ten sentences. The report was out-of-date and he guessed that the trail was already going cold. There was speculation that the boys had been engaged in some misadventure that had resulted in their tragic deaths. Farm accidents were not uncommon.

'Can you talk about the DNA?' asked Gus.

'Eugene Connor is long dead. It can do no harm. Hopefully, the opposite. My laboratory friend said that he'd never seen a DNA structure like it before. He hasn't been able to pinpoint its origin. It's very strange. He went on to examine the thread. It's approximately two hundred years old – can't say for definite without tests which could prove ruinous on such a small sample. Says he was lucky to get anywhere with it.'

'How did he know that it came from a military coat?'

'He's done a lot of forensic work in the last thirty years for the police and the British Army. Some quite specialised. He gained such a good reputation with them that the Ministry of Defence in London reopened many old cases and asked him to look at their samples. The thread was traced to a traditional military tailors in the West End of London.'

'I don't suppose he's received any more visitors recently – apart from Father Murphy?'

The latter's visits are purely routine – part of his duties as the local curate. We have his number in the office if you want to contact him.'

'Thanks. I'd like to do that. I'm very grateful for everything you've done. Is there an outside line I could use? I'd like to try him now while I'm still in the area.'

'There's one at Reception. Think nothing of the help. I'm sorry I can't tell you any more than I have. I'm fascinated by the case myself. It's been nice to see you again. I will be in touch.'

Gus phoned Father Murphy and explained his interest in George Connor.

'My role has been purely pastoral. I've only been here a year. George is content to receive Holy Communion but there's never been any meaningful verbal contact. The person you *should* talk to is the ex-parish priest for the area – Father Campbell. I'll ring him if you wish. I'm sure he'll be happy to talk to you.' He rang back with the address and said that the man would be content to meet him in the afternoon.

He had a gap of three hours to fill and think about the laboratory analysis. He extracted his map and calculated that the North Coast Road was only a short drive from the hospital. He could visit the priest on his return.

A back road with no space to pass another car took him past a series of small rural farms and new bungalows. Many flew red, white and blue flags. He came through a small village with the edges of the pavements painted in the same colours.

26

A dual carriageway bypassed the town of Larne and brought him to the sea. A two hundred year old thread, he thought, as he drove along the spectacular Coast Road with the car hood down. Despite the cold clear air, his mind had fogged over. He could see no explanation for the laboratory results.

The Ballygally Hotel provided him with an opportunity to stop for lunch. He ate scrambled eggs with smoked salmon and wheaten bread. There was a small beach at the front that was almost deserted. In the States at this time of year such a spot would be crowded with daytrippers. He knew that the main vacation season had not yet arrived here.

On the way back, the drive took him inland past the omnipresent flags. Occasionally, there was an islet of other colours. At two o'clock, a housekeeper showed him in to visit the old priest.

'You are very welcome. Would you like some tea or perhaps something stronger?'

'Tea will be fine – unless you're having a nip of something yourself?'

'A couple of small ones will do us no harm.'

Gus explained some of the background and his interest in George Connor. 'So George is in a sense your cousin. Just let me think this all through for a while.' He paused and sipped from his glass of Powers. 'My father told me all about the terrible tragedy when I was young. What happened was this. The family, William and Jane Connor with the two sons – Eugene and George – had moved to Belfast some months before the incident. With the First World War looming, there was plenty of work to be found in places like the shipyard. The Titanic had been built there two years previously, you'll recall.' He stopped again to drink his whiskey.

'The linen mills were also major employers of both men and women. However, after the incident, Mrs Connor – always an odd woman according to my father – found life in Belfast unbearable. There was the additional problem of visiting George who had been committed to where he is now. And so they moved back here.'

'After some years, they tried again for a child and Mike Connor was the result. In fact, we were about the same age and grew up together. We lost touch when I entered the priesthood. Do you know what happened to him?'

'He worked in an administrative capacity for the US Army. I understand that he was doing very well and was sent to Vietnam as an advisor. My father was told in 1969 that he had been reported missing.'

'Tell me again about your relationship with them?'

'Bill Connor was Mike's son. In 1964 we met for the first time in hospital. I had a kidney problem and he had an appendix removed. It was Bill who told me all about the tragedy. It's always bothered me as to what actually happened that night.'

'Nobody ever got to the bottom of it,' interjected Father Campbell. 'Then when the War started, the authorities had enough on their plates and the case was forgotten. I'm one of the few people left round here who could tell you anything about it.'

'What happened the parents?' asked Gus.

'Oh, they lived to a ripe old age. She died around 1950 I think and he went three years later. I don't believe Mike ever came back to see them although I know he wrote regularly and sent money.'

Gus waited for him to finish his whiskey. 'I must tell you that I have an ulterior motive.' He told him about Ed's problem. 'George may be the only possibility, and apparently there was a son.'

Father Campbell looked up warily. 'Yes. I believe there was a child. We can look up the records for you later. I think we need some fresh air. As a matter of fact, Eugene Connor is buried in a churchyard not too far from here – on the Ballygowan Road. I'll drive you over if you like.'

Despite his age, he drove nimbly and swore if a car dawdled in front of him. Ten minutes later, he took a sharp turn up a steep hill. An ancient stone wall surrounded a graveyard at the summit. The graves encircled an old building with a white cross ensconsed at the peak.

The doors of the small church were locked but Father Campbell produced a collection of keys. 'I always kept a spare set. There's been a big population change here over the years. The chapel is only used once a week – on Saturday evenings for Mass.' He led Gus out to the plots at the rear.

Many of the graves had no headstones. 'Everyone was poorer in those days and could not afford anything other than a basic burial. However, our own parish records tell us where the bodies are interred.'

Four poplars towered above the cemetery wall alongside which the boy's plot lay. Gus tried again. 'Wasn't George out of hospital for a short time?'

'Yes. In the nineteen thirties it would have been. I understand that he came back to the area and worked on a farm. By then I had entered the seminary in Belfast. After leaving there, I went to Maynooth and then Rome. When I returned from the continent, the bishop sent me to a parish in Longford. I was in my fifties before they gave me a parish priest's post near my birthplace and I've been here ever since.'

'That's how you met George Connor again?'

'Well, initially it never occurred to me that he would still be alive. It never even entered my head after the long years away from home. My parents had died long since. On top of that, it wasn't my duty to do the hospital visits. That was a job for a curate. Until one day when he fell ill I visited the mental home. Like yourself I was dumbfounded to find George…and still in the same situation. It's absolutely tragic.'

'You haven't seen him recently?'

'Remember I'm retired. In any case, that's Father Murphy's duty. And there's no point visiting him for friendship – not in his state.' He rested his hand on the cemetery wall. The rear end backed onto a farmer's vegetable fold.

'They say round here that the fecundity of his produce – cabbage, turnips, leeks and God knows what else – is due to his graveyard neighbours. The fat juicy earthworms travel like submarines and enhance his soil no end.' The old man smiled. His wintry blue eyes looked at Gus and turned away. 'I suffered from tuberculosis in Italy and lost a lung. Don't know how I survived this long.' He grasped the area to the left of his chest and rubbed it. 'My turn will come soon…as will yours in time.' He looked back at the plots.

Gus saw that the priest was becoming tired and decided to press no further. He had intended asking about the terrorist link but felt unsure of himself. Something told him that such a line of questioning would not be welcome. They drove back to the priest's house. Gus thanked him.

'It was pleasant to talk to you. I don't get much company these days. I'm sorry to hear about your own son.' He stumbled as he crossed the front step and turned. 'I'll see what I can find out for you. My memory's not what it was.'

It had been a long day. The old priest had been cautious at the end. Perhaps he'd heard some rumour. At his age, he wouldn't want any bother. Probably had his own sympathies and would not want to inform on someone. And yet Gus felt he had made a friend. Additionally, he felt he could rely on Canavan to produce the necessary data. He drove straight home.

There was an e-mail from Tony Hamilton. He reminded him that he had examination meetings for the rest of the week and hoped that they could meet again on the following Monday.

Gus spent the remainder of the week preparing for his forthcoming lecture in Holland. In truth, there had been no dramatic developments in the last year since the Blair/Clinton satellite Conference. Most of his slides up to then could be recycled if necessary. If there was only some way in which the Genome project could help his own son, he thought.

On the Thursday evening, a second e-mail message arrived from Tony. He had managed to contact Arna Breen. Although not enthusiastic, she had agreed to meet Gus. If he called at David's house around six o'clock on the following Friday evening, she would talk to him. The address was provided – a detached villa three miles to the north of the University backing onto the River Lagan.

CHAPTER 5

JET-BLACK hair streamed back from her pale face. The violet eyes betrayed suspicion. 'Come in. I've just got back,' said Arna Breen. She led him down a hallway stacked high with ribboned manuscripts. They exuded a pleasant smell of must. 'Would you like a drink? I only have wine.' She removed her brown leather jacket. He noted the well-pressed Levi jeans.

'That would be fine.'

She poured two large glasses of Californian Chardonnay. 'Hamilton told me that you wanted to talk to me about David.'

'If you don't mind. I met him on a number of occasions many years ago and would have enjoyed meeting him again.'

'You know he's gone to Italy and I don't know when he'll be back.'

'Yes. However, I'm planning to visit there later in the summer. I have friends who live near Naples.'

'Well then. You might be in luck. He's staying near Ravello. I suppose Hamilton has filled you in about me. Nothing good, I assume?' She looked at Gus and raised her eyebrows.

'Tony told me something of what he'd heard. Don't blame him. David and Tony were friendly.'

'Anything you've heard about our relationship is bullshit. I know what they've been saying about me...that I led him on, that I've got my hands on his money.'

'It's none of my business or anyone else for that matter. I wanted to tap David's brain about something.'

Arna relaxed and offered more wine. 'You realise how unpredictable he is – more so lately. I do have a telephone number where a message may be left. There is no guarantee that he will get back to you.'

'What are you working on yourself?'

'My research funding expired. I've taken a routine laboratory job.'

'You don't mind if I ask what research David was doing before he left.'

'That's a long story. I don't mind telling you if you have the time. I was about to make something to eat.'

'If you're not doing anything this evening,' Gus suggested, 'perhaps you'd like to go out for a meal. My treat.'

'I'm doing nothing. I test blood samples, come home, read and go to bed. That's about it these days. So I'll take you up on that. Let's go.' She suggested a restaurant that looked over the river. They left and she led him through the back garden. A large ash loomed over a little gate at the end.

The path along the river was narrow and on one side the grass spilled over from the adjoining fields. It twisted and turned every few hundred yards to match the flow of the River Lagan. On the other side, meadows stretched as far as the eye could see.

'How long is the towpath?' asked Gus. 'And where does it end up?'

'This part runs for about ten miles. The river widens about three miles from here and then meets Belfast Lough. Don't worry. We're not going that far.'

'How did you come to work for Burgess?'

'I saw his advertisement for a research fellowship in DNA sequencing. He knew the mathematics but needed someone with all the current knowledge of molecular biology. I had just completed a PhD in the subject and fitted the bill. As a matter of fact, mine was the only application.'

'Did his reputation frighten students?'

'Perhaps, but the area is so specialised. I don't know anyone else in this country who would have been qualified.' She stopped to point a finger at a large white building set among the fields to their left. 'That's the Agriculture Research Unit of the University. I'm hoping to get a job there. They've advertised for a molecular biologist.' They continued along the towpath.

'Wild Atlantic salmon used to leap in this river,' she went on. 'Pollution in the upper and lower reaches clogged it up and prevented the completion of their life cycle. There's been a drive to reverse the trend – as you can see in the clear water. Their DNA cycle is fascinating. Burgess was always emotive on that particular subject.' She suddenly grabbed his arm and ducked as a stray bramble caught her face.

'He was interested in everything to do with DNA,' she continued. 'Initially I knew more about it than he did. After a few days, he set me some problems and left me alone. In the first year, I only saw him twice. Of course his genius was obvious to me and I worked hard to impress him.' They reached the restaurant.

They ordered fillet steaks, potatoes roasted with garlic and a Caesar salad. He chose a bottle of Rosemount Shiraz.

'So how did things go with Burgess after the first year?' enquired Gus.

'In the second year, I helped him with an important breakthrough and we became friendlier. He lived with his mother who was always ill. We began to work together in his home. Then his mother died. My funding was drying up. He asked me to move in. I did not want to go back to live with my parents and so I accepted.'

'How did that work out?'

'Don't get the wrong idea…like everyone else. There was no sexual relationship. He is asexual – as far as I'm aware. His only outside interest is music.'

'Yes…that's how I became friendly with him. He told me about his habit of buying new records but not playing them for exactly three months. Towards the end of the period, he said that he found the build-up of tension exquisite.'

'He still has the habit. Anyway, I was beginning to find it difficult to guard my independence in a different way. Apart from his foreign travels, he had always lived with his mother. Often, there was little food in the house – he'd never had to look after that kind of thing. He gave me money. I had to be careful I didn't end up as a hired help.'

'What about the research work?' asked Gus.

'I said that he was a genius – with one caveat. Once a problem had been solved in his own mind, he tended to move onto something else without publishing what he'd found.'

'Tony told me about the damage to his reputation. Work not published is work not done.'

'He was very interested in the development of Monte Carlo algorithms which are widely used in protein structure calculations. You will know that these methods make use of random numbers to search for the minimum of a complicated function.'

'Yes – the name was invented by Von Neumann. He took it from the name of the famous casino.'

'In our research work, Burgess needed the technique to locate the minimum energy of a protein as a function of the variables that define its conformation. If we wish to predict protein conformation, the calculation is controlled by the effective temperature, T. When the latter varies, you need to use a technique referred to as *simulated annealing*. Firstly, T is set high to allow efficient exploration of conformations, then it is reduced to drop the system into a low energy state.'

'Yes I know about that. I wanted to discuss it with him. Some scientists regard the refinement as a waste of time,' Gus butted in.

'Burgess didn't…and with my help in the understanding of the biological problem, he developed a particularly elegant refinement of

33

the methodology. As I said before, he should have published his findings. Instead, he moved onto a different problem. Our discussions led us into the whole area of cloning. Are you up on all that work?'

'A nucleus is transferred from an adult cell into an egg cell. An electrical current or chemical stimulation is applied which produces a reprogramming whereby the adult nucleus is reset and becomes the nucleus of a single-celled embryo. What was his particular interest?'

'The transformations involved in the whole process. David became very excited about new developments in cloning and attended a Conference at Trinity College, Dublin. Only supposed to be there for two days but stayed for a month. When he returned he was secretive. All he said was that he had discovered neglected research that had been carried out by an Irish scientist in the nineteenth century.'

'Who was that?'

'Wouldn't tell me the real name. Let's just call him *Diogenes* he said when I asked.'

Over coffee, Arna went on to explain that Burgess then appeared to lose all interest in their joint work. She had found a job but remained in the house with Burgess. He was working on a new project but would not reveal its nature.

'What happened next?' asked Gus.

'Essentially we lived separate lives. The job which I have is in a Veterinary Science Laboratory. Some of the most exciting work in science is being done with collaboration between medical and veterinary scientists – and in strange places like Korea. It's good experience. However, all I'm doing is fulfilling the role of a laboratory technician. It's very frustrating. They call us bottle washers. Anyway, it's a nine to five job. I leave at eight and get back at six.'

'And Burgess. What was he doing?'

'He'd got his lecturing schedules down to an absolute minimum and he never got landed with any administration. The very idea made everyone laugh. Sometimes he didn't even turn up for lectures which got him into a lot of hot water with the corporate suits. They were always threatening him. Research was all that mattered to him. If he'd published, that would have been fine. They'd have left him alone. At the end of the day, that's where a substantial amount of the money comes from.'

She sipped her coffee and stared across the river. 'However, you wanted to know about his routine. He went back to the ways of the pure

34

mathematicians. There was no sign of him in the mornings nor often in the evenings either. You'd hear him rumbling about throughout the night. If he didn't need to go into the University, he stayed at home. Occasionally, he had to go to the library to stock up on books and research papers. I didn't see what he had for it went straight into his study – a closed shop for me. In any case, I was too tired to bother anymore.'

'What about weekends?'

She sighed. 'Ships in the night. Often in the past, I'd give in and make dinner. Now he was too erratic and I couldn't be bothered. I needed a break from work. I started exercising more – swimming and running. We're very near all the University sports grounds and facilities.'

'Not quite Burgess's cup of tea, I imagine,' Gus grinned.

'Hardly. It's probably what he needed. I did worry about him though. I tried to encourage him to get out and take his mind off things. That's on the rare occasions when I could get his attention.'

'What preceded the flight to Italy?'

'When I did catch him in the evenings or at weekends, he often reeked of whiskey and he sometimes initiated what usually turned out to be a rambling conversation.'

'Still no hint of what he was working on?'

'Not really. One Sunday afternoon, he started talking about the Michelangelo frescoes on the ceiling of the Sistine Chapel in Rome. Did I know, he asked, that the serpent offering Eve the fruit of the tree of knowledge is represented with its legs coiled around the tree in the form of a double helix.'

'I didn't know that,' said Gus

'Nor did I. One evening, I found him reading FERMAT'S LAST THEOREM by Simon Singh. He had told me before how depressed he had become after the proof of the theorem was published by Andrew Wiles in 1995. He knew that Wiles had achieved the only kind of immortality that matters.'

'In mathematical terms, the equivalent of finding the structure of DNA,' commented Gus. 'The double helix.'

'Or splitting the atom like Walton. Well, the drinking worsened as did his personal appearance. He stopped shaving. Once, sitting opposite me, I noticed a big gap in the crotch of his trousers. He had previously been fastidious in these matters. Then, one morning, I found a short note to say that he'd gone to Italy to finish his work.'

'Did the letter tell you much else?'

'It was paranoiac. He suspected that some colleagues had found out about his new project and were going to steal his ideas. Then I received a letter telling me about the telephone contact.' She looked at her watch.

'It's getting late. Let's go back.'

The sky darkened as they returned along the towpath. A pale rose sheen glowed behind the elms and alders of the Lagan meadows. The river narrowed and they reached the rear entrance of the house.

'You'll come in for a nightcap?' she asked. 'I'll see what I can find for you on your annealing problem.'

'You must be tired. Don't go to any trouble.'

'That's OK. I've enjoyed the conversation. It's taken me out of myself.' She twisted an old fashioned key in the lock of the back door and pushed it open.

She poured two nips of brandy and made more coffee. 'I've found the file for you. You may borrow it for as long as you like but don't lose it.'

'Thanks. I'll take it home with me.'

'I suspect there's something else preying on your mind.'

'As a matter of fact you're right.' He hesitated and then gave her an outline of the story of the lost boys, Ross and the visit to Ballypalady. 'So you can see how important all this is to me.'

'Why don't you contact the police?'

'I suspect that they have enough on their hands in this country without reopening a ninety year old case. There have been many murders here over the last thirty years which remain unsolved.'

'Old crimes – if it was a crime – are sometimes solved using the new DNA techniques.'

'Only with high profile histories. I don't think I'll bother them just yet. Our conversation this evening has suggested some other possibilities. Think about it!'

Gus thanked her for the drink and the files. 'I'll not keep you any longer.'

'Keep in touch. I might be able to help you.' As he drove away, neither noticed the solitary blue Rover sitting on the opposite side of the Avenue.

CHAPTER 6

THE SOUND of fifes from a procession reached Gus as he tested the broadband connection with the laptop. He spent Saturday researching historical material on the ancient Greek philosophers and famous Irish scientists from the nineteenth century.

At seven o' clock, he barbecued a fillet steak, mixed a salad and opened a bottle of New Zealand Pinot Noir. Afterwards, he put on a recording of Maria Callas singing from Tosca with Tito Gobbi, lit the peat fire and wrote down his findings. The Greek list was large and the Irish one small. He watched the News, finished the wine and slept late.

On Monday morning, he met Tony early and, before they began their work, gave him an account of his visits of the previous week. 'On Monday, I went to see Canavan who was of great assistance. Although he couldn't give me the medical data which I need, I suspect that he wants to help. That meeting led to a meeting with an ex-parish priest from the area. An old guy called Father Campbell. He knew quite a bit about the background to the story. His father was acquainted with the Connor family and he grew up with my father's cousin – Mike Connor – George's younger brother.'

'Slow down,' said Tony. 'I had exam meetings all last week. My head's still buzzing.'

'Sorry. He brought me out to see where Eugene Connor was buried – in a lonely churchyard way out in the country from here. I think the priest knows a little more than he told me – got edgy when I mentioned George's son. However, he knows the problem I've got and his conscience should get the better of him.'

'You got my message about Ms Breen?'

'Thanks for that. I went to see her last Friday night. Had quite a night.'

Tony raised an eye. 'Well, tell me!'

'She's not as bad as some loose tongues have made out. Rather the opposite. You're familiar with how Burgess was behaving before he left for Italy?'

'To some extent. I didn't see him that much. He was beginning to look rather dishevelled. He didn't attend staff meetings but that wasn't unusual. A pity for they were much more amusing when he did go to them. The Dean, George Smyth, was boring us on one occasion when David suddenly stood up and yelled. Smyth looked over in fright but Burgess apologised and said that his leg had gone stiff. He then left the room and didn't come back.' Tony laughed at the memory. 'I'm digressing. Go on with what you were going to tell me.'

'Apparently he was worse at home. Was hitting the sauce quite hard. She said she didn't see much of him. Wouldn't tell her what he was working on after a mysterious trip to Dublin.'

'I heard something of that,' said Tony. 'He became very interested in cloning research.'

'All he would tell her was that he had discovered the work of an Irish scientist from the nineteenth century. He referred to him as Diogenes.'

'The Greek philosopher?'

'There were two of them called by that name. The first one was Diogenes of Sinope who died around 324 B.C. He belonged to the School of Philosophy called the Cynics – founded by a Greek called Antisthenes. The latter was an adherent of Socrates. He admired the latter's independence of character, which led him to act in accordance with his convictions, no matter what the cost.'

'And our friend Diogenes. What did he believe?'

'Diogenes of Sinope felt that Antisthenes had not lived up to his own theories and called him a 'trumpet which hears nothing but itself.' Banished from his country, Diogenes spent most of his life in Athens although he died in Corinth. He called himself the 'Dog' and held up the life of animals as a model for mankind. His objective was what he called the 'recoining of values' and, opposed to the civilisation of the Hellenic world, he extolled the lives of animals and barbarians.'

'Sounds like quite a character. I can see why Burgess would be attracted to the name,' said Tony.

'There's plenty more. Apparently he advocated community of wives and free love, while in the political sphere he declared himself a citizen of the world. Diogenes advocated a positive asceticism in order to attain freedom. His philosophy led to a flouting of all convention. He would do in public what it is generally considered should be done in private – and even what should not be done in private!'

'Sounds like...'

'Rather worse I think. Diogenes liked to live up to his reputation and the public idea of a Cynic. He enjoyed entering the Athenian marketplace at midday carrying a lighted lamp. Searching for the truth, according to him. He also liked to stand in a barrel wearing no clothes and holding out the lantern.'

'What about the other Diogenes?' asked Tony

'Diogenes Laertius lived much later – in the third century A.D. He wrote a Lives of the Philosophers. This book is a compilation of material taken from various sources. Very untrustworthy according to the historians. Much of the biographical content is based on anecdotes and unverified legends. However, like most good liars, there was an element of truth in most of his stories. Many of them were corroborated by other sources. Much of his information is regarded as valuable as it helps to elucidate the opinions and lives of the Greek philosophers.'

Tony thought for a minute. 'I doubt very much whether Burgess chose the name at random. He would have admired the unconventional behaviour of the first Diogenes and despised the mendacity of the second. There must be some correlation – however tenuous – with the research that he was doing.'

'I agree with you. Of course, he may have just admired the guy – as you've said – and liked the idea of the grand search for truth. He would have found the tale of the lighted lamp in the daylight amusing.'

'What about Arna Breen? Are you sure she knows nothing else?'

'When we relaxed over drinks and a meal, she was very helpful. She's doing some boring job in a laboratory and is hoping to obtain a proper research post near where she lives. Although she worries about Burgess, she's getting on with her own life – lonely though it is at the moment.'

'Then there's the other angle,' said Tony. 'The scientist himself – never mind the name. You said you'd been doing some research on great Irish scientists of the nineteenth century.'

'I can only speculate. The most famous Irish scientist of the nineteenth century was probably William Thomson.'

'Who later became Lord Kelvin. He spent his early life in Belfast. Indeed, there is a statue of him in the Botanic Gardens – only a few minutes walk from where we are now.'

'I'll look at that later. Well, you probably know as much as I do about him.'

'His father, James Thomson, was a Professor of Engineering in Belfast and he later moved to Glasgow for a Chair in Mathematics. His son attended the University there at the age of ten. However, I haven't studied physics for a long time and can't remember much about his subsequent career.'

'In those days, physics was called natural philosophy. He began what we would consider university level work in 1838 when he was only 14 years old. He studied astronomy, chemistry and natural philosophy, including courses on electricity and magnetism. His Professor encouraged a unified view of all the branches of science.'

'Unlike today when everyone tends to specialise,' said Tony.

'Thomson went on to Cambridge and graduated in 1845. He worked in Paris with the French mathematician Liouville and attempted to bring together the ideas of Faraday, Coulomb and Poisson on electrical theory. Concepts of 'action at a distance', properties of the 'ether' and ideas of an 'electrical fluid' were difficult to unify. He returned to Glasgow in the following year to take up – like his father before him – a Professorship.'

'Nepotism,' grinned Tony.

'Maybe. However, William Thomson was certainly at that time a top class mind. He became famous for his proposal of an absolute scale of temperature in 1848.'

'Still known today as the Kelvin absolute temperature scale.'

'His theories later led Maxwell to develop his new theory of electromagnetism. However, Thomson did not agree with Maxwell but was eventually proven wrong. Watson, in a biographical sketch, put forward the view that during the first half of Thomson's career he seemed incapable of being wrong while during the second half of his career he seemed incapable of being right.'

'No doubt you have the examples.'

'He refused to accept the existence of atoms, opposed Darwin's theories and Rutherford's ideas on radioactivity.'

'Many people still don't accept Darwin's theories.'

'I know. However, Thomson seemed to lose an increasing number of scientific arguments as he grew older. His reputation as a lecturer was also patchy but he continued to attract the top students of the time to his classes. Additionally, the best research staff. We'll come back to that. I was going over all this on Saturday evening when something else in his later life attracted my attention.'

'Don't draw any conclusions from insights when you're tipsy.'

'I realise the dangers. Let me run it past you before we finally get started.'

'We're in no hurry. This sounds more interesting.'

'In the mid 1850's, Thomson joined a group of industrialists on a project to lay a submarine cable between Ireland and Newfoundland. He played several roles in this project, being on the Board of Directors and also an advisor on theoretical matters of electricity. In particular, he designed and implemented a mirror-galvanometer that was used in the first successful and sustained telegraph transmissions on transatlantic submarine cable. There was a dispute with an electrician called Whitehouse who had tried to use his own devices in order to effect successful transmissions. On this occasion, Thomson was triumphant. His instruments were fully used for the third attempt at laying a cable in 1865 and this proved highly successful. This made his fortune and it was for this work that he was created Baron Kelvin of Largs in 1866 – Kelvin being also the river which runs through the grounds of Glasgow University and Largs being the town on the Scottish coast where Thomson built a mansion.'

'You still haven't said what made you focus on this later part of his life,' said Tony with an air of exasperation.

'Listen. Thomson – or trusted colleagues – must have visited Newfoundland at some point. The latter is only a short boat trip away from Nova Scotia. There may have been contact of some kind with the capital, Halifax – where Ross is buried in the church called St. Paul's. He's bound to have been interested in the life of his fellow Ulsterman.'

'That's assuming he or a friend went to visit Halifax.'

'He almost certainly knew about Ross and his adventures. At this stage, the General had only been dead for about fifty years. He was well regarded among the Establishment as a great hero of the Peninsular and Anglo-American Wars. The successful invasion of the White House was well documented. Additionally, his father James Thomson – who became a Professor of Mathematics in Glasgow – was born in 1786 in Annaghmore which is only a few miles from Rostrevor. He was brought up on a farm near the Spa in Ballynahinch. This was at that time a fashionable meeting place for the rich from all over the North of Ireland. Accordingly, it is thought that James Thomson was able at an early age to acquaint himself with the wider world and probably explains his rise in the world despite his humble rural upbringing.'

'What are you trying to imply?'

'I'm inferring nothing. All I'm saying is that it's intriguing. Thomson and his pupils had all types of interests. How do we know that one of them didn't take a closer look at the problems of biology? They were well aware of Darwin. A unifying view of nature was often the target of these mathematical scientists.'

'Are you suggesting that one of them almost stumbled upon the secret of DNA but did not publish it?'

'You never know. Think about how the structure of DNA was finally discovered in 1953. Others came close. Only Crick and Watson realised its helical nature with all the biological implications.'

'If someone in the nineteenth century did make significant progress with DNA, they kept it very quiet.'

'Which brings us back to where we started earlier this morning. The *Diogenes* project of Burgess. Supposing a scientific genius associated in some way with Thomson comes across the story of Ross, i.e. how he died, was preserved and buried. I've suggested connections. He obtains samples. There would be no shortage of those – given how Ross had been mortally wounded and transported to Nova Scotia. This person – and we're assuming it's a 'he' – keeps notes which reach an archive in Trinity College, Dublin.'

'Burgess discovers the notes,' gasped Tony. 'He immediately realises the full implications.'

'Yes. And think on. If the mysterious scientist discovered the structure of DNA, what else did he discover before anyone else?'

'Surely you're not suggesting the secrets of cloning?'

'Why not? Leonardo da Vinci almost invented the aeroplane – hundreds of years before the first successful flight. By the way, did Burgess ever discuss Michelangelo with you?'

'I'd have remembered it if he did,' replied Tony.

'Arna Breen mentioned something odd to me.' Gus repeated what she had said. 'Just a coincidence? Or the fantastic insight of a genius?'

'Let's get down to some work,' said Tony. 'Before we get carried away.'

'That reminds me. I've brought a file which Arna Breen gave me. You remember that, at one time, I was very interested in Monte Carlo methods and the more advanced technique of simulated annealing. I couldn't concentrate on the file yesterday but she said that Burgess had developed a very elegant refinement of the annealing process.'

'He didn't publish anything.'

'I doubt if he'll ever bother. He'll not object to us having a look at what he's done as long as we don't publish it. It might provide us with fresh insight into our own problem. Perhaps we could get the PA here to copy the material for us?'

'That should be fine. We'll leave it with her and grab an early lunch. Let's take a walk over to the Botanic Gardens.' They left the Department and strolled out through the front of the Lanyon building. The manicured lawn was deserted with the examination season over and graduations not yet commenced. They walked up the University Road, past the Graduation Hall. Tony directed Gus to his left and they entered the Gardens. They were confronted immediately with the imposing statue of Lord Kelvin.

'I don't think he really regarded himself as a Belfast man,' said Tony. 'Not like his father. He thought of himself more as a Scot from Glasgow. However, if you look across the way, you will see the Physics Building. They're very proud of him there, I believe. If you need any more information on that front, I could put the word about.'

'Thanks. I'm not sure if that will lead anywhere. I have a hunch that *Diogenes* was from the South and studied at Glasgow with Kelvin.'

'What makes you think that?'

'Between 1840 and 1896, Thomson contributed a large number of research papers to the Dublin Mathematical Journal and was a regular visitor to Trinity College, Dublin. He could easily have attracted a bright student from there.' Gus paused and then snapped his fingers. 'I was falling asleep on Saturday night as I read over the last years of Kelvin's life – the stuff I got on the Internet. It's come back to me again. In 1884, Thomson – or Kelvin as you call him – gave a set of prestigious lectures in America and subsequently travelled widely across Canada. I'll need to check an official biography in order to get more detail.'

'Whereabouts in America did he give the lectures?'

'Baltimore.'

CHAPTER 7

A HARD voice slurred on the answering system. 'Keep your fucking nose out of what's none of your business. Otherwise, I'll get you.'

Gus had tested all the new computer connections at the weekend but had not checked his voicemail. The sinister call had been made in the early hours of Sunday morning when the phone had been on call minder. Gus listened again.

'We do not have the caller's number to return the call.'

He contacted the phone company. The number in the directory was listed in his aunt's name. Although they acknowledged the menacing nature of the call, it was suggested that he may have been rung by mistake. It was also possible that it was a prank by drunks who rang numbers at random to frighten a hapless recipient. Nevertheless, they advised him to report it to the police.

He poured a large glass of Bushmills and splashed in from the kitchen tap an almost equal measure of water. Half was cleared in a few seconds and he calmed down. It had to be a sick joke, he thought. He added another dash of whiskey and left out the cold water. It was fortunate that he hadn't answered at the time. A three a.m. call like that could wreck your nerves even though you were the wrong target. Not in a mood for cooking, he microwaved tandoori chicken with pilau rice and washed it down with two ice-cold Budweisers.

The Baltimore Lectures came back to him. He would have to obtain the transcripts and see if he could identify the itinerary which Thomson had followed. Also, the dates of his visits to Trinity College. Who had he met there? Perhaps, more importantly, who had followed him back and been inspired to do great things? Scientists could be as twisted and ambitious as anyone else. He thought of Dr Mengele and the Nazi scientists who were prepared to do anything to further their careers. The experiments on Jewish twins, for example. Even after the Second World War, other scientists had ignored the ethical issues and made use of their research.

Then there was the invention of the atom bomb. Many ex-Nazis had worked on the Manhattan Project at Los Alamos. I'm getting paranoiac, he thought. The call had unsettled him.

After coffee, he went for a walk to unblock his mind. Although now past midsummer, the evenings were long and clear. Traffic was light as he strolled along the Antrim Road away from the city. The last rays of sun glowed behind the Cavehill. A late jet headed for the airport behind the mountain. He halted and turned at Bellevue Zoo which was located on the lower slopes of the hillside. The sky was yellow as he returned home.

He watched television with a glass of whiskey and went to bed. The serpent from the Michelangelo fresco came to him as he attempted to sleep. The devil had offered Eve the apple from the Tree of Knowledge. What she did with it was up to her. How was she made? From Adam's rib. Snakes multiplied in his dreams.

On his way to the library on the following morning, he stopped at the nearest police station – Fortwilliam. He found a parking space. It was nine- thirty. This was no ordinary police station. During the Troubles, he guessed that they had had to be fortified in this way.

Huge concrete walls stood behind a watchtower. He was reminded of the Alamo. A cop stared out at the view beneath. Reluctant still, Gus walked across the road and pressed an elaborate buzzer. A disconnected voice asked him to state his business and he was admitted through a steel door. A sign directed him to Reception.

'I tend to agree with the phone company,' said the duty sergeant with a yawn. 'You say that you've only been here for a short time. Not long enough to annoy anyone I hope.' He grinned. 'And you weren't mentioned by name?'

'It's just as I said,' said Gus, realising that the conversation was going nowhere. 'I'd still like to make an appointment with your Chief.'

'We've got our hands full in this place. I'd advise you to keep a record of any more incidents and report them to us. There's nothing we can do at the moment,' said the sergeant dismissively, 'But I'll log the incident and your request.' Gus glanced up at the watchtower as he left the station. Perhaps he was wasting everyone's time.

He drove into the city and found a space to park behind Belfast Central Library. The swing doors led him into a grand entrance area. A library assistant advised him to try the specialist Irish Department on the top floor. This was reached via a magnificent staircase.

'I'm looking for a recent biography of William Thomson – who later became Lord Kelvin,' he asked the young librarian.

'Are you sure he was Irish?' she enquired. 'I've never heard of him.'

'I'm sure.' Gus smiled. 'I'm also trying to find a biography of a Major-General Robert Ross who was from Rostrevor.' She checked.

'Ah yes. We do have a biography of Kelvin. It's called *Energy and Empire*. The authors are C. Smith and M.N. Wise. I'll see if I can find it.' She disappeared into a back room and did not return for some time. When she did, both hands supported a large tome. 'This is the only copy we have so it can't be taken out of the library.'

'I'd like to consult it. I don't have a library pass.'

'I could fix you up with one if you like.'

'You're very kind. I think I'm going to need one while I'm here. I work for Ohio State University and I'm over here on sabbatical for a year.'

'I'll see what I can find on the other man. You said his name was Ross?'

Gus found a clear desk and scanned through the biography of Kelvin. Nearly a thousand pages. Weeks of reading. He hadn't the time. The era on which he needed to focus was well researched but there was a substantive amount of cross-analysis. The librarian tapped him on the shoulder.

'We don't have anything on this Ross,' she said. 'There are quite a few famous people with that name. However, I don't think any of them is the same one. For example, there's a famous explorer called Ross.'

'Thank you for trying. Do you have a photocopier?'

'I'm afraid it's broken this morning. I thought you might be interested in borrowing a book I found when I was searching for Ross of Rostrevor.'

'What's it called?'

'*Village in Seven Hills* by W.Haughton Crowe. It seems to be all about Rostrevor. Hasn't been lent out for many years. It may contain something on Ross.'

'If you can get me a library pass, I'd like to take you up on that. This other book is huge and I had been hoping to photocopy some of it.' He flicked through the middle of the biography. All the details of the transatlantic cable project were there. Then he looked at the section on the mid 1880's. The Baltimore Lectures had been well-received. Kelvin had travelled all over Canada. No record of a visit to Nova Scotia. Then again, who had joined him on these trips? The biography could not be expected to cover every single detail. He would have to return on another day. The librarian lent him Crowe's book on Rostrevor – a slim green-backed paperback.

In the evening, he phoned home but did not mention the threat.

'We'll be arriving late morning on August 15,' said Lucia. 'For two weeks. I'd like to get to Dublin at some stage also. How will you be fixed around that time?'

'That will be fine. I'm going to the Conference in Amsterdam next Wednesday and then on to see Primo in Italy. I'll be back late July.'

'Any news from Dr Canavan? I was very excited when you told me. It all seems to have gone flat. By the way, I haven't told the kids anything about this. I don't want to raise any false expectations.'

'I saw the doctor last Monday. He was very sympathetic but still no clearance, I'm afraid. He put me in touch with an old priest who knew the Connor family. Took me out to see the grave of Eugene Connor. He was very friendly but I feel he was holding something from me regarding the son of George Connor. Said he would call me sometime if he had any more. How is Ed?'

'Well, in a way, I'm glad you rang. He misses you. It's a pity he's out at the moment. There's something bothering him, I feel. He's not eating properly and not taking much in the way of exercise. If he's not playing games on his computer, he just watches television. I don't know how we'll handle it if the whole kidney business blows up again.'

Gus found it difficult to cheer her up. 'Look, honey. Don't fret about it. I'll e-mail him and see if I can tease out how he's feeling.' He had been about to tell her about Burgess and Arna Breen but thought better of it in her current mood.

'I'll tell him to expect it,' said Lucia. 'Maybe you'll turn something up over there.'

'Anything positive and I'll phone immediately. I can't wait for your visit in August.'

The menacing call still troubled him. He wondered could it have anything to do with his search for information about the boys. Perhaps he had disturbed a very nasty can of worms and attracted the attention of the wrong guy. Everyone seemed hospitable in this country. Nevertheless, if they were all so saintly, why all the wars over the years?

He told Tony about the warning when they met on the following day.

'I cannot believe that there is a link. I agree with the police that it's probably some hoax. Forget it. We need to plan our schedule for the next three months. As you know, next Wednesday is the eleventh of July – the beginning of the major vacation season here. I'm taking the family to Donegal and won't be back until early August. I know you have other arrangements.'

'A lecture has to be delivered in Holland. I really need to get down to organising it. My photographic slides for the talk are in good shape. I just need to tighten up on everything.'

Tony looked at him with concern. 'Look. Forget that call. I know the Connor business is important to you. Wait until you hear from Canavan again.'

Gus had wanted to talk about the Baltimore angle but held back. Perhaps Tony was right. Additionally, he didn't have time to read a huge biography and follow up further leads. The book by Crowe would suffice for light reading. 'I'll try to take your advice. When I'm finished in Holland, I told you that I'm going to see a friend in Naples. As you know, Burgess is not too far away from there and I hope to catch up with him when I'm in Italy. That will depend on Arna Breen. I'm going to ring her this evening.' They made another appointment for later in the week and agreed a schedule for August.

When he returned home, he checked his voicemail. There was a message from the phone company to say that they had traced the threatening call to a public telephone box near the University. Therefore, the caller could not be identified. He could change the number and also have a special monitoring device placed on his system. After a Bushmills, he rang Arna Breen.

'I'll leave a message for him,' she replied when he made his request.

'When will you be in Italy?'

'I'm flying to Naples from Amsterdam on July 16. I plan to spend a few days with my friend Primo Conti – the one who worked with me in Ohio. Then I'm coming back via London on July 23. I should be back here a couple of days later.'

He was settling down with a second Bushmills when the doorbell rang. The neighbours never bothered him and, as he swallowed his whiskey, he was surprised to see three cops on the doorstep. Gus invited them to come in.

'You wanted to talk to me,' said Inspector Townsend, stooping slightly as he entered. The two younger cops were armed and stood by the front bay window.

Townsend refused a drink and sat down awkwardly. 'You haven't had any more calls or threats of any kind? We don't like to see visitors intimidated.'

'There's been nothing else. The phone company traced the call to a public telephone box near Queen's University. If the warning was for real, there's only one business which could be of any possible interest – even though it's a long shot. If you have the time, I'll be happy to tell you.' The Inspector nodded and Gus told him the story of the lost boys.

The other cops fidgeted as Townsend listened attentively. He took off his cap and placed it on his knees. The top of his head was shiny and the hair at the sides closely cut. 'Such a link is too far-fetched,' he commented when Gus had finished. 'My staff don't have the time to go back and check all these old cases just because these new tests are available.'

'I accept that my contact Dr Canavan was fortunate in being able to get a friend to perform the tests.'

'It doesn't give us anything to go on. I would remind you that the deaths occurred in 1914. We were in an entirely different political system. Record keeping was poor. Much has been lost forever.'

'I understand. I plan to go down there again when I return from Italy in late July.'

'Keep me informed if you are bothered again,' said Townsend as he left. Gus wondered why someone of his rank had taken the trouble to make a personal call. Did they know something that they weren't revealing? On the other hand, he had not told them everything he knew.

Later that night, Arna Breen rang. 'David has been in contact. He is willing to meet you and discuss any mathematical problems that you have. Nothing else. I wish you luck.' Gus thought of inviting her out to dinner again before he left. However, he had not mentioned her to Lucia and did not want to risk any trouble again on that front. His Dutch lecture had also to be finished.

In the evenings, he read Crowe's book. On page 28, he found again the comment:

'Americans may not like what I have written here, or, for that matter, many of my fellow-countrymen but, like it or not, it is part of the history of this land, and from its history no land can escape, no matter how it may attempt to obliterate the past. The fighting man may no longer be surrounded by a glamorous halo, but no matter how history may view the ideas for which men fought, one cannot but admire the tremendous sense of duty to country, home, and family which appeared to be the driving force and inspiration behind such men as Major-General Robert Ross.'

Ross had become a Major in the 20th Regiment in 1799 and had then seen significant action in Africa and Europe. The obelisk clearly indicated 'distinguished service' in Holland and Italy. Gus e-mailed Primo and his colleague in Amsterdam – the scientist who had invited him to present the lecture. Jan Schukken replied that he would see what he could do in the short time available. There was a second message for Gus on the computer.

I've warned you once. The cops won't protect you.

CHAPTER 8

THE EASYJET flight from Belfast International Airport to Amsterdam was delayed by a security scare. Aldergrove was crowded with families anticipating their annual two week vacation. The bar and restaurants were packed with delayed travellers. Gus's mood was still edgy after a sleepless night. He ordered a bottle of Miller and sipped it as he stood at the bar.

'I thought we'd seen the end of all this,' said a wiry man sitting on the stool beside him, the broken veins of the heavy spirit drinker pulsating at the side of his nose and cheeks. 'I only fly once a year and this is what happens.'

'I'm going to Amsterdam,' said Gus. 'I've been here in Belfast for the last two months and never met any security problems before.' He thought again of the threatening e-mail.

'You going on holiday?'

'Not really. I'm giving a lecture in Holland and then I'm going to Italy,' said Gus.

'Sounds like a holiday to me. What are you going to talk about?'

Gus always felt awkward in these situations although he did not want to patronise the man. 'It's a scientific lecture on DNA and the Human Genome Project,' he replied.

The man edged off his barstool and finished his glass of Powers in a single gulp. 'Listen. There's an announcement that we've got the all clear and we'll be moving off soon. Nice to talk to you.'

Gus waited for a few minutes, finished his beer and joined the check-in queue at the EasyJet desk.

Dr Jan Schukken welcomed him at Schipol airport and they drove to Wageningen University. 'I'm afraid that I haven't been able to find out very much about that query you sent me,' he said in his impeccable English. 'I managed to speak to a friend in the History Department and he has arranged for photocopied material to be ready for you at Reception tomorrow. You're not staying for the week?'

'Unfortunately not. I'm going to Italy on Monday to spend a few days with friends.'

'You are speaking first thing in the morning so you can relax after that.'

When his presentation had finished, Gus answered questions and stayed for the rest of the morning session. In the afternoon, he attended a session on the role of computing in molecular biology. Arna Breen had asked him if he could provide her with any notes on current developments in the use of bioinformatics to control the spread of dangerous epidemics.

'Suppose a biological virus creates the possibility of a new zoonotic disease,' opened Professor Dietz. 'For example, in the 1997 avian flu outbreak in Hong Kong, there occurred limited transmission between people of H5N1 virus. It is quite possible that this virus could mutate through a porcine route. Since pigs can catch viruses from humans or poultry, it is not unlikely that such a mutation could occur. The probability may be low but, if the virus did mutate, the implications are frightening. The world would have on its hands something like the Spanish flu epidemic of 1918 – when millions died as a result.

'In such a situation, laboratory scientists will isolate its genetic material – a molecule of nucleic acid consisting of a long polymer of four different types of residue – and determine the DNA sequence. Computer programs will then take over. Screening the new genome against a database of all known genetic messages will characterize the virus and reveal its relationship with viruses previously studied. The computer analysis will continue with the objective of developing antiviral therapies.'

During the afternoon break, Gus checked the Conference Reception Area and found a brown envelope addressed to him. Schukken's friend from the History Department apologised for not being able to do much in such a short time. He enclosed a short precis of the background to Ross's arrival in Holland and what he had done there.

Gus skipped the late afternoon sessions – usually the most boring – and went back to his room. He was still coming down from his own lecture and was also trying to distill what Dietz had said. The Professor would be a useful contact for the future. Gus extracted a silver flask of Bushmills and looked at the information on the General.

1799 - Anglo-Russian force lands in North Holland
In 1799, during the Wars of the French Revolution, a British expedition landed in Holland as the opening move in a campaign to drive the Dutch and their French allies from the Low Countries. The landing force of 10,000 men was commanded by Sir Ralph Abercromby. He determined to land on the North Holland peninsula. His first objective

was to capture a Dutch arsenal and naval depot at Helder, at the tip of the North Holland peninsula just north of the landing beaches.

The British fleet arrived off the Dutch coast on 21 August but was unable to land for six days because of the weather. During that time, the Dutch commander, General Herman Willem Daendels, gathered 6,000 infantry, cavalry, and artillery nearby at Callantzoog, where they were protected by sandhills from the guns of the British fleet. The landing began at dawn on 27 August. It was described by a contemporary, Sir Henry Bunbury:

[The fleet] threw a storm of shot upon the beach, while the boats, heavy with soldiers, were rowing to their landing place. But the only boats were those of the men-of-war, ill calculated for such a service and incapable of conveying more than 3,000 men at a time. To the officers of our navy this kind of operation was entirely new; nor did they understand the details, or feel the importance of arrangement on which military order and military success must greatly depend. Thus parts of regiments were conveyed to the shore, while parts were left behind. Battalions were intermixed; and companies had to find their proper places after they had landed and were under the fire of the enemy. The soldiers had to wade and scramble out of the surf as well as they could, and look out for their comrades, and run to their stations in the line which was growing slowly into shape along the beach.

Although disorganized, the landing was well covered by naval gunfire, and Daendels did not try to attack the landing force as it was coming ashore and forming up. Only after Abercromby had properly deployed his troops and advanced inland did the Dutch attack. After a fierce battle that cost the British 500 casualties, the Dutch withdrew southward, leaving Abercromby in control of the northern end of the peninsula. The next day, 28 August, he occupied the arsenal at Helder, which had been hastily evacuated. On the 30th, the Dutch fleet, anchored nearby, surrendered to the British fleet, and on the 1st of September Abercromby repulsed a counterattack by a French and Dutch army.

The landing had been a clear success, but the subsequent attempt to achieve the objective - to sweep the French from Holland - failed. Bolstered by Russian reinforcements, the Allied army of about 30,000 men, now under the command of the Duke of York, took the offensive. It fought three bloody but indecisive battles (19 September, and 2 and 6

October) but fell back when confronted by the Franco-Dutch army in entrenched positions. The expedition reembarked on 30 November, having suffered 50 percent casualties during the campaign.

This campaign revealed the difficulties in conducting landing operations in the age of sail, as well as the decline in British amphibious skills since the Seven Years' War and the War of American Independence. The landing force was not well organized and would have been very vulnerable had the Dutch counterattacked early, before the British could form up on the beach. Fortunately, the caution of the Dutch commander and the gunfire support of the fleet provided the British infantry with the time it needed to deploy properly. Abercromby learned the tactical lessons, which he applied with success two years later in an assault landing at Aboukir Bay, Egypt.

The campaign was largely devoid of strategic results. Ultimately, the Russo-British expedition failed because of an inability to build up and support a sufficient force in time to achieve a decisive victory, probably for lack of transports, logistic supports, manpower, and other resources. Major Ross had been sent to Holland with his regiment immediately after his promotion on August 6th 1799. It formed part of the Anglo-Russian army. Three quarters of the men were volunteers from the militia. They established themselves as 'a regiment that would never be beaten.' At Krabbendam on September 10th, Ross and his men repulsed a sustained attack by the central column of Brune's army. The Ulsterman distinguished himself in the action and was marked out by his courage. His tenacity in leading from the front – the quality which was to prove his final undoing – was noted by his superiors and his men. On this occasion, he was severely wounded and sent home to recuperate.

Gus sipped from the flask and his mind went back to the second threat. The message had originated from a University mailbox. The prefix had been a general one – AGRI. His immediate reaction had been to lift the phone and contact Townsend. Then he had held back. The warning said 'won't'. It depended what you read into it, he thought. He had not slept well on the previous two nights. The flask was emptied and he fell asleep.

On Friday, the morning session was followed by a visit to tulip fields and the home of Vermeer.

'What Delft has to offer is the prettiest light in all Holland,' said the guide. 'So pure, so fine – something both intellectual and palpable, neither pearl nor petal, but their visible souls. The whole of Vermeer is dissolved in this moist, bright atmosphere. In no other place is there more intimate intercourse between the view and its image; the picture is impregnated with his minute contemplation. In the line of gables, bridges and bell towers we still recognise the same ethereal appearance, the same geometry, the same frigid, precise charm.' Gus purchased prints for Kay and Lucia. On the tour bus back the reference to bell towers resonated in his mind. The lost boys had heard a bell. Was it St Bronach's Bell? It had existed for fourteen hundred years. It was still there in the Roman Catholic Church of Rostrevor. George Connor was still alive. Gus had no doubt that there had to be a connection between his search and the threats.

At the Conference Dinner he was placed beside a Swedish scientist whose company Schukken thought he might enjoy. It did not turn out that way.

'We will soon be able to perform DNA tests at birth which will tell us the risk of the development of a wide range of diseases.'

'That's a long way off for practical purposes,' said Gus cautiously. The man reeked of vodka. 'In any case, if the parents find out something bad, what are they going to do?'

'The same as they do with embryos when something like spina bifida is detected in the womb.'

'You're not suggesting infanticide?'

'Of course. Why not? What's the difference? The child is only going to be a major burden to its parents at some stage. Get rid of it early and stop the pain. The child will be no wiser.'

'I don't wish to insult you but your views hardly differ from the Nazis.'

'Many liberal Westerners subscribed to such a view long before the rise of Hitler. Many still hold such views privately. This country practises widespread euthanasia – the legal killing of older people whose lives are not worth living.'

'Those people get a say in the matter. They want to die.'

'Not necessarily. They may be in a coma. Their children decide to end their lives. Why not the other way round?' Gus slipped away after coffee was served.

He dreamt of the boys. Visions of Ross on a white charger came to him – protecting his family and countrymen from what the Connors might do in the future. His yellow lantern eyes pierced the darkness slashing wildly at all his enemies. The air was acrid with smoke. He would never be beaten.

On Saturday morning, he woke with that refreshed feeling you sometimes get. The Conference featured lighter lectures until lunchtime and more tours were offered in the afternoon. He had decided to spend the night in Amsterdam. The arrangement suited Jan Schukken as he would be busy with administration. He arranged transport and accommodation at a hotel.

Gus spent the early evening walking along the canals. He broke off for a beer in a 'brown' café. The smell of cannabis drifted from a corner where two young boys drank coffee. Schukken had agreed to send him on any more information which his friend could find about Ross's time in Holland. He had a meal in an Indonesian restaurant, wandered around the Red Light district and returned to his hotel. Something Professor Dietz had said came back to him as he fell asleep. A virus which could mutate and could cause a serious epidemic in the human population.

On Monday, he caught a cab to Schipol. The KLM flight left for Naples mid-morning and arrived at lunchtime five minutes ahead of schedule. Primo greeted him at Naples Airport. 'You look tired.'

'It's been a rough few days,' replied Gus. 'I'll tell you all about it this evening.' Primo had not changed much since leaving Ohio five years ago. Although in his early forties, he had the young-old face of the ageing hippy. The hair, tied back in a ponytail, exaggerated the lines in his cheeks. Gus's stomach muscles tightened as the tiny Fiat weaved through the heavy traffic at breakneck speed.

'How's life back in Italy?'

'It has its moments. Gina's parents look after our daughter during the daytime. We run a small business teaching English to Italians. We get by.' He grinned. 'I wasn't suited to the scientific life – especially as it operates in America. The constant drive to publish research papers no matter whether the work was important or not. Then, as you know, the political correctness was not congenial for me. Nor the fanatical health lobby.' Primo lit a cigarette.

'Fanatical is rather hard. There's a strong anti-smoking lobby. Nothing the matter with that. You know you'll give yourself lung cancer.'

'Not necessarily. No scientist has actually proved cause and effect. It may be due to stress. Life here is more relaxed. We take time to eat and enjoy our food as you'll see.'

That evening, they went to dinner at a restaurant near Herculaneum.

'I hear you've been having a bad time,' said Gina. 'Do you want to talk about it?' He told them about the lost boys and the threats to himself.

'Don't forget what Belfast used to be like. I know the Troubles appear to be over but I've heard that there's still a lot of gangster activity.'

'You've still got the Mafia here.'

'Yes... and we know when to keep our mouths shut,' said Primo.

'Relax. Here comes our food. You fancy some salted chilli squid with garlic?' The meal was long and relaxed. 'Have some grappa to open a hole in your stomach. It'll help you to sleep.'

'Thanks. I feel a lot better. I've listened to what you've said. I still can't get the business out of my mind. It can't do any harm to do a little more historical research on Ross. I feel safe here. Did you manage to find anything for me?'

'As a matter of fact, I have. There's a North African in my class who used to live in Spain. Shoukri found the material that you requested. I'm not allowing you to see it until the morning. You need a good night's rest.'

In 1800 Ross went with the regiment to Minorca, and helped to persuade the men, who were engaged for service in Europe only, to volunteer for Egypt. The regiment landed in Egypt in July 1801, when Menou was still holding out in Alexandria; and it distinguished itself on 25th August by storming an outpost with the bayonet only, and repelling the enemy's attempt to recover it. A few days afterwards Menou capitulated; and at the end of the year the 20th went to Malta.

Ross had been made brevet lieutenant-colonel on 1st Jan 1801 for his service in Holland; but he was still regimental major when he succeeded, in September 1803, to the actual command of the 20th, which was now reduced to one battalion. He exercised the regiment indefatigably:

'We were repeatedly out for eight hours during the hot weather; frequently crossing the country, scouring the fields over the stone walls, the whole of the regiment acting as light infantry; and the best of the joke was that no other corps in the island was similarly indulged.' (STEEVENS, *Reminiscences*, p39)

In November 1805 the regiment went to Naples as part of the expedition under Sir James Henry Craig, but there was no fighting. Two months afterwards, upon the news of Austerlitz and the approach of the French in force, the expedition withdrew to Sicily. In July 1806 the British troops, now under Sir John Stuart, landed in Calabria, and met the French at Maida. The 20th had been sent up the coast to make a diversion, and disembarked in the bay of St. Euphemia only on the morning of the battle. The French cavalry and skirmishers were turning the British left, when Ross, who had hastened up with his regiment, issued upon them for a wood. He 'drove the swarm of sharpshooters before him; gave the French cavalry such a volley as sent them off in confusion to the rear; and, passing beyond the left of Cole's brigade, wheeled the 20th to their right, and opened a shattering fire on the enemy's battalions. The effect was decisive. Reynier was completely taken by surprise at the apparition of this fresh assailant; he made but a short and feeble effort to maintain his ground.' (BUNBURY, *Narrative*, p247)

Stuart, in his general orders, spoke of Ross's action as 'a prompt display of gallantry and judgement to which the army was most critically indebted.' Ross received a gold medal for this battle. The 20th took part in the storming of Scylla Castle, and then returned to Sicily. In the following year it was included in the force under Sir John Moore, which was meant to anticipate the French at Lisbon, but which, finding itself too late, went on to England.

Ross had established himself as a hero of the regiment, thought Gus. Even before his attacks on America, he had carved a name for himself in the annals of British military history. If you intended to clone a hero, here was the ideal man. Gallant, brave beyond the bounds of common sense. Ready to 'do or die' for his comrades and his country. It was time to make contact with Burgess.

CHAPTER 9

SWEAT stung his eyes as the Alfa Romeo brought him along the crowded road towards Ravello. He had showered before leaving for the Amalfi coast but his hair was greasy from the stifling heat.

'Was Shoukri's material much use to you?' asked Primo when they had met for lunch on the previous day. 'He's a very good student and a keen user of the Internet.'

'It enhanced the background to what I already know of Ross,' replied Gus. 'He and his regiment were sent to Naples in 1805 and then withdrawn to Sicily. In the following year, they were dispatched to Calabria in the build-up to a major battle with French troops after which they returned to Sicily.'

'So he spent quite a bit of time in southern Italy.' Primo scratched his chin. 'It's a small world.'

'It's not the Italian background itself that is so fascinating,' said Gus. 'His behaviour in charge of his regiment was entirely consistent with what I already knew about him. An extremely brave man – perhaps to the point of foolhardiness. It's surprising that he wasn't killed earlier. He was always leading from the front – he was no armchair strategist. Always wanted to be in the thick of the action.'

'Not a man to get on the wrong side of.' Primo smiled.

Gus changed the subject. 'I told you about my friend Burgess. I've managed to get in touch with him by telephone. He says he will see me tomorrow lunchtime.'

'Near Ravello you said. If you're going to drive there, you may as well spend a night or two in the region. I'll fix something up for you if you like. And a car will need to be hired. The old times can wait until you come back.'

He had arranged to meet Burgess in a restaurant overlooking the main square. Gus ordered an ice-cold Peroni and waited.

Half an hour later, he saw Burgess come out of a side street and march towards the bar below. 'I am happy to see you,' he said. He took off his spectacles and smiled. 'I enjoy my own company but I have been isolated up here for some time.' He ordered Campari. The healthy tan did not disguise the depressions beneath his eyes. A black tee shirt hung from his thin frame.

A waiter brought culatello. They shared a salad of small fish with lemon and black olives. 'Arna sends her regards,' said Gus.

'I owe a big debt of gratitude to her. She sustained me when my mother died. As you are aware, I have few friends and no relatives.'

'Would you like to order for us?'

'I recommend the pan-fried kidneys. There is a faint tang of urine but don't worry about that. Perhaps we can push the boat out on the wine. We might never meet again.' Burgess ordered a bottle of Montepulciano. The soft and succulent wine smelt of crushed red berries. They relaxed in the sunshine and drank their aperitifs.

Gus saw that it was not going to be easy to extract from Burgess any details of his research. He waited for an opening.

'No doubt Arna will have told you something of how I came to be here,' said Burgess abruptly. 'But I don't want to talk about any of that. Nothing personal. Fill me in about why you're here.'

'She didn't tell me too much,' said Gus, his attention straying to a commotion across the square. An American in check trousers seemed to be having difficulty in settling his bill. 'I understand. I'm in the North of Ireland on a sabbatical and I'm also taking the opportunity to attend Conferences in Europe. Also, it's good to meet up with old friends like yourself and Tony Hamilton.'

'Tony is a good guy – unlike quite a few other bastards in that Department. What have you been doing with him? Anything interesting?' Burgess finished his Campari and drank a glass of water.

'Oh, we're just tieing up some loose ends on research work we did some years ago. Purely computational problems. You know how it is in the States. Everything you do has to be published. Otherwise, your career is finished.'

Burgess smiled. 'Don't get me onto that subject.'

'I did want to talk to you about simulated annealing. However, Arna took the liberty of showing me non-confidential files on your recent work and they have cleared up the difficulties which I faced. Don't worry. I'll not use them in any way without your approval.'

'I know you wouldn't do that. Many have. Let's eat. This wine was a good choice.' They tasted their kidneys and drank the Montepulciano. Someone inside the restaurant switched on a recording of Pavarotti. Gus thought of Lucia. 'How are your family?' asked Burgess. 'I met them briefly once in Ohio many years ago.'

Gus sighed. 'My wife is fine. My daughter Kay is studying literature in Boston. My son Ed is not so good. He had a major kidney operation last winter and Lucia suspects the other one is starting to play up. We were warned about the dangers at the time.'

'I hope that I haven't offended you with my choice of meal.' Burgess looked at him anxiously.

'That's OK. That kind of thing doesn't bother me. It's the kind of coincidence that James Joyce would have enjoyed.' Gus saw that Burgess was on the defensive. Despite his acerbic reputation, he guessed that he had never set out to hurt or embarrass anyone.

'What else have you been doing apart from your work with Hamilton?'

'Well, now that you mention it, there is something which has been taking up a lot of my time. I told you about Ed's problem with only one remaining kidney. I need a potential donor. It turns out that I do have relatives in Ireland who could possibly help. However, the whole situation is complex.'

'Tell me. I've got plenty of time.'

The commotion across the square had ceased – apparently to everyone's satisfaction. They drank their wine and Gus embarked again on the story of the lost boys. Burgess fidgeted with his spectacles and appeared not to register any great interest. However, as the full story unfolded, he listened with a more acute attention.

'Since you don't believe in ghosts, are you suggesting that a clone of Ross killed the boys?'

'What do you think of the story?' asked Gus.

'I admit that it's a fascinating one,' replied Burgess. 'However, even if someone had produced a clone, how could it know that a descendant of one of the boys might go on to kill British soldiers?'

'I can't explain that part of it, apart from supernatural foresight. Quite apart from that aspect of the matter, I'm puzzled by these threats.'

'You don't know that they are linked. Some people just don't like Americans. There are a lot of students from the Middle East attending Queen's University – especially in the last few years. They are often very skilled in the use of information technology. Many of the major virus attacks originate from there and North Africa.'

'That hadn't occurred to me.'

'However, whatever the truth of your matter, I am working on a subject related to cloning.' Gus saw his opportunity.

'Arna mentioned that you'd started a new research project that you referred to by the name *Diogenes*.'

'I thought she might have told you something about that. Did she tell you the background?'

'Yes. You want to tell me *anything* about it?'

Burgess finished his wine and suggested some cognac. 'It's not that I don't trust you or Arna. I just think it's better that you don't know too much until I've written up my work. I don't intend to become deflected. That's why I'm up here. There'll be no more visitors. I became tired of life at the University and the way in which my later career had drifted. There was no satisfaction in teaching. My research had dried up. I've read the life of G.H Hardy many times. I saw the writing on the wall.'

'Hardy. The great number theorist. He spent some time at Princeton before the Second World War.'

'That's him. When his mathematical powers began to desert him, he became clinically depressed. He felt that the creative life was the only serious one for any man. Physical and mental illness was followed by a botched suicide attempt although he died shortly afterwards. I was heading the same way. The work with Arna kept me going for a while. The interface between Biology and Mathematics is a fruitful area – similar to that which had existed between Physics and Mathematics in the nineteenth century. Although she didn't seem to realise it, Arna provided the last vital spark for me. Something she said to me one evening set me off on a research problem connected with cloning.'

'I can tell you that she didn't tell me much,' said Gus

Burgess's eyes glowed. 'I read everything there was to know about the subject. I obtained all the recent research papers and information about important Conferences – including the one in Dublin.' He paused to sip his cognac. 'I thought I'd made a mistake by going there. Largely a waste of time and no good contacts – apart from one. I met a scientist from the University of Melbourne – more of a philosopher of science than a real scientist – who provided me by chance with a link to some work done by an Irishman over a hundred years ago. The Australian said that Trinity possessed the key archives on his research. Original manuscripts from the time. Out of curiosity, I found the scripts, became fascinated and skipped the rest of the Conference. The man was a genius, but there were too many gaps and leaps of the imagination in the documents. It was strange that the great scientists of the time did not recognise his ability – for he seemed to know them. There was also a substantial correspondence with many of them clipped in at the back of the manuscripts. If a veteran of the subject had taken him under his wing, it might have made a big difference. His career appeared to evaporate.'

'Had he a connection with Lord Kelvin at any time?' asked Gus. Burgess knocked over his glass of brandy. He recovered and smiled.

'I've told you. He knew everyone that mattered. Kelvin's life spanned most of the nineteenth century. It would have been most unusual if they had never met. Diogenes was far younger and with a completely different bent to Kelvin. That's all I'm going to tell you. Let's have one for the road.'

Gus had hoped for more and made a second attempt. 'Let's go back to my tale about Ross. Initially, it just all seemed far-fetched. Ross dies in bloody circumstances attacking the US in 1814. The boys die a hundred years later. Logic indicates no possible causal link. However, suppose a top-rank scientist obtains samples of blood or skin from the preserved body of Ross – either in Baltimore or Nova Scotia. The same person is way ahead of his time in his understanding of biology and DNA. He manages to clone Ross and persuades a childless couple to co-operate. A child is produced – probably in the late nineteenth century. For arguments sake, we will say 1890. The clone is only twenty-four when the boys are killed in Rostrevor. OK, I haven't explained the supernatural foresight angle but at least we have a tenuous link. Before we had nothing.'

'Who would believe such a story?' asked Burgess.

'You're living in a Roman Catholic country here,' said Gus. 'Millions of Catholics for the last two millennia have believed in the Virgin Birth and still do. Not only that. The offspring is the Son of God himself.'

'Touché' grinned Burgess. 'I'm very tempted to open up to you. I can't do it today. I need more time to think about all this. By the way, if there was a supernatural interference, how come it killed the wrong boys?'

'In the world of the supernatural, there are two forces – good and evil. If a ghost of Ross came to frighten and kill George Connor, perhaps a hostile spirit arose in order to prevent him. Don't forget also that the person who has truly suffered as a result of this tragedy is George.'

'You know I'm an atheist and so can't sign up to any of this.'

'If you're an atheist, why are you driving yourself to an early grave with your work?'

'I think you know why. We've mentioned a Greek philosopher. I forget which one said that you must lead your life as if everything matters but knowing in your heart that nothing does.'

'I'll look it up when I get back. So you want to achieve immortality by publishing a great discovery before you die?'

'General Ross wanted to achieve an immortal reputation. I'll say that for him.'

'He partially succeeded. There are substantial dedications to him in Ireland, Canada and in St Paul's Cathedral, Westminster. He made his mark over half of Europe, North Africa and America.'

'I think we've had enough.' Burgess drained his glass. 'I've enjoyed your company today. It gets lonely up here. I have your number. I will ring you or Arna sometime soon.'

The Alfa passed him as he walked unsteadily down the hill. Like a fly on a cream cake, Burgess was doing what he wanted to do but knew that it couldn't last. Gus feared for him. If this final creative surge did not work out, there was only one answer.

He spent four more days in Italy. On Sunday, he toured Pompeii with Primo. He noted the bodies preserved in ash from A.D. 69. In the late afternoon, they approached the summit of Vesuvius. The Bay of Naples stretched out before them.

'There's some tremendous archaeology still being done round this area,' said Primo. 'I was talking to a scientist from Rome last month. They think that they may have identified the remains of a villa where Augustus Caesar lived before the time of the volcanic eruptions.'

'I should have arranged to spend more time in Italy. I'd like to have visited Rome.' Gus told Primo about the Michelangelo frescoes in the Sistine Chapel.

'Leave it for another day,' said Primo. 'The heat would be unbelievable especially with all the tourists. The Pope himself will be living in his summer villa. If he wasn't, I'm sure he'd have liked to listen to your story about the serpent.'

Gus left on the following afternoon to catch his plane to London. He had arranged accommodation for two days in University College.

He spent the morning checking references in the UCL library and had a pub lunch near Whitehall. It took some time to locate the military tailors in an alley which ran from Regent Street.

A contact at the College had made arrangements for access to Westminster. After his visit there, he walked to St Paul's Cathedral. The inscription was checked, as were the entries for Ross in Hansard.

He returned to the West End in the late afternoon. It was packed with shoppers and tourists. Gus pushed through the crowded streets. He began to sweat and his mouth was dry again. The open doors of the Prince of Wales attracted him. He sat with a light ale and studied the digital imprint of the engraving.

ERECTED at the PUBLIC EXPENSE
to the MEMORY of MAJOR GENERAL ROBERT ROSS
who having undertook and executed an ENTERPRISE against
the CITY of WASHINGTON the CAPITAL of THE UNITED STATES
of AMERICA which was crowned with complete success
was killed shortly afterwards while directing a successful attack
upon a superior force near the CITY of BALTIMORE
on the 12th DAY of SEPTEMBER 1814.

In the evening, he travelled by Underground to Gloucester Road and ate chicken jalfrezi in the Bombay Brasserie. He washed it down with three glasses of Cobra beer. Afterwards, he returned to his rooms, drank a last Bushmills and went to bed.

He arrived back in Belfast on July 25th. After his time in Naples, the streets seemed deserted. A clean, well-lighted place, he thought. He ate a solitary dinner, opened a new bottle of Bushmills and checked his e-mail. There was only one message. **Don't come back.**

CHAPTER 10

HE ARRANGED to meet Townsend on the following afternoon. There was no other choice. The sergeant showed him into the Inspector's office.

'You say the first message on your computer was sent on the afternoon of July 10th. And the second one in the middle of the following week.'

'That's correct. There was no time to do anything about the first one as I was going to Amsterdam.' Townsend raised an eyebrow.

'The messages came from a computer at Queen's University. How do you know that?'

Gus showed him the printouts of the messages. 'AGRI@QUB.AC.UK,' Townsend read aloud. 'Yes. OK. I'm no expert on these matters but you say that we should be able to trace the computer from which the threats originated?'

'Or at least the central computer unit,' replied Gus. 'I suspect, since there was no name, that the latter is the case. The person would hardly be foolish enough to identify themselves.'

'How would they know your e-mail number?' asked Townsend.

'If you accept that these warnings are no random hoax, the person probably knows where I'm living and my actual name. Also, my contacts with the University. Since they know how to use electronic mail, it would not be difficult for them to guess my e-mail number.'

'As for the second computer message, why would they send it to your home when it seems they knew you were away?'

'They assumed that I had carried the laptop with me and would check my messages abroad. In fact, that's what I would usually do.'

'I'll initiate a preliminary enquiry in order to track down the computer at Queen's. That will take a little time. We can't jump in with both feet. I still don't believe that this affair can be connected with your interest in those boys. Any other ideas?' Gus told him of Burgess's suggestion about students from the Middle East.

'That sounds more plausible. If that turns out to be the case, we will crack down very hard on them. We've had some problems before with foreign students.' They shook hands and Gus left the station. At least, some progress would be made. Perhaps it *was* anti-American feeling.

There were no messages on the answering machine. He had given his portable computer to the police. There was still the worry of his personal safety. Townsend had agreed that his men would keep a discreet eye on his home. Gus rang the States but there was no reply.

He phoned Arna Breen to tell her about his trip and the meeting with Burgess. 'You would have enjoyed the Conference. I have made extensive notes for you on the use of molecular biology to control the spread of new biological viruses.'

'I appreciate that very much,' Arna replied. 'I've have an interview coming up soon – in the research station I pointed out to you when we were walking along the towpath to the restaurant.'

'I'll put them in the post to you.' Gus was unsure about offering to deliver them personally as he would have liked.

'That's fine. You said you met Burgess. How was he?'

'In some ways better than I expected. I thought that he might be rather more restrained than he was. We had a very good lunch.'

'Did he open up about what he was working on?' she asked.

'He made it clear at the start that he couldn't do that. However, I managed to draw him out a little about Diogenes. It seems he found out all about him from an Australian whom he met at the Trinity Conference. He said that he would keep in touch. I wouldn't guarantee it.'

'Are you sure you're telling me everything?'

'His general mood worried me. We talked about the great pure mathematician G.H. Hardy who made his name in Number Theory. In his sixties he became ill and tried to kill himself. He had wider interests than Burgess, but once his career was finished, he lost the will to live. That's all I can tell you, I'm afraid. There's a call coming through. I'll have to go.'

'Thank you again for the lecture notes. If I have any questions, do you mind if I ring you?'

'No problem. I'll give you any help you need. It was good of you to put me in touch with David.' He rang off. No mention had been made of the threats. He also felt guilty about not telling her that his family would be arriving to stay with him in August.

The phone rang. It was Lucia. 'I got your message. I've just got in. We've a lot to talk about.'

'How is Ed?'

'There is no change. He's been complaining that you haven't e-mailed him. What happened?'

'I've had a problem with the laptop which I hope to get fixed within the next few days. I didn't bring it to Holland with me as I had quite a load to carry.' He told her about the Conference. 'Primo and Gina send their regards.'

'What about Dr Canavan. No news?'

Gus gave a guilty sigh. 'I didn't want to push too much. You can't do that over here.'

'Some days I'm climbing up the walls. We've got to find out.'

'I'll ring him now and get back to you.'

It was late afternoon before he got through to the hospital. A nurse informed him that the consultant always took his annual vacation in July but was expected back on Monday, the sixth of August.

Townsend rang him over the weekend. He could have his portable computer back.

'Any progress yet?' asked Gus.

'I told you that the investigation will take time. These University people can be very litigious.' Gus continued to feel that something was being withheld.

On Monday, he visited the specialist Irish section of the Belfast Central Library.

'We have all the newspapers from that era catalogued,' said the young assistant. 'If you can give me a better idea of dates, I'll get them out for you myself.'

A yellowing copy of the Irish News from August 1914 provided him with what he needed. The incident had made front-page headlines despite the imminent war. There was enough information for him to identify the location of the deaths. He decided to go back to Rostrevor.

Early on Tuesday morning, he removed the top from the MX-5 and drove to Newry. He stopped at the tourist office in Warrenpoint.

'I remember you. You were here some weeks ago, weren't you?' said Theresa. 'We have a set of new brochures if you'd like them.'

'You are very kind.' He left and photographed the giant obelisk again. There had been no attempt by anyone to cut the grass surrounding its base. A large collection of flies swarmed around a turd at the side of the monument.

He parked the car in the Central Square and tightened the tarpaulin despite the absence of rain. Theresa had asterisked a map in nineteen different places - remarkable for a small town.

He sat at the focal point. In the fourteenth century, a castle – built by a Rory McGuinness – had stood on its south side. The town had at that time been called 'Caisleann Rhudri'.

Two hundred year old oak trees dominated the Square and many of the buildings were from the same era. Five of the houses had once formed a Hotel called Sangster's. A couple called the Yelvertons had stayed there prior to an infamous marriage in 1857.

He entered the deserted Kilbroney Parish Church and studied again the inscription to Major Ross. A clock chimed eleven o'clock. Dust mites floated in the rays of light that streamed through an upper window.

His map indicated that there were three other churches in the town. A Scottish Regiment had been based here in the mid nineteenth century and this had resulted in the erection of a Presbyterian Church built in the gothic style.

The great Methodist, John Wesley, had also visited the area in the nineteenth century and a church had been constructed in 1890 for his followers.

There stood adjacent to it a row of terraced houses called Syenite Place – Syenite being a local rock. They had been built as homes for the workers in a nearby quarry. Your importance was recognised by the size of the house and Gus noticed that these became smaller as he walked along.

At the top of the steep hill running from the Square, he found St Mary's Star of the Sea Roman Catholic Church – built in 1850 through the efforts of a Father Mooney who had been intricately involved in the Yelverton affair. He studied the ancient Bell of St Bronach. It was time for something to eat.

'It was concealed in the ivy-covered fork of a tree,' said the man in the pub. 'Tradition has it that it rang for a thousand years across the surrounding valley. It signified a message of either doom or gloom. When it stopped ringing after the start of the First World War, minds were filled with superstitions and forebodings.'

'What happened after that?' asked Gus. He remembered again the notes which Dr Canavan had shown to him. These recorded George Connor's memory of the muffled ringing of a bell.

'It must have been around 1920. The tree had to be felled. When the branches were being dismembered, they found the bell with its tongue detached. Its sudden cessation, like so many other mysterious happenings in this world, had a rational explanation.' When Gus mentioned the deaths of the boys, the man said that he had never heard of the incident. He looked away, finished his pint of Guinness and left.

Gus drove along the Shore Road. The Irish News article indicated that the deaths had happened approximately three miles along this route. He passed an elegant Square of terraced houses surrounding a broad Green. The brochure commented that, in Victorian times, the residents had used it for cricket and croquet on warm summer afternoons.

Before leaving the town, the next stop on the tourist map was Rostrevor Quay which dated back to 1745. Although built for commercial purposes to land coal from schooners, it had also been the site of the Mourne Hotel adjacent to which had stood a skating rink. Victorian tourists travelled to Warrenpoint by train and then continued their journey to the Quay on Ireland's first horse drawn tramway. Gus noticed the remains of the track. An inscription on the wall of a nearby building recorded that the Quay had been built by a Robert Martin.

Something nagged at the back of his mind as he reached the area where the boys must have crossed through fields to the house where they slept. He could only speculate about the exact location where two of them had met their Maker. In the distance stood a white bungalow. The surrounding fields were still protected by barbed wire. Plump Friesians grazed the long lush grass. They whisked their tails at blow flies and stared at him with vacant interest. He turned the car around and returned. The conversation with Burgess came back to him. There was something he had to check back in town. If a clone of Ross had killed the boys, why had he missed the right one?

The penultimate asterisk on the map – for again there was no time to see everything – highlighted Kilbroney Graveyard. It contained the remains of the 12th century Church of St Bronach and he recalled again the story of the Bell. Ask not for whom the bell tolls, he thought.

The final asterisk gave him what he was looking for. Beside the cemetery stood Kilbroney House – house of the Martin family. One brother, Robert, had been responsible for the Quay. However the most famous resident of the house had been his brother John – referred to as 'Honest John' Martin. The latter's fame was derived, according to the notes, from his friendship with a man called John Mitchel. Both had been members of the 'Young Irelanders' movement in 1848. They had subsequently been tried for treason and deported to Australia, or Van Diemen's Land as it was then called. John Mitchel had returned home via America. Elected MP for Tipperary, he was prevented from taking his seat at Westminster by Disraeli – for he was a convicted felon.

It hardly mattered for the years of hardship had taken their toll and he died in Newry shortly afterwards in 1875. His friend had caught influenza at the funeral and died a few days later.

Gus drove back to Warrenpoint.

As he parked the MX-5 beside the Square, the tricolour caught his attention again. He called back with Theresa at the tourist office in Warrenpoint and thanked her for her brochures.

'Is there anything else I can help you with?'

'I was just finishing my tour at Kilbroney House when the information regarding John Martin and John Mitchel caught my attention.'

'I can find you plenty about both but especially John Mitchel. If you're going back via Newry, there's a statue of him in St Colman's Park. Also if you have time, you could visit his grave in the Presbyterian Old Meeting House Green. The graveyard is enclosed by the Convent of the Sisters of the Poor Clare. Anyone in Newry will be able to direct you to it.'

'Any other historical material?'

'There's no shortage of that available but I don't have it here. Any good library should be able to find out more for you. He wrote a famous book called *Jail Journal*. I haven't read it myself.' She went into a back room and returned with a framed inscription and a photograph. 'Here's a picture of Mitchel. It's not for sale nor is this inscription but I could photocopy it for you.'

'If you don't mind.'

Gus returned to the car and studied the words from a page of Mitchel's book.

But why do we not see the smoke curling from those lowly chimneys? And surely we ought by this time to scent the well-known aroma of the turf-fires. But what (may Heaven be about us this night) – what reeking breath of Hell is this oppressing the air, heavier and more loathsome than the smell of death rising from the fresh carnage of a battlefield. Oh, misery! Had we forgotten that this was the *Famine Year*? And we are here in the midst of those thousand Golgothas that border our island with a ring of death from Cork Harbour all round to Lough Foyle? There is no need of enquiries here – no need of words; the history of this little society is plain before us. Yet we go forward, though with sick hearts and swimming eyes, to examine the Place of Skulls nearer. There is a horrible silence; grass grows before the doors; we fear to look into any door, though they are all open or off the hinges; for we fear to see the yellow chapless skeletons grinning there; but our footfalls rouse two lean dogs, that run from us with doleful howling, and we know by the felon-gleam in the wolfish eyes how *they* have lived after their masters died. We walk amidst the houses of the dead, and out at the other side of the cluster, and there is not one where we dare to enter. We stop before the threshold of our host of two years ago, put our head, with eyes shut, inside the door-jamb, and say, with shaking voice, 'God save all here!' – No answer – ghastly silence and a mouldy stench, as from the mouth of burial vaults.

The sky darkened and it began to rain. He pulled up the convertible hood and secured it. Before driving off, he looked at the photograph of Mitchel. A pale, gaunt man with his chin firmly clenched. Here was the other side of the coin.

CHAPTER 11

MITCHEL, JOHN (1815-1875), Irish nationalist, the third son of the Rev. John Mitchel of Dromalane, Newry, a Presbyterian minister, by his wife Mary Haslett, was born at Camnish, near Dungiven, Co. Londonderry, on 3 Nov. 1815. He was educated at Dr Henderson's School at Newry, where he became acquainted with his lifelong friend John Martin (1812-1875) [q.v.], and in 1830 matriculated at Trinity College, Dublin. According to his biographer, Mitchel took his degree in 1834 (DILLON, i. 15), but his name does not appear in the 'Catalogue of Graduates.' Though intended by his father for the ministry, Mitchel began life as a bank clerk at Londonderry, and subsequently entered the office of John Quinn, a solicitor at Newry. At the close of 1836 he eloped with Jane, only daughter of Captain James Verner of Newry, a school girl of sixteen. The fugitives were captured at Chester, and Mitchel was taken back in custody to Ireland, where he was kept a few days in prison before being released on bail. Their second attempt was, however, more successful, and on 3 Feb. 1837 they were married at Drumcree. Mitchel was admitted a solicitor in 1840, and commenced practice at Banbridge, some ten miles from Newry. In 1842 he became acquainted with Thomas Osborne Davis [q.v.], the friend who, in Mitchel's own words, 'first filled his soul with the passion of a great ambition and a lofty purpose' (ib. i. 70). In the following year Mitchel joined the Repeal Association, and in the autumn of 1845 abandoned his profession and accepted a place on the staff of the 'Nation' under Charles Gavan Duffy. In June 1846 Duffy was prosecuted for publishing in the 'Nation' for 22 Nov. 1845 Mitchel's 'Railway Article', which was described as a seditious libel. Mitchel acted as Duffy's attorney, and the jury was ultimately discharged without coming to an agreement. Mitchel took a leading part in the discussions on the 'moral force' resolutions in Conciliation Hall, Dublin, and seceded from the Repeal Association with the rest of the Young Ireland party on 28 July 1846. Under the influence of James Finton Lalor [q.v.], Mitchel's political views became still more advanced; and at length, finding himself unable any longer to agree with Duffy's more cautious policy, he retired from the 'Nation' in December 1847. As the Irish Confederation failed to concur with his views, Mitchel shortly afterwards withdrew from any active part in its proceedings, and after the Limerick riot resigned his membership.

On 12 Feb. 1848 Mitchel issued the first number of the 'United Irishman,' a weekly newspaper published in Dublin, in which he wrote his well-known letters to Lord Clarendon, and openly incited his fellow-countrymen to rebellion. On 20 March following he was called upon to give bail to stand his trial in the Queen's bench for sedition. The charge, however, was never proceeded with, as the juries could not be relied on to convict, and on 13 May Mitchel was arrested under the new Treason Felony Act, which had received the royal assent in the previous month. He was tried at the commission court in Green Street, Dublin, before Baron Lefroy and Justice Moore, on 25 and 26 May 1848, and was sentenced on the following day to transportation for fourteen years. The sixteenth and last number of the 'United Irishman' appeared on 27 May 1848. In June Mitchel was conveyed in the Scourge to Bermuda, where he was confined to the hulks. In consequence of the bad state of his health he was subsequently removed in the Neptune to the Cape of Good Hope. Owing to the refusal of the colonists to permit the convicts to land, the Neptune remained at anchor in Simon's Bay from 19 Sept. 1849 to 19 Feb. 1850. In the following April Mitchel was landed in Van Diemen's Land, where he was allowed to reside in one of the police districts on a ticket of leave. Here he lived with his old friend John Martin, and in June 1851 was joined by his wife and family.

Gus had arrived early at Belfast Central Library and found Mitchel's name in the National Biographical Dictionary. There were a number of references which he could not locate.

'You will need to go to the even more specialist Linenhall Library,' said the assistant. 'Ask for Mr Baker, who is an expert in the field.' He photocopied what was available and walked the short distance to the other Library. It was the end of July and the streets were quiet.

'Mr Baker is in a meeting,' said the girl. 'I'll do what I can to help. Yes, we have a lot of material on John Mitchel but you would be better speaking to Mr Baker for a judgement on its significance. You should probably begin with Mitchel's *Jail Journal*. It details all his prison experiences and reflections.'

The book opened:

'**May 27th, 1848** – On this day, about four o' clock in the afternoon, I, John Mitchel was kidnapped, and carried off from Dublin, in chains, as a convicted 'Felon'.

Gus flicked through the 320 densely packed pages of the Journal. The man had a fine rebellious mind. This was clear from the account of the reasons for his capture, his subsequent internment and deportation to Van Diemen's Land. It was difficult to imagine a more fevered opponent of the British Empire – and one born a year after the death of Ross. Additionally, a dedicated member of the Fenian Brotherhood buried only a few miles from the obelisk. Two excerpts chosen at random displayed his feelings.

September 11th 1849

'The British transportation system is the very worst scheme of criminal punishment that ever was contrived: and I seriously think it was contrived by the devil, with the assistance of some friends.' This piece had been written between Bermuda and the Cape of Good Hope.

September 12th 1849

'Thoughts like these come upon me when I hear at night, rising from the Ship's forecastle, some Irish air that carries me back to the old days when I heard the same to the humming accompaniment of the spinning wheel; and then I curse, oh! How fervently the British Empire. Empire of Hell! When will the cup of abominations be full? But I always check myself in this cursing; for there is small comfort in unpacking the full heart with indignant words. Indignant thoughts must be stifled and hushed to rest for the time. These things must not be thought after these ways. So, it will make us mad.' These musings had been recorded as he listened to the mournful songs of his fellow Irish convicts. Gus looked again at the inscription that he had been given in Warrenpoint. The second half began:

'Ah! They are dead! They are dead! The strong man and the fair dark-eyed woman and the little ones, with their liquid Gaelic accents that melted into music for us two years ago; they shrunk and withered together until their voices dwindled to a rueful gibbering, and they hardly knew one another's faces; but their horrid eyes scowled on each other with a cannibal glare. We know the whole story – the father was on a 'public work', and earned the sixth part of what would have maintained his family, which was not always paid him; but it still kept them half alive for three months, and so instead of dying in December they died in March. And the agonies of those three months who can tell? – The poor wife wasting and weeping over her stricken children; the heavy-laden weary man, with black night thickening around him – thickening within him – feeling his own arm shrink and his step totter with the cruel hunger that gnaws away his life, and knowing too surely that all this will soon be over. And he has grown a rogue too, on those public works, with roguery and lying about him, roguery and lying above him, he has begun to say in his heart that there is no God; from a poor but honest farmer he has sunk down into a swindling, sturdy beggar; for him there is nothing firm or stable; the pillars of the world are rocking around him; 'the sun to him is dark and silent, as the moon when she deserts the night.' Even ferocity or thirst for vengeance he can never feel again; for the very blood of him is starved into a thin, chill serum, and if you prick him he will not bleed. Now he can totter forth no longer, and he stays at home to die. But his darling wife is dear to him no longer; alas! And Alas! There is a dull stupid malice in their looks; they forget that they had five children, all dead weeks ago, and flung coffinless into shallow graves – nay, in the frenzy of their despair they would rend one another for the last morsel in that house of doom; and at last, in misty dreams of drivelling idiocy, they die utter strangers.

Oh! Pity and Terror! What a tragedy is here – deeper, darker than any *bloody* tragedy ever enacted under the sun, with all its dripping daggers and sceptred palls. Who will compare the fate of men burned at the stake, or cut down in battle – men with high hearts and the pride of life in their veins, and an eye to look up to heaven, or to defy the slayer to his face – who will compare it with this.

No shelter here tonight, then; and here we are far on in the night, still gazing on the hideous ruin. O *Boetho*! A man might gaze and think on such a scene, till curses breed about his heart of hearts, and the *hysterica passio* swells about his throat....'

Gus felt a tap on his shoulder and turned to see a tall man with thick glasses.

'You were looking for me earlier,' said Baker. 'I was told that an American was looking for information about John Mitchel.'

'I think I have found enough here to keep me reading for a month,' replied Gus. 'Hi. I'm Gus McWilliams. This is some Journal.'

'Carl Baker. Yes. You've begun with the right book. If I can be of any assistance, you need only ask.'

Gus looked at his watch. 'I was just going for a bite to eat. Perhaps you might like to join me?' Baker suggested the Crown Bar.

'A famous film was shot here,' said Baker as he wiped the froth of the Guinness from his mouth. '*Odd Man Out*, starring James Mason. Carol Reed made it just before *The Third Man*. He practised a lot of the film techniques in the earlier film. This place hasn't changed since. That's why I like it. Not many Americans are interested in guys like Mitchel. How did that come about?'

Gus sighed. 'It's a long story. I was in Rostrevor yesterday and visited Kilbroney House.'

'John Martin's home?'

'Exactly. And that's how I homed in on Mitchel. So I thought I'd do some historical research. Mitchel's a fascinating character. And I see he spent most of his later life in the States. I'd appreciate any help you can give me. I'll tell you the whole story some other time.'

'You will need to know a little more about the political background to Mitchel's time,' said Baker. 'It will explain his subsequent life. I don't want to go too far back. We'll start at the turn of the nineteenth century. In 1801, The Act of Union dissolved the short-lived Irish Parliament which had existed from 1782 to 1799. It seemed to dash all hopes of Irish Independence from England. From its introduction, Irish nationalists concentrated on its Repeal. However, many did not subscribe to violence in order to achieve their objective. Rather, they were persuaded by the oratory of the man they called the Liberator – Daniel O'Connell. He insisted that violence must be eschewed at all costs and quoted the disastrous example of the failed 1798 Rebellion which only served to set back the cause of independence. O'Connell argued that nationalists should put their trust in the English Parliament and rely on their powers of peaceful persuasion rather than violence. He was credited with being the instrument which forced the British Government to grant Catholic Emancipation in Ireland in 1830.'

'From what I've read so far about Mitchel I gather that he didn't sign up to this approach.'

'He regarded the Emancipation as an underhand measure to calm nationalist feeling. The Carthaginians – as he called the British – gave with one hand and picked the Irish pocket with the other. For example, they abolished the franchise whereby landowners had found it expedient to guarantee security of occupancy to their tenants in order that they could commandeer their votes at election time. As a result of the abolition, wholsesale eviction of tenants began. Mitchel felt that the overall aim of the British was to dispossess the native Irish – even as *tenants* of the land – and, by stealth 'reduce the surplus population', in the words of Scrooge. Indeed, tenants were often told to 'starve or emigrate'. The farmhouses of the dispossessed were subsequently beaten into clay and agrarian land turned over to pasture. Then came the Famine in the 1840's. Mitchel would have been in his early thirties by then. He was savagely indignant about the mass starvation of these times and he blamed the British. He took an increasingly harder line, set up his own newspaper – the *United Irishman* – and openly advocated violent resistance to the British Government.'

'I've been reading about his trial and subsequent deportation to Australia. The odd thing to my mind is the fact that he was a Presbyterian,' said Gus.

'Yes. Many Presbyterians from his time – before and after – were fervent Irish nationalists and dedicated themselves to getting the British out of Ireland. For example, Henry Joy McCracken from the 1798 Rebellion. He is buried in a small cemetery between where we are now and where you said that you were living. You should visit it and also McArts Fort – at the top of Cavehill. A famous proclamation of republicanism was made there before the 1798 Rebellion.'

'Do I detect a certain sympathy with these guys?'

'I'm only stating the facts as I know them. I have no sympathy with their modern descendants. At the height of our current Troubles, they tried to burn the library down.' He smiled ruefully.

'Thank you for taking the time to talk to me,' said Gus.

'No problem. But I'll have to be getting back. You must keep in touch.' They strolled back to the library. Gus added *Jail Journal* to his growing collection and returned home.

He did not stop at the cemetery. However, he had meant for some time to make the climb to the top of Cavehill. The Guinness at lunchtime had made him feel sluggish and he decided that now was the time to make the attempt. Baker had said that he should begin at Belfast Castle which was a ten minute walk away.

An approach track brought him through a forest thickly populated with beeches, elms, oak and chestnut trees. These were broken up by carpets of moss. The route rose steeply as the trees thinned. Then the great black rock reared up above him. The path turned to the left past a large cave and onto Napoleon's Nose. To his right he saw a bomb crater sprinkled with stunted brambles. The approach to the top was nothing more than a wide dirt track surrounded by dark green heather and thick grass.

The view from the summit was spectacular. His sweat dried in the cold air. The Lough sparkled blue and he saw Scotland in the distance. His head cleared. He sat down and scanned the remains of the fort.

Mitchel had been in America from 1853 onwards – until just before his death in Ireland in 1875. He had landed in San Francisco from Australia and had later made his way to New York. Had he met *Diogenes*? If he had, where and when did they meet? He thought of the three Presbyterians with their Rostrevor connections.

Trinity College, Dublin, lay also like a golden thread between the lives of the three men. Ross had graduated in 1789, pursued a distinguished military career before being mortally wounded at Baltimore. Mitchel had been born in 1815 and studied at Trinity between 1830 and 1834. From the 1840's on, he had followed a determined path in support of Irish Republicanism – a life which would have been repugnant to Ross had he survived the Anglo-American Wars.

Thomson, born in 1824, had been a frequent visitor to Trinity and published his work in the Dublin Mathematical Journal throughout the latter part of the nineteenth century. He had been at the peak of his fame in 1865 – playing a significant part in the laying of the first transatlantic cable between Cork and a site near the burial place of Ross.

Gus walked from the summit and thought of possible links between the soldier, the politician and the scientist. The blue waters of the Lough had changed from blue to grey. As he entered the forest, rain began to drip through the evergreens.

CHAPTER 12

ARNA BREEN woke at 4.00 am to find the tips of her toes touching the bedroom wall. The room was black. She remembered afterwards that there had been no moon.

She reached out to her left to find the pepper pot that she kept in the drawer beside her bed. As she did so, she smelt the stale breath and saw two cat-like eyes stare from a balaclava.

The pepper caught the eyes as the phone erupted downstairs. The attacker cursed, withdrew and ran away. She heard a door crash. She phoned the police. In the half-hour before they arrived, she lay trembling beneath the bedclothes.

'Probably a burglar,' said the policeman. 'Realising you were the only one here, he got carried away. Anything missing?'

'I haven't looked. I was too terrified to go downstairs until you came.'

'We'll have a look round.' She lit a cigarette.

'He broke in at the back door. The glass has been shattered. Probably came up by the river. Left by the front door. Apart from the glass, there's no sign of any other disturbance. You were very lucky. Do you know who phoned?'

'I'll check.' She rang the messaging service. 'A friend from Italy,' she said. 'He owns the house. Sometimes doesn't realise what time it is here.'

'When will he be back?'

'Nobody knows – not even him.' The two policemen exchanged looks.

'We'll do a tour of the area and return later. Try and get some rest.' They did not come back but phoned mid-morning to say that they had not been able to find anything suspicious. 'Some of the bars near the University don't close until 3.00am on Saturday morning. There were some drunken students roaming the streets. They don't normally wander up this far. We stopped to talk to them but it was unlikely that it was any of them. No, whoever did it would return home and lie low. We'll keep in touch.'

Gus was sitting in the back garden on Saturday afternoon when he heard the faint noise of the telephone. He placed the Journal of John Mitchel on the ground.

'It's Arna Breen here. I'm sorry to disturb you but I didn't know who else to talk to. There's been a break-in here and I was attacked in my bedroom. I could have been raped.'

Gus could hear the shake in her voice and sensed her terror. 'When did this happen?'

'In the middle of the night. I phoned the police. They thought it might have been a burglar who got too excited. I don't know about that. I've heard that they watch a place first for a time to see who lives there. They would've known I was alone.'

'Casing the joint as we call it in the States,' said Gus. 'Would you like me to come over?'

She paused. 'If you don't mind. I have to talk to someone. I don't want my parents knowing anything about this. They'll put more pressure on me to move back with them. I don't want to do that and I've nowhere else to go.'

The sun shone in a blue sky as he entered her Avenue again. The large detached houses sat in silence. Somewhere a lawnmower hummed. A curtain twitched in the neighbouring house as he walked up the path to the front door. It opened immediately after he rang the bell. He could see she was in bad shape. The depressions beneath her eyes were accentuated by the whiteness of her face.

'The police called again. They'll be round later this afternoon to take more photographs and swab my bedroom. Thank you for coming over so quickly. I feel a bit of a fool now for asking you.'

'Think nothing of it. I'm glad to be of help...even if it's only to listen. I suspect you feel there's something else behind this?'

'You've guessed right. I'll come back to that. Would you like some coffee?'

'That would be fine.' He sat in the front living room and she left to prepare it. Gus noticed the ash-tray with the half-extinguished cigarette. A faint smell of whiskey lingered in the air.

She returned carrying a tray with a coffee pot and a quarter bottle of Bushmills. 'I need another drop of this. Would you like some?'

'Just a nip in the coffee. Thanks. I read until late last night and had one glass too many. Anyway, tell me all about it.' Gus sipped his coffee and waited. She offered a cigarette which he refused. Her hand trembled as she put it to her lips.

'I never told anyone – not even the police. I've had an eerie feeling this past few weeks. As if someone has been watching me. Perhaps it was my imagination. I've noticed strange cars in the Avenue at odd times of the evening. Most people round here park their cars in the garage at night.'

'Have you anything else to go on?'

Her hand shook as she added more whiskey to the coffee. 'I don't know much about cars but on more than one occasion I've seen a dark blue car...a Rover I think...parked about fifty yards away on the other side. One evening I went out for a walk. As I left by the front gate, the car started up, did a rapid three point turn and accelerated away. That made me even more suspicious.'

'You didn't get a number?'

'No. I didn't get close enough and it hasn't been back. There is something else. I have a gut feeling that this attack is somehow connected with your last visit here.' She stared at him directly and looked away.

Gus was startled. He had told her nothing of his own threats but decided that he could not hold back. 'I don't want to frighten you even more,' he said. ' But it's only right to tell you that I've been getting telephone warnings and strange messages on my computer.'

'When did these begin?'

It had not occurred to Gus before. 'We met on Friday June 29. The first warning came in the early hours of July 1st although I had callminder in place and I didn't check until the evening afterwards. Then, before I left for the Conference in Amsterdam, I received an e-mail message.' He gave her the essence of the two messages.

'And after that?'

'When I returned from Italy on July 25, there was another message on the PC...sent when I was away...telling me not to come back. Naturally, I didn't mention anything about it when we last spoke. I did not imagine that it would be anything to do with you. And still find it hard to credit.'

She finished her coffee and inhaled again. 'It's an intuition. I could be wrong. You can see I'm rattled although I feel a little better. Let's talk about something else. You don't mind me smoking?'

'No. I brought the lecture notes with me. The ones you asked for on virus spread. You'll not be in any mood for it today.'

'Thanks. When my nerves settle, I'll have to concentrate on the interview. It's coming up in a fortnight's time. I have to get the job. The boredom in the one I have is killing me.' She paused. 'It can wait. I told you about the phone call from David. Tell me more about your trip. What else did you talk about?'

'I'm afraid it may bring us back to what we've just been discussing. I've told you some of what he said. However, I told him about the first two threats. Recall that the second one came just before I left for Amsterdam. I did not know whether to be reassured or not by what he said.'

'What did he think? He often has good insight.'

'He thought it might be students from the Middle East who saw me working at the University, picked up on my accent and were motivated by malice. I reported the incidents to an Inspector Townsend from my local police station. He thought it plausible although he seemed to be cagey about everything. I thought the threats just might have been somehow connected with my story about George Connor but he pooh-poohed that idea.'

'You told him about Canavan and the DNA?'

'Yes but his reaction was as I expected. As I said to you last time, the police don't have time to be digging up old cases like these unless there is something very firm to go on.'

'Burgess could be right,' she said, stubbing out a cigarette. 'That's the last of those. I hate them really. Anyway, there are quite a few students from the Middle East at the University. There's one other thing you need to be aware of. Quite a few students have sympathies with the Palestinians...mostly the radical ones who also have IRA sympathies. You wouldn't want to get on the wrong side of either of those two groups.'

'I haven't done anything to annoy either.'

'You don't know that for sure. Who knows what you've stumbled on.'

'I can take care of myself. I'm more concerned about you.'

'Maybe it was a burglar – nothing to do with anything. A random break-in.'

'Perhaps. May I use your bathroom?'

'Of course.' When he came back, she had fallen asleep. He found a blanket and placed it over her. There was nothing else to be done. Security seemed OK. The glass in the back door had been covered and nailed with hard cardboard.

He decided to wait until the police returned. He took the tray to the kitchen, washed the cups and put the bottle in a cupboard. There were some garden chairs outside and he sat in the late afternoon sunshine.

Everything is getting out of hand, he thought. The most logical explanation could be that a student with Palestinian sympathies had targeted him and even followed him to her house at the end of June. Decides to have a little malicious fun with him. But burglary and rape? Gus lifted his face to the sun and closed his eyes. The e-mail address floated into his mind.

A hand shook his shoulder. 'The police are here,' she said. 'Maybe you'd better go. I fell asleep. Thanks for staying. I'll be fine. Don't worry. I've told them who you are.'

'Did you tell them about my own threats?'

'I'll leave that up to you. Maybe you better talk to this guy Townsend first. He'll be a higher rank than these two men. In any case, they're interested in forensic evidence and are keen to begin. You can phone from here if you like.'

The Inspector was dealing with an urgent piece of business. Gus left a message and then spoke briefly to the two policemen. 'Ring me this evening or tomorrow.' She thanked him again and he drove home.

Townsend rang him back at ten o'clock. Gus told him about the attempted rape.

'I'll check the details with our men on the other side of town,' replied Townsend. 'I very much doubt that there is any link. You haven't had any more problems yourself?'

'No. Any progress with the origin of the computer?'

'We're still pursuing it. More pressing matters have taken up my time. It's not a good time of year for us with all these marches.' He rang off.

Gus expected more calls over the rest of the weekend but nothing came from anyone. He slept late on Sunday. The skies were grey and the summit of Cavehill was shrouded in mist from early afternoon. He roasted a chicken with garlic potatoes and roasted parsnips. The Bushmills was left on the shelf and he stayed with the wine from Puglia.

On Monday morning, the Linenhall Library was just opening when he arrived. He found a desk and planned his schedule for the week ahead. Tony was back from vacation later in the week. Canavan was expected to return that same day but he had to be patient. The man would be inundated with urgent work after the long break. This gave Gus a little time to explore possible links between Ross, Mitchel and *Diogenes.*

He stopped for coffee and met Carl Baker. 'If you've got time, I'd like to tell you more about the background to all this.'

'We're not too busy this morning. I'd like to help you if I can. I told you that.' Gus told him as much as he knew.

'I've heard of Ross,' said Baker. 'And the defacement of his monument by republicans. Ross. Yes. He wouldn't be as famous as Mitchel is around certain parts of this city. I'll see what I can find for you. You said that you were interested in his exploits between his departure from Southern Italy and his final expedition in America.' He returned shortly afterwards.

On 21 Jan. 1808 Ross became lieutenant-colonel of the 20th, and six months afterwards embarked with it for Portugal. Vimiera had been fought before he landed, though part of the regiment was engaged there; but he was with Moore during his advance into Spain and subsequent retreat to Coruña. The 20th formed part of the reserve, and was for some time the rear-guard of the army. It was repeatedly engaged, but owing to its excellent discipline it lost fewer men than any other regiment. Ross's knowledge of French and Spanish proved very useful in this campaign. As part of Paget's division (the reserve), the 20th had a share in the turning movement which decided the battle of Coruña. Ross received a gold medal for Coruña. In August 1809, having been brought up to its strength by large drafts from other regiments, the 20th was sent to Walcheren. It was not engaged; within a month two-thirds of the men were in hospital, and on its return to England the regiment had to be once more reformed. To restore its condition it was sent to Ireland. There the men were again drilled by their colonel as in Malta, 'every conceivable contingency of actual warfare being carefully and frequently rehearsed.' About 1809 a sword was presented to Ross by the officers of his regiment in honour of Maida. On 25 July 1810 he was made brevet colonel, and in the same year aide-de-camp to the king.

At the end of 1812 the 20th was again sent to the Peninsula, and was brigaded with the 7th and 23rd fusiliers in the fourth (Cole's) division. In the spring of 1813, shortly before the campaign opened, Ross applied for the command of a brigade. Wellington gave him the fusilier brigade, of which his own regiment formed part, and on 4 June he was made major-general. At Vittoria, Cole's division was in support, and played only a secondary part; but it was foremost in the series of actions by which Soult's attempt to relieve Pampeluna was frustrated. This attempt began on 25 July with a direct attack on Byng's brigade, twelve miles in rear, while Reille, with sixteen thousand men, moved round its left flank. Ross's brigade hurried up in support of Byng, and on reaching the main ridge of the Pyrenees, above Roncesvalles, encountered the head of Reille's column. To secure the advantage of ground, Ross ordered the leading troops to charge at once; and Captain Tovey, with a company of the 20th, dashed at the 6th léger with the bayonet. Other companies followed; and though they were soon forced back by overwhelming numbers, time enough was gained for the rest of the brigade to form up and secure the pass. In the night the British troops fell back, and the army was gradually concentrated in front of Pampeluna. In the battle of Sauroren on the 28th (as Wellington wrote in his despatch of 1 Aug.), 'the gallant fourth division, which had so frequently been distinguished in this army, surpassed their former good conduct. Every regiment charged with the bayonet, and the 40th, 7th, 20th, and 23rd four different times. Their officers set them the example, and Major-General Ross had two horses shot under him.'

Ross was at the battle of the Nivelle (10 Nov.), and his services were mentioned by Cole in his report. At the battle of Orthes, 27 Feb. 1814, he carried the village of St. Boës on the French right, and five times attempted to deploy beyond it to attack the heights, in face of an overwhelming fire of artillery and musketry. He received a wound which nearly cost him his life, but of which he wrote cheerfully a fortnight afterwards: **'You will be happy to hear that the hit I got in the chops is likely to prove of mere temporary inconvenience.'** It disabled him, however, for the rest of the campaign. He was among the officers who received the thanks of parliament for Orthes. He was given a gold medal for Vittoria, and the Peninsula gold cross.

They met again for lunch. 'Ross was an outstanding officer. His record in the Iberian Peninsula mirrors his earlier career. Always leading from the front – determined never to be beaten.'

'It doesn't elucidate your search,' said Baker. 'By the way, I've found the newspaper from the late nineteen seventies that you asked for this morning – the Warrenpoint tragedy where the British soldiers were killed.'

Gus examined the identikits of suspects. The hairs stood up on the back of his neck. The newspaper showed three men and a woman. He had only seen George Connor twice – a man in his nineties. There was no mistaking the resemblance between him and one of the men.

CHAPTER 13

FROM JAIL JOURNAL, October 26, 1849:

'Last July, the 'government' got up a very horrid massacre in the County Down. There was a great Orange procession of armed men: they marched with banners displayed, through a district chiefly inhabited by Catholics; and there, at Dolly's brae, between Castlewellan and Banbridge, a collision took place, of course: a large force of police and military was present, and they took part, also, of course, with the Orangemen: five or six Catholics were killed, five or six of their houses burned; only one Orangeman or two seriously hurt; - and the procession went on its way in triumph. Lord Roden, it appears, had feasted the Orangemen at Bryansford, and excited them with 'loyal' toasts; and afterwards, when informations were sought against the orange rioters at the hands of the said Lord Roden, presiding at a bench of magistrates, he refused. Very properly, for there is no law in Ireland now. I know no reason why Orangemen should not burn Papists' houses now.'

GUS barbecued a slice of Aberdeen Angus. He ate it with dauphinoise potatoes and peas in their shells. As he drank a second glass of claret, he saw Townsend and two constables come up the driveway.

They came into the living room and the Inspector sat down. He apologised for his tone on Saturday evening. 'These marches cause us a lot of extra work at this time of year and keep us away from what we would like to be doing.' The other two betrayed no facial expression as they stood by the window. Gus noticed their packed holsters.

'That's fine. I've been here long enough to realise that,' said Gus. 'However, you requested me to inform you personally if anything strange happened.'

'I've spoken to my colleagues on the other side of town. They suspect a burglary which got out of hand. It's a coincidence that you knew Miss Breen.' Townsend smiled briefly. 'That's not what I've come here to talk to you about. There are two other matters which we need to discuss.'

'Too many coincidences,' said Gus. 'Well. Go on. I take it that you've traced the computer.'

The Inspector continued. 'Yes. The threats were logged on a personal computer belonging to an Agriculture Research Unit – an outlying Department of the University.'

'Who owns the computer?'

'It actually belongs to the University and is on their official inventory. Their Central Unit had allocated it to a Dr Kenneth Jones who was advised on the use of passwords. Also, to keep it under his direct control. They have strict guidelines against the use of their computers for improper purposes – mainly to guard against the use of pornographic sites on the Internet.'

'Have you spoken to Dr Jones?'

'When we got the call this morning, we moved rapidly. These academics can be difficult to find at this time of year but fortunately he was there. We caught him on the hop.' He paused as if something had just occurred to him. 'Our friend Jones ignored all the warnings about the risks and provided access for his postgraduate students. Apparently they all knew the passwords and, at different times, used the computer without any supervision.' Townsend sighed. 'Big brains sometimes don't correlate with common sense.'

'Is there any way of homing in on a more likely suspect?'

'We're working on that. He has a mixed bag of students from home and abroad. Four of them are still there and we are seeking clearance to interview them as soon as possible. However, the other two have left the country – only temporarily Jones assured me. One is on vacation – a local boy. The other has gone home to Serbia.'

'Serbia? Do we know anything about him?'

'It's not a he. It's a she. A Muslim with radical views according to Dr Jones.'

'That could tie in with our previous Middle East theory,' said Gus.

'Wrong country. Right religion.'

'She won't be back until mid-September. It wouldn't be usual for a girl to do this. However, it could have been a friend. She was living in the Residential Halls – approximately halfway between the main site and the Agriculture Unit. We're going to have to interview the Warden.'

Gus burst in. 'Is the Research Unit a large white building set back less than a mile from the river?'

'Yes. That's it. I see what you're thinking. The penny has just dropped with me as well. Miss Breen must live quite near it. When I phoned my colleague, I wasn't thinking of the geographical connection. I apologise. This throws a different light on the affair.'

'As a matter of fact, she told me on Saturday that she has an interview for a research job there in a fortnight.'

'I'll brief my colleague about this development.' His upper lips closed in a tight parabola. 'We'll have the house watched for the next few weeks.'

Gus told him about the blue Rover. 'You wanted to talk to me about another matter?'

'Yes. This business of these lost boys. We have no current access to the original files on that incident – apart from the newspapers which you have already located. But we did manage to get a hold of records for the Warrenpoint atrocity in the late seventies. Some terrorists were caught and there were many additional suspects. There was nobody called Connor. Of course, if George Connor had a son, he may have been adopted at an early stage of his life and taken the name of a stepfather. Alternatively, he may have used an alias.'

Gus grew excited. 'I was in the Linenhall Library this afternoon and found reports and photographs related to the tragedy. Wait a moment.' He returned with the clippings. 'One of these guys here bears a striking resemblance to George Connor.' Gus pointed him out.

Townsend retrieved his spectacles from his top pocket and examined the photographs. 'Well, well,' he said. 'You've been doing quite a bit of detective work.' He looked over at Gus and pursed his lips. He looked down, paused and then stared closely at Gus. 'It's not only Mr Connor he resembles. There's a certain likeness to yourself. It's a small world isn't it?' He smiled, his eyes cold.

Gus studied the prints again. There *was* a resemblance. It made sense. This guy was his cousin.

'We should be able to find out who this is,' said the Inspector. 'I advise you in the meantime to be very cautious. You don't know what you're dealing with over here. Many terrorists were freed early under the Good Friday Agreement in 1998. In my opinion, most of them should still be locked up. The leopard does not change its spots.' He rose and they shook hands. 'We'll get back to you soon.' He glanced at the green backed book lying open on the coffee table. Gus could not tell whether he had been able to see its cover.

When they left, he made some coffee. Townsend had given him plenty to worry about. If the threats had originated from the Serbian route, he had better warn Arna. She had applied for a job in the same Unit. If successful, that could prove dangerous. He knew that Lucia would be anxious about the return of Canavan but he had decided to leave it until Wednesday.

He rang Arna Breen and told her about his conversation with Townsend. 'You will probably see a police Landrover touring the Avenue occasionally. The Rover car will hardly come back if the person who drove it is implicated in the attack.'

'I'm still feeling shattered. I rang the laboratory and told them that I would be off until Thursday. Perhaps we could talk again before then. There's something else I forgot to tell you but it can wait.'

'How about dinner tomorrow night? Maybe you can suggest somewhere.'

'Thanks. I'd like that. I know a good Chinese place downtown.'

'Let's meet in the Crown Bar about six-thirty.'

Gus poured a small glass of Bushmills and looked again at what he had on Mitchel. There was nothing he could do about the Serbian. His son was more important. Baker had said that John Mitchel had been much admired by the Republican Movement in Belfast. It seemed to Gus that, despite Townsend's warning, he would eventually have to make contact with someone from that background. He needed to understand the mindset. Mitchel's Journal had given him no shortage of clues. He picked up his notes and read through them again.

Mitchel had been convicted as a felon and had spent a considerable amount of time being transported to Australia. He had arrived there in April 1850 where he had met again his old friend from Rostrevor, John Martin.

April 6th 1850

'The mountainous southern coast of Van Diemen's Land! It is a soft blue day; soft airs, laden with all the fragrances of those antarctic woods, weave an atmosphere of ambrosia around me. As we coast along over the placid waters, passing promontory after promontory, wooded to the water's edge, and 'glassing their ancient glories in the flood,' both sea and land seem to bask and rejoice in the sunshine. Old Ocean smiles – that multitudinous rippling laugh seen in vision by the chained Prometheus. Even my own sick and weary soul (so kind and bounteous is our mother earth) feels lightened, refreshed, uplifted. Yet there, to port, loom the mountains, whereunto I am to be chained for years, with a vulture gnawing my heart. Here is the very place: the Kaf, or Caucasus, where I must die a daily death.'

A long way from Dolly's Brae, thought Gus. Mitchel had lived in Bothwell, Tasmania from 1850 to 1853. He kept an intermittent diary, sometimes with breaks of many months. Although a great lover of nature, he was always aware of the difference between Australia and his native land.

July 30th 1850

'The birds have a foreign tongue: the very trees whispering to the wind whisper in accents unknown to me; for your gum-tree leaves are all hard, horny, polished as the laurel – besides, they have neither upper nor under side, but are set on with the plane of them vertical; wherefore, they can never, never – let breeze pipe or zephyr breathe as it will – never can they whisper, quiver, sigh or sing, as do the beeches and the sycamores of old Rosstrevor. Yes, all sights and sounds of nature are alien and outlandish – suggestive of the Tropic of Capricorn and the Antarctic Circle – save only the sparkle and the music of the streams. Well I know the voice of this eloquent river: it talks to me, and to the woods and rocks, in the same tongue and dialect wherein the Roe discoursed to me, a child; in its crystalline gush my heart and brain are bathed; and I hear, in its plaintive chime, all the blended voices of history and prophecy and poesy from the beginning. Not cooler or fresher was the Thracian Hebrus; not purer were Abana and Pharpar; not more ancient and venerable is Father Nilus. Before the quiet flow of the Egyptian river was yet disturbed by the jabber of priests of Meroe – before the dynasty was yet bred that quaffed the sacred wave of Choaspes, 'the drink of none but kings' – ere its lordly namesake river, in Erin of the streams, reflected yet upon its bosom a Pillar Tower, or heard the chimes from its Seven Churches, this river was rushing through its lonely glen to the southern sea, was singing its mystic song to these primeval woods.'

In June 1851, he was joined by his wife and family who had landed in Adelaide in the previous month. His journey to Bothwell to meet them had not been without incident – including a night in the cells of Launceston jail, having annoyed an official by his 'haughty manner' and travelling without a passport.

He goes on to record his meetings with other 'Young Irelanders' and deportees from home, including William Smith O'Brien. Gus flicked through the pages in order to find any more clues to his character. Despite his reputation as a felon, Mitchel continued to come across as gentleman and lover of nature. There was also no doubt about his love and affection for his wife and family. A considerable amount of time was spent riding the countryside with John Martin.

October 18th 1851
'We still ascended, the mountain becoming wilder and steeper at every mile, until we were full two thousand feet above the plain of Ross. Here an opening among the trees gave us a view over the low country we had left, wide, arid, and parched in aspect, with ridge after ridge of rugged-looking wooded hills stretching far towards the Pacific eastwards. High and grim, to the north-east, towered the vast Ben Lomond; and we could trace in the blue distance that valley of St Paul's, where we had left O'Brien wandering on his lonely way.'

After three years in Van Diemen's Land, Mitchel had had enough and decided to escape to America. Travelling under a range of aliases from Henry Miller to Father Macnamara, he eventually found a captain of a vessel called the Emma willing to transport him and his family to Sydney. From there, he made his way on the *Orkney Lass* to San Francisco. His family travelled on a different American ship, the *Julia Ann*.

The following day was sunny and Gus walked again to the summit of Cavehill. He wondered had Mitchel ever walked this path as had his compatriots from 1798. The family had arrived in San Francisco in October 1853, Mitchel having transferred to the *Julia Ann* near Tahiti. Most of the rest of his life was spent, from 1853 to 1875, in America...the key crossover period with Kelvin's laboratory corps.

The walk had given him a sharp appetite. On his return home, he showered and left for the Crown Bar. He had just taken his second gulp of Guinness when she entered. She looked refreshed. The black shadows had disappeared. 'What would you like to drink?' he asked.

'A glass of Chardonnay will do nicely. I'm feeling better since you saw me on Saturday although it's going to take me some time to get over it.' They stood for a moment in silence.

'Have the police spoken to you again?'

'No but I've noticed the police Landrover and there's been no sign of the mystery car. Let's get something to eat before we talk. It's only a short distance to the Sun Kee. I think you'll like it.'

They ordered noodles with king prawns and Gus ordered a bottle of Chiroubles. 'Aren't you worried about the possible Serbian connection?' he said. 'After all you might be working there soon.'

'Even if I get the job, it'll probably be in the New Year before I start. I hope that this business is resolved before then. We'll see what happens when the girl returns.'

'You wanted to talk about something else?'

'It's maybe not unconnected,' she replied. 'You remember that it was Burgess who phoned me and interrupted the attacker the other night. In my panic, I didn't listen to the entire message, it was the police who caught on when they double checked. After his initial ramblings, there was a pause and then he spoke again...about you.'

'What did he say?'

'He said that you should concentrate on the loose thread. I remembered your story and thought it was important that you should know.'

Gus sighed and sipped his wine. 'The thread. Yes. When I returned from Italy, I spent some time in London. The military tailor still exists.'

'I'd like to help you.'

'I'll think about what Burgess said. I've been pursuing another line of inquiry.' He told her about his research on Mitchel.

'I've heard of him. Perhaps I could do something.'

'Well...if you could get me a safe contact in nationalist circles it might help.'

'I'll see what I can do.' They went back to his car and he drove her home. She said that she was tired. He took the hint. He had not said anything about the coming visit.

On the following morning, he rang the hospital and got through to Dr Canavan.

'I'm afraid it's bad news,' said the doctor. 'Just came through yesterday. We cannot tell you anything about George Connor's personal details for legal reasons. That's all the letter says. I think you should appeal the decision. Why don't you come and see me again and we'll talk about it.'

'My wife arrives here next week. It would be valuable if you could meet with her as well.'

CHAPTER 14

A LETTER arrived from Carl Baker. It contained additional information about Ross after he had been wounded at Orthes in February 1814. The hit in the chops had indeed proven to be of mere temporary inconvenience. There was also some information about his wife and family.

Ross had married a lady called Elizabeth Glascock in December 1802. They had several children, of whom two sons and one daughter survived infancy. After being wounded at Orthes, Ross convalesced in St Jean de Luz. Elizabeth Ross landed by ship from Ireland at Bilbao. She then made her way over the snowy mountains from Spain to nurse him. Three months later, when he and his regiment were sent to America, he promised her that it would be his last campaign. And so it had turned out. She herself died in May 1845, just as the Famine was beginning to take its toll.

He caught Lucia on the phone as she was leaving for work. 'I'm afraid the news is not good. The authorities have not granted permission for Dr Canavan to reveal anything in George Connor's records.'

'Is there nothing we can do?' He heard the disappointment in her voice.

'He's willing to see us together when you're in Ireland in order that we can prepare an appeal. Bring anything with you that you think may help. For example, Ed's medical records and any additional proof of who I am.'

'I'll have to go. That's my day shattered. I'll ring next week before we leave.' She rang off.

He resigned himself to the further delay. Even if the records were released many problems remained. His head throbbed in frustration

The phone rang. It was Arna. 'You said you'd be at home today,' she said with a shake in her voice. 'I wanted to thank you for last night. Sorry if I was rather abrupt when you dropped me off. I was ready for bed.'

'I understand. I should tell you that I've had some bad news this morning.' He told her about the call from Canavan. 'I'm going to have to appeal it. I've spoken to my wife.' He paused. 'She and the kids have confirmed that they'll be flying over next week – August 15th. We're going to go up and see Canavan again to see what can be done.'

'I said that I would do what I could to help. I contacted an old friend from my undergraduate days. She's from a place called Ardboe but teaches biology in a school in Belfast. When I spoke to her at lunchtime, she agreed to help.'

'I'll be honest with you,' said Gus. 'It's not just Mitchel. I need to get a lead on George Connor's son. It may be my only hope.'

'I guessed that. I'll ring you back after I've spoken to my friend again.'

At least he had squared with her, thought Gus, in more ways than one. He rang Tony Hamilton who had said that he would be back from Donegal to prepare for students undertaking resit examinations.

'Good vacation?'

'Terrific. Patchy weather but the air up there would wake up the dead,' replied Tony. 'How's everything with you? We haven't spoken since you left for Amsterdam.'

'There's a lot to tell you. Would it be okay to meet you early next week?'

'Let's make it Monday morning. I'm busy later in the week.'

'That would be great. I think I told you that Lucia is coming over next week.'

'I remembered. Emma is looking forward to meeting her. I'll have to go. Bloody students. See you on Monday.'

When Gus returned from his walk that evening, he checked his telephone messages. No threats. A message to ring Arna Breen.

'My friend Colette rang back with a useful contact. A history teacher called Basil McLean. He knows all about Mitchel. She's spoken to him and he said that you could ring him if you wish. I have the number here.'

'I'll do that now. Thanks.'

McLean's wife answered the phone. Gus heard a cry in the background. 'Basil…Basil! An American is on the phone for you. Hurry up.'

'Colette told me about you. We could have a drink together. How about Friday night? I use my local social club in West Belfast. Don't worry. It's safe.'

'I appreciate your help.'

'It's nothing. I'll tell you how to get there. Ask for me at the front door. Come about nine.'

Gus spent Friday preparing for his meeting with McLean. He reviewed the notes from the biographical dictionary and extracts from *Jail Journal*.

Mitchel had spent three weeks in California and then sailed on the Cortez and subsequently the *Prometheus* for New York. Gus laughed and slapped his knee when he learnt of the destination.

November 1st 1853

'Three weeks in California. We have been the guests of the city, and more than princely are the hospitalities of the Golden City; we have spent a week at San Jose; cantered through the crack-openings at the base of the coast range, and penetrated the Santa Cruz Gap, amongst wooded mountains, where our senses were regaled with the fragrance of pine woods, - unfelt for five years.'

November 16th 1853

'The *Prometheus* arrived this evening, but will not take us on board till tomorrow. So, the innkeepers of Greytown are to have twenty-four hours harvest more. We keep our rooms in Lyon's Hotel, but can neither eat nor drink there. By researches in the town, we have found a little restaurant, adorned all around with uncouth pictures, kept by a Frenchman, who makes eatable omelettes, gives a good dinner, and keeps good claret.'

December 29th 1853

'This morning, the heights of Nevisink, then Sandy Hook, Staten Island, Long Island. We steam rapidly up the outer harbour. My wife and I are walking on deck, enjoying and admiring the glee of some of our New York acquaintances on board, as the great ocean avenue to native city opens before them, after years of absence in California. They eagerly point out every well-known feature in the vast bay; and ask us to admit that it is the most beautiful bay in the world. I answer that it is the most useful.'

The nights had started to draw in but it was still light and the air was fresh. Gus drove up the Falls Road. The graffiti caught his eye. He felt nervous as the road seemed to go on forever. He had been told to keep to the left when he reached Andersonstown police station...a fortress worse than the one that he had been in recently.

A football stadium – Casement Park – told him that he was close. He turned right, then left and breathed a sigh of relief. One more hurdle to cross. The word social was not a good description of the exterior of the bar. He rang a bell and was admitted. A small man with pulsing veins in his cheeks asked him to sign a visitor's book and sent a young man to find McLean.

The soft voice on the phone had not betrayed this bear of a man with thick red hair. He had an infectious smile and asked Gus what he would like to drink.

'It's warm tonight. I'll try a pint of Smithwicks.'

'So you're one of us,' grinned McLean. Gus wondered what he meant. 'If you'd ordered Guinness I wouldn't have been able to tell for sure. Sorry, it's an old joke. What can I do for you?'

Gus had no desire to reveal everything at this stage and had decided that it would be better to stay with the subject of Mitchel. He outlined again a description of the trips to Rostrevor and the background to his curiosity.

'I was attracted by the fact that he spent the last twenty years of his life mainly in the States. Also, I've explained to you my own Irish-American history and I'm always interested in such links.'

'I understand,' said McLean. 'I have many friends and relatives in Canada and America. How far have you got in your knowledge of John Mitchel? You can speak freely in this place.' The club was becoming crowded with drinkers and many of them were packed around the bar.

'I've been to the Linenhall Library and a man called Carl Baker has been very helpful. I have *Jail Journal* and other biographical information. It's great to meet someone with the same interest.'

'I know Carl. Great guy. Well, you already know quite a bit. I have some other fairly obscure references which I have had photocopied for you. These are mainly from the late nineteenth century.'

'Excellent. I'm building up quite a library with material which is more interesting than my own study area.'

'Colette said you were some kind of mathematical biologist.'

'Bioinformatics,' said Gus. 'An unfortunate name. Anyway, if you were presenting a pen-portrait of Mitchel, how would you describe him?'

McLean stroked his chin. Then he pulled out notes from an inside pocket. 'In 1885, a journalist called O'Shea collected some pieces together and entitled the result *Leaves from the Life of a Special Correspondent*. He knew Mitchel well and described him as an honest, but hopelessly impractical man. He possessed considerable force of character but O'Shea thought that he was deficient in judgement and with his whole mind warped by an implacable hatred of England...or Carthage as he called it.' McLean looked around him and grinned as he looked away from his notes. 'He would be popular in the bar tonight. O'Shea provides a useful physical description. In appearance Mitchel was 'tall and gaunt, his eyes were grey and piercing, his expression of countenance self-contained, if not saturnine, his features bony and shallow, with an inclining to the tawny tint, high cheeks and determined chin.' Mitchel was a writer of some force. He was also a quick and incisive speaker. Everyone who knew him commented that, in his domestic life, he was one of the gentlest men you could meet.'

'The contrast is puzzling,' said Gus. 'On the one hand he incites violence and yet is a good family man.'

'You would not find it strange if you had lived your life over here. And I'm not just talking about the Republican side. The Rev. Ian Paisley, who many here would say incited men to violence in the early part of the Troubles, is noted for his domestic civility.'

'I'm sure we've had *our* politicians who match in the two categories.'

'Let me go on. Thomas Carlyle, the historian and essayist, met Mitchel in September 1846 and referred to him afterwards as 'a fine elastic-spirited young fellow, whom I grieved to see rushing on destruction palpable, by attack of windmills, but on whom all my persuasions were thrown away.' He also told Mitchel that he would most likely be hanged, but 'they could not hang the immortal part of him.' Recognition I think of an immortal spirit.' McLean laughed. Gus grimaced.

'You can have all these,' said McLean. 'When you've had a chance to look through them, get back to me.' His glass was empty.

Gus rose to order more beer. The bar was thronged with men clutching pints of Guinness. They looked at him with curiosity as he fought his way through to the bar. He felt uncomfortable here but he had to maintain a good relationship with McLean. He sensed that the man knew that there was something else on his mind but Gus had decided to leave it for another time.

'You asked me about *my* interest in Mitchel,' said Gus. 'What attracted you?'

'I've always been curious about Presbyterians who espoused nationalist politics. You don't see it so much these days. Carl Baker will have told you all about them. Men like Henry Joy McCracken – also a freemason by the way – and Thomas Russell, the Man from God Knows Where as he was called. They had a burning sense of injustice and literally spent their lives in the pursuit of freedom from the Brits.'

They finished their beers. McLean offered again but Gus said that he was nervous about being stopped on the way home – something which had not previously worried him. 'You don't mind if I contact you again?'

'Not at all. I must say that I've enjoyed your company. This place can be very parochial. If there's anything else you'd like to talk to me about, give me a call anytime.' They shook hands and Gus left. The bars along the Falls Road were crowded and some drinkers sat outside on the narrow pavement. Gus arrived home and swallowed a glass of Bushmills. He poured another and read to the end of *Jail Journal.*

'In truth, we can hardly speak, for now we pass the Narrows, leave Staten Island behind, and straight before us looms the dense mass of the mighty city, fringed on both sides with forests of masts that stretch away into the blue distance. Hardly less magnificent, the City of Brooklyn crowns its heights, and lines for miles the shores of Long Island with stately buildings. Williamsburg on this side; Jersey City on that – a constellation of cities! – a ganglion of human life!

We come up to the pier. My brother and Meagher step on board to welcome us – we go into a boat, which takes us to a steam-ferry; without entering the city at all, we pass straight over to Brooklyn, where my mother awaits our arrival; and here ends my Journal.'

Gus looked through McLean's file. In early 1854, Mitchel had founded a newspaper in New York. He called it *'The Citizen'* and continued to publish his reflections intermittently until 1866, although his role as general editor had ceased after a year. Thereafter, he had concentrated on farming and lecturing.

Gus rubbed his eyes. Enough of Mitchel for one day. He tried to concentrate on the thread again. Why had Burgess meant him to focus on it? Whoever attacked Eugene Connor had been wearing a military overcoat. Gus tried to establish a connection. Diogenes discovers how to clone humans in the nineteenth century. On a visit to Canada or America, he obtains preserved samples of blood and/or body tissue from Ross. Possibly in Baltimore or Nova Scotia. The latter is freezing for most of the time with icebergs near Halifax throughout the year, apart from mid-summer.

Diogenes is clever enough to know how to transport samples and keep them preserved. He finds a childless couple and persuades them to co-operate. Implantation is successful, the embryo survives to full-term and the woman gives birth. If Diogenes was rich, he might even have brought her with him to Halifax and conducted his experiment in Canada. For whatever reason, he has concentrated on Ross. A military hero. He hopes that the clone will turn out the same.

The child grows up. The clone would not be absolutely identical. The tissue surrounding the nucleus of the egg still belongs to the mother. Diogenes does not know how matters will turn out.

He takes an interest in the boy – assuming it was a boy. Provides him with clothes – second hand perhaps. Military clothes to encourage him to progress in a certain way.

The clone is still alive when the boys make their visit to Warrenpoint. However, everything has not turned out as planned. The new Ross grows up with a sadistic streak which can be misdirected. This leads to the tragedy. Gus drank his last Bushmills.

He turned to Mitchel again. He reminded himself of his twofold interest. The relationship with McLean could lead him to George Connor's son. Another thought struck him. Perhaps Diogenes was more sophisticated than his previous idea of him. Maybe he had cloned Mitchel as well. The Irish Republican was egotistical enough to see the benefits. The scientist had established a helical dance. Two clones with antipathetic backgrounds. Fighting it out on their local patch. Maybe the same woman had even been used twice, thought Gus. Hostile clones with the same mother.

CHAPTER 15

TOWNSEND rang on Saturday morning. 'We've interviewed the four students. Two of them were at home over the period when the threatening messages were sent. Both admitted that they had open access to the computer. We knew that from Jones.'

'And the other two?'

'Both were in the research station when the warnings were sent but say that they were engaged on experimental work at the time and can prove it. They have alibis. Although nervous, it struck me that they were innocent of anything.'

'No progress then?' asked Gus.

'I wouldn't say that. The last student who was interviewed was an exuberant talker. He said that the Serb and the other student – a local fellow called Whitley – were heavy computer users. It could have been either of them.'

'Where is Whitley? I remember you said that the girl was expected back in mid-September.'

'That's correct. She left on July 18th. Whitley has actually finished and been awarded his doctorate. We've found out that he's gone to Australia for three months. Jones has some more funding for him when he comes back in November. Unless we check with his relatives, we won't find out exactly where he is.'

'Are you going to do that?'

'That's rather heavy-handed and could cause all sorts of legal problems. As for the girl, there's nothing we can do about her. No, I think we'll have to sit tight. Let's see if you get any more threats. If you do, we'll track down their source. As for the Serb, we'll probably have to wait for her return.' He rang off.

Gus put down the phone and went to make coffee. He would have to remain in limbo. Lucia knew nothing about the threats and he was worried that they might be followed up when the family was with him. Ed would want to use the computer. Maybe the whole thing was a malicious prank by an anti-American student who wouldn't be back in Ireland for some weeks. It was a small consolation if that was indeed the case.

Last evening's spirit driven thoughts came back to him. There was a blind alley wherever he looked. He needed to find out who Diogenes was. It might be useful to look again at the life of Thomson, *Energy and Empire*. His head cleared as he drove to the Central Library. He found a clear desk, opened the book and looked for connections between Thomson and Darwin.

The index showed two Darwins. There was the more famous Charles Darwin but also George Howard Darwin. The latter was the second son of the distinguished naturalist. G.H. Darwin had been born in Kent in 1845 and died in 1912.

He had graduated from Trinity College, Cambridge in 1868 as Second Wrangler and Second Smith's prizeman. Later that year he was elected a Fellow. By 1873, he had settled in Trinity, having abandoned attempts to read for the Bar as his health deteriorated. Two years later, he noted in his diary that a 'paper on equipotentials was much approved by Sir W.Thomson.' George Darwin's academic activities had come much closer to Thomson's than to his father's.

Soon afterwards, Thomson had reported favourably to the Council of the Royal Society on young Darwin's first major memoir. The physicist's method of assessing research work was sometimes unconventional by modern standards. He liked to meet the author, if it proved convenient, and discuss everything at a personal level.

The two men, Thomson and Darwin, had met for the first time in 1877 and had become good friends. Indeed, the younger man had subsequently become an adopted intellectual son of the eminent natural philosopher.

What he had read so far demonstrated Kelvin's ability to inspire and work with the brightest of research students. If he could do it here, he could do it with anyone.

Gus returned to the older Darwin. An important scientific debate had arisen between the two great men. Charles Darwin's *The origin of species by means of natural selection* had been published in 1859. Darwin had elucidated his theories by a discussion of the valley, known as the Weald of Kent, lying between the North and South Downs of Southeast England. He had assumed that it had resulted from the encroachment of the sea upon the line of chalk cliffs at a rate of one inch in a century. The consequent estimate of geological time provided a specific target for attack by Thomson.

In an article in *Macmillan's Magazine* in 1862, he challenged the theory of natural selection by disagreeing with Darwin's estimate of geological time. He was supported in his attacks by the physicist James Prescott Joule who wrote:

'I am glad you feel disposed to expose some of the rubbish which has been thrust on the public lately. Not that Darwin is so much to blame because I believe he had no intention of publishing any finished theory but rather to indicate difficulties to be solved...It appears that nowadays the public care for nothing unless it be of a startling nature. Nothing pleases them more than parsons who preach against the efficacy of prayer and philosophers who find a link between mankind and the monkey or gorilla – certainly a most pleasing example of what muscular Christianity may lead to.'

The 'denudation of the Weald', as Thomson referred to it, required an estimate of geological time of 300 million years for Darwin's theories to be correct. The physicist believed such an estimate to be a major overestimate. His belief was based on his calculations of the age of the sun's heat and the secular cooling of the earth.

Throughout the period from 1861 until his death in 1907, William Thomson remained staunchly committed, on both religious and practical grounds, to his theories which set time limits to human habitation of the earth. Speaking on the sun's heat to the Royal Institution in 1887, he gave implicit expression to his own underlying regrets that his devotion to science in other fields had diverted him from such grand questions:

'The sun, a mere piece of matter of the moderate dimensions which we know it to have, bounded all round by cold ether, has been doing work at the rate of 476×10^{21} horse-power for 3000 years, and possibly more (than this rate), certainly not much less, for a few million years. How is this to be explained? Natural philosophy cannot evade the question, and no physicist who is not engaged in trying to answer it can have any other justification than that his whole working time is occupied with work on some subject or subjects of his province by which he has more hope of being able to advance science.'

The younger Darwin, while not falling out with Thomson over the controversy, eventually sided with his father on the issue. Despite the strong support of some fellow physicists, the weight of scientific opinion gradually moved away from Thomson – one of the many disputes which he lost in the second half of the nineteenth century.

The first major critique of Thomson's estimate of the sun's age came in 1894-5 from a former pupil John Perry (1850-1920), who had served as a member of Sir William's laboratory corps in the mid-1870's. Perry attacked Thomson's theories regarding the secular cooling of the earth. A lengthy debate ensued in the pages of *Nature*. Perry cited the full support of his friend G.F.Fitzgerald – a physicist from Dublin.

The library closed at midday on Saturday and Gus went home. *Energy and Empire* jumped back and forward in time. Characters such as Fitzgerald flitted in and out of the biography dependent on the latest controversy.

George Francis Fitzgerald had published his first major paper in Nature in 1855 and so must have been approximately the same age as Thomson. This, along with the fact that he was a physicist, probably disqualified him from consideration as Diogenes. However, it again demonstrated the close linkage between Trinity College, Dublin and Glasgow College which became the University of Glasgow in 1870.

Gus fried two eggs and made a sandwich. He washed it down with a mug of tea. Something Arna Breen had said when they first met came back to him. The leaders in current work on cloning comprised a joint team of veterinary and medical scientists in Korea.

There were only seven universities in the United Kingdom and Ireland which provided courses and performed research in veterinary science. At one time, there had been an eighth – Trinity College, Dublin. There were two in Scotland – Glasgow and Edinburgh. The latter had produced Dolly in 1997: a lamb created from a body cell taken from an adult ewe.

Due to the nature of the development of annual production science throughout the twentieth century, it was not surprising that veterinary scientists should lead the way in cloning research. They would not be inhibited by ethics in the same way as medical scientists who wished to develop human clones.

Something else now came back to Gus. The story of Burke and Hare. Gus finished his lunch and switched on the laptop. No messages. No threats. Put it out of your mind, he said to himself. He found an article on the Internet that had been extracted from the London Times.

Trade in cadavers was murder on your health

Trading in the deceased has a long and dishonourable history in Britain, involving grave-robbing and murder. The demand from the early anatomists was for whole cadavers rather than mere parts.

Nowhere was the demand greater than in that foremost centre of medicine, Edinburgh, and no suppliers were more efficient than Burke and Hare.

In the early 19th century the law allowed only the bodies of executed criminals to be used for autopsies. But with the advance of medical research, demand far outstripped supply.

The obvious answer was grave-robbing. Those who practised it were labelled 'resurrectionists' and the graveyard of St Cuthbert's Church in Edinburgh's West End still has examples of the iron cages erected by grieving relatives to ensure that their dearly departed remained in the ground.

But the quality of the merchandise from robbed graves was highly variable, and there was no guarantee of freshness. William Burke and William Hare, two Irish labourers who had come to Scotland to dig canals, had a much better idea. Murder.

They took over a lodging house in the city's West Port area and during the year 1827 claimed 16 victims among the lodgers and visitors. Their technique was simple; ply them with whisky, then suffocate them. Result – a fresh and undamaged corpse.

They found a ready customer in Dr Robert Knox, professor of anatomy at Edinburgh University, who paid them seven pounds ten shillings for their first delivery – considerably more than the £4 rent arrears the hapless victim had owed Burke. For subsequent bodies, the price rose to £10.

Burke and Hare found the trade to be remarkably easy money. They grew greedy: lodgers, prostitutes, beggars were all lured into the boarding house. Greed was their undoing. Neighbours began to notice that several well-known faces from the street had disappeared. Burke and Hare lured two prostitutes into their house; one managed to leave and summon the police, who arrived to find the other's body in a back room awaiting delivery to Dr Knox.

Burke and Hare were arrested. Hare turned King's Evidence and was freed, while Burke was hanged after making a full confession.

Knox was never charged, but he was a marked man; the Edinburgh mob rioted outside his house. His students gradually deserted him, and his reputation so collapsed that he was driven to the ultimate indignity – he moved to Glasgow.

It was mid-August and the evenings were beginning to cool. He lit the peat fire and found Tosca again. The heart-rending voice of Maria Callas soared throughout the room. He fried calf's liver with bacon, boiled cabbage and mashed Kerr's pinks with garlic.

He looked over the Lough and drank the Pauillac which Celia had bought in 1982. Three months had passed since he had arrived in Ireland for the second time. Despite his recent problems, he had decided to stay – perhaps for good.

The idea would have to be sold to Lucia when she arrived in the following week. Apart from that problem there was much to be done. George Connor's son would have to be found. McLean was the guy who could give him the lead. He and his wife must meet with Dr Canavan as soon as possible. The claret glowed in his stomach as the peat died in the hearth. He needed an early night and plenty of fresh air on Sunday.

There was a heavy downpour of rain which drenched the flowerbeds in the quadrangle as he entered the Lanyon Building on Monday morning. Tony Hamilton sported a deep tan. 'I've bought you a present,' he said as he pulled out from underneath his desk a bottle of straw-coloured liquid. 'We were shopping in Dungloe at the weekend when I found this rare bottle of Midleton whiskey from Cork. You don't often see it and I know you like a drop.' He grinned. 'Tell me what you've been up to. This is our only opportunity this week.'

'I don't know where to begin,' said Gus. 'Thanks for the whiskey. I will return the favour.' He told Tony about the e-mail threats. 'The first one came just before I left for Amsterdam. The second one came when I was in Italy. As I hadn't my laptop, I didn't see it until I returned. We'll come back to that problem.'

'Did you meet Burgess?'

'Yes. He sends you his best wishes. I stayed in Italy with my old friend Primo Conti. I managed to establish contact with Burgess and we had lunch near Ravello. He was in better shape than I had expected.'

'Did he give you any indication of what he was doing?'

'Not really,' replied Gus. 'I told him my story about the lost boys. At first, he looked bored and then came alive when I mentioned Kelvin. I never found out the reason. After cognac, we parted. He later sent me a message through Arna Breen. I must concentrate on the thread, it said.'

'Have you seen her again?'

'We'll come to that later. I caught a plane from Naples to London and stayed there for two days. I verified the inscription on Ross in St Paul's Cathedral. Also, I found the military tailors behind Regent Street. When I arrived home, I found the second e-mail threat telling me not to come back. I called the police.'

'What did they think?'

'A guy called Inspector Townsend has been taking an interest. They eventually traced the computer to an Agriculture Research Unit of your University – about three miles from here. In fact, near Burgess's house.'

'I know the place although we don't mix with that crowd. They have a strange reputation.' Tony grinned.

'This brings me back to Arna Breen. At the beginning of August, someone broke into the house and almost raped her. She lashed pepper into his eyes. Also, Burgess rang her. The attacker panicked and fled. She called me and I went over to see her.'

Tony looked surprised. 'Watch yourself. What did the police say this time?'

'Different guys of course. But I told Townsend all about it. Arna Breen is convinced that the attack was linked to my visits.'

Tony groaned. 'You've been having quite a time of it. Anything else?'

'The police think the messages may have been sent by one of two students. One is local. Guy called Whitley. He's finished his thesis and is travelling in Australia. Won't be back until November.'

'What about the other one?'

'A girl from Serbia with a radical reputation. She's gone home but will return next month. The cops will do nothing until they come back.'

'Let's finish this research paper,' said Tony. 'I've done bugger all since Donegal.'

'Hold on for a minute. There's some other stuff I have to tell you. I went down to Rostrevor again and discovered this guy called Mitchel. You remember we talked about a hostile force coming to prevent a Ross clone attacking George Connor?'

'Vaguely yes.'

'I'm only speculating. I've done quite a bit of research on the guy. I've also met a guy called Basil McLean who's helped me with it.'

'Where is all this leading?'

'I said previously that I was speculating. However, chance has led me to someone whom I think can help me track down George Connor's son.'

'You will have to be very careful.' Tony grimaced.

'Everyone tells me that. I have no choice. My boy's life may depend on it. By the way, the family are arriving on Wednesday.'

'I told Emma. When they've had a chance to settle in, you'll have to come out for dinner. Perhaps Saturday evening?'

'That would be fine. OK. Let's start.' Gus had decided not to discuss any more of his recent theories with Tony. Not until he had something more to go on. They worked throughout the afternoon to finish their research paper. When he got home, Gus checked his voicemail. A message to ring Townsend.

'We called late this afternoon but you were out,' said the Inspector. 'I had wanted to speak to you personally. However, I'm tied up with another matter for the rest of the week so I'll have to tell you now. I wanted to talk to you about that other business.'

'George Connor's son?'

'Yes. We believe the suspect who bears a resemblance was going under the name of Patrick Tohill. I shouldn't really have told you that. But you'd have probably found out anyway from what I've been hearing about you. I must warn you again to be careful. This is not a game.'

CHAPTER 16

LUCIA was standing by the luggage carousel. He appraised the white trainers, blue jeans and white blouse. Her hair had been dyed a lighter shade of blond and was cut short. Gus came up behind her and put his arms around her waist. Startled, she turned and smiled.

'Sorry I'm late,' he said. 'One thing you will notice about this country is the amount of roadwork on main routes. The cabdriver was on fire. He said that they are put in place automatically when you're behind schedule. Where's the kids?'

'They've gone to the bathroom,' she replied. 'You're looking more Irish since I last saw you.' She inspected his corduroy trousers, brown brogues and faded blue shirt. 'Here they come.'

Gus hugged them both. Kay looked older and resembled her mother. Ed seemed to have grown taller. His face was thin and he looked drained.

At the exit to the terminal he hailed a cab. Rain pelted from a grey sky as they hurried inside.

'What you notice about this country is the green everywhere,' said Kay as they drove towards Belfast. 'Quite a change from Ohio.'

'Everyone says that on their first visit,' said the cabdriver beside her. 'It's all this rain we get.'

The roadworks had disappeared and they arrived within half-an-hour.

'Would you like me to make you something to eat?' asked Gus. 'I've got everything in.'

'I think we all need a rest,' said Lucia. 'We didn't sleep much on the overnight plane from New York. I was seated beside this guy from Manhattan who never stopped talking.'

He showed Kay and Lucia to their bedrooms. Ed checked out the television. Gus demonstrated the computer system. 'How you feeling?' he asked. 'Mom said you'd had a few problems.'

At first, his son did not answer and then mumbled 'I'm OK. I'll just try this out for a while and then lie down and get some rest.' His eyes drooped after a few minutes and Gus told ordered him to bed.

The house was silent. Gus fried bacon and crumbled it with softly cooked onions. He mixed in diced potato leftover from his evening dinner, whisked fresh eggs and cooked them gently until they set. He added wild parsley and chives.

Nobody stirred until late afternoon. He heard the shower being switched on. Shortly afterwards, Lucia entered the room, her hair wet and combed back.

'The house has great views,' she said. 'I woke with a start and sat looking across the bay after the rain had stopped. I'm not surprised you've settled in here so well. Too well I think.' She glanced across at him and then at the simmering fire. 'That's a beautiful smell.' The wind blew down the chimney and the peaty smoke whooshed across the hearth.

'We'll maybe go out later and I'll show you around.' He could see what was on her mind.

'You haven't spoken again to Dr Canavan?'

'I'm going to do that first thing in the morning. But we'll have to tell the kids what we're doing. We can't keep hiding it any longer.'

'I realise that,' said Lucia. 'I always feel guilty that this is the only way forward. That there's nobody on my side of any benefit.'

'We've been over this a million times. You only found out that they weren't your real parents after your mother died.'

'After Dad passed away, she could have told me.'

'People get themselves in a major bind with their secrets. The longer it goes on, the harder it becomes to tell the truth. I know it was harsh finding it all out from a document hidden in the back of a cupboard.'

'You know how I feel. How anyone would feel about it. The trail had gone cold. I'll never know who my real parents were.'

'Maybe someone will come forward one of these days,' sighed Gus. 'I know we can't depend on it.'

'OK. I'll try and be positive. We'll tell the kids this evening and you arrange for us to meet Dr Canavan.' Her eyes dulled. 'Perhaps it will all be a waste of time.'

'You're jet-lagged,' said Gus. 'I'll make you some tea. It'll revive you.'

'How's everything else over here?' she asked. 'I sense you've been preoccupied and you're not telling me everything that you've been doing.'

Gus thought of what he had said earlier, but he didn't want to ruin their vacation. 'I admit that I sometimes forget to tell you things. But I've told you everything that's important. I think I've got a lead on George Connor's son.'

'I know you said he might be a terrorist of some kind. Where's that going to get you?'

'It may be our only chance. What else can I do? I have to take the risk.' He told her about McLean and what he had found out from the police. The full story was kept back. 'You said to *be* positive. Let's be positive.'

'I'm sorry. I guess you're right.' She finished her tea. 'As a matter of fact, I did check out some things for you about this guy Ross. The man who is supposed to have attacked your cousins. I caught the train to Washington last weekend and visited friends in Maryland who were helpful. They faxed me some stuff before we left. I have it for you upstairs.'

Gus smiled. 'It can wait. Let's wake the kids. We'll take a stroll. I've prepared something to eat for later. Just needs warmed up.'

'You've become very house trained.' Lucia brightened and smiled. She went upstairs and knocked at their bedroom doors. Then Gus took his wife for a stroll around the neighbourhood. When they came back, Ed was on the Internet and Kay lay sprawled in front of the peat fire.

They all had beers and Gus prepared dinner. He had not given Ed password access to his own e-mailbox so that, even if a threat came through, only he would know. That morning, he had prepared a stew with baby lamb chops, small onions, carrots, stock and organic potatoes from the Glens of Antrim. He heated it up and added parsley and chives.

'Would you like some Italian wine?' he asked. 'Aunt Celia's favourite.' The kids stayed with beer and Lucia chose wine. Afterwards, Kay watched television and Ed returned to the computer. Lucia and Gus finished the wine by the fire. The three went to bed and Gus scanned the file on Ross.

Clipped to the front was a faxed letter addressed to Lucia from a friend called Laura in Maryland. He read that Laura's father was a veteran from the Second World War and had always been interested in military history.

The clippings had been cut and pasted from different sources. Gus rearranged the material to fit chronologically with his previous knowledge of Major-General Robert Ross.

In May 1814, the British government had decided to send four brigades of infantry from the Duke of Wellington's army to America and

Canada. Three went to the latter and an expeditionary force, commanded by Ross, was to attack the coasts of the United States. He embarked on June 1st 1814. His mission was 'to retaliate upon the Americans for the outrages which they had committed upon the frontiers.' The force consisted of three battalions, to which a fourth was added at Bermuda, bringing up its total strength to 3400 men.

The combined naval and military force entered the Chesapeake, sailed up the Patuxent, and on August 19th the troops were landed at Benedict. Including a strong battalion of marines, their total number was about 4,500 men; they had three light guns and some rockets.

An American flotilla had taken refuge in the upper water of the Patuxent, and an attack upon this flotilla served to cover an approach to the capital. While the boats of the fleet moved up the river, the troops marched up the right bank to Upper Marlborough. The American commodore, having no means of escape, blew up his vessels. Ross then struck inland, and marched on Washington by way of Bladensburg, a distance of about twenty-eight miles. At Bladensburg he found the United States troops drawn up on high ground behind a branch of the Potomac – 6,500 men, mostly militia, with twenty-six guns, worked by the sailors of the flotilla. There were about five hundred dragoons; while Ross had no horsemen except some fifty artillery drivers who had been mounted on such horses as could be found. His troops had to defile over a bridge swept by the fire of the enemy's guns. But he attacked without hesitation. After three hours' fighting the Americans, pressed on both flanks as well as in front, broke and fled, taking shelter in the woods, and leaving ten of their guns behind. The British loss was 250 men, and Ross himself had a horse shot under him.

The same evening (August 24th) he pushed on to Washington. On his approach to reconnoitre a few shots were fired, and he again narrowly escaped, his horse being killed. Otherwise no resistance was made. 'So unexpected was our entry and capture of Washington,' he wrote, 'and so confident was Madison of the defeat of our troops, that he had prepared a supper for the expected conquerors; and when our advanced party entered the President's house, they found a table laid with forty covers.' In the course of that night and the next day all the public buildings – the halls of congress, the supreme court, the public offices, including the national archives and library – were burnt. The arsenal and dockyard, with the vessels under construction in it, had already been set on fire by the Americans themselves. Their destruction was completed; and the great bridge over the Potomac was also burnt. Private property was scrupulously respected, with the exception of the house from which the shots had been fired. The following night the troops began their march back to their ships. It was not interfered with, and they re-embarked on the 30th.

Of this expedition, an historian of the time, Jomini wrote: 'To the great astonishment of the world, a handful of seven or eight thousand English were seen to land in the middle of a state of ten million inhabitants, and penetrate far enough to get possession of the capital, and destroy all the public buildings; results for a parallel to which we should search history in vain. One would be tempted to set it down to the republican and unmilitary spirit of those states, if we had not seen the militia of Greece, Rome, and Switzerland make a better defence of their homes against far more powerful attacks, and if in this same year another and more numerous English expedition had not been totally defeated by the militia of Louisiana under the orders of General Jackson.' The United States government had had ample warning that an attempt on Washington was contemplated. General Armstrong, the Secretary of War, who had made light of it, was forced by the subsequent public outcry to resign. Changed times, thought Gus.

He stirred in the early morning light. For the first time in three months, they lay together. Lucia tossed and turned. He sensed that she was half-awake. A tentative hand reached out and he reciprocated. They knew each other well after all these years and the movements, though familiar, were still exciting to them. They made love and the climaxes came quickly for it had been a long time.

Gus made breakfast and took it to her on a tray. 'Ed didn't react too much when I told him,' he said. 'It'll sink in today. Kay got a little excited.'

'He needed to know that there was some hope if things got bad,' said Lucia. 'But we're not out of the woods yet by a long chalk.'

'I'll ring Canavan's office now and see if I can obtain an appointment.' He returned to say that the doctor would see them on Monday afternoon.'

'I hope that we can get some progress before we go back in two weeks.'

'Remind me of your arrangements.'

'We're leaving here on August 27th and are flying to New York from London Heathrow two days later. You said you could arrange accommodation for us in London.'

'No problem. I'll fix something up.' He woke Ed and Lucia but nobody surfaced until midday.

In the afternoon, he showed them around Belfast. They were apprehensive but thawed when they saw that it was thronged with shoppers and workers going about their business. They admired the City Hall and they called on Carl Baker. 'Mr Baker has been a great help to me.' Gus stood behind them and put a forefinger to his lips.

In the evening, Gus barbecued fillet steaks and Lucia mixed a Caesar salad. He took them on his evening walk as far as Bellevue Zoo. 'I guess you're a little old now for a visit,' he said smiling. 'I always intend paying it one but I've never managed it. They thought that the setting of Belfast was magnificent and determined to make a trip to the summit of Cavehill. On their return, they went to bed early. Gus finished the wine and on an impulse phoned McLean.

This time McLean answered. 'Sorry to call you so late,' said Gus. 'But you did say that you wouldn't mind meeting again.'

'Call up tomorrow night if you like. I suspect there's something else you'd like to talk about.' Gus admitted that there was and that he would appreciate it if McLean could help. They agreed to meet as they had done on the previous Friday night. Gus had hoped that a change of venue might be suggested but McLean did not offer. He appeared reluctant to leave his own neighbourhood.

At breakfast, he told them that he had an appointment that evening on a research matter. Lucia looked at him suspiciously. 'It's that guy I was telling you about,' he said. Ed and Lucia did not appear interested. In the afternoon they walked up Cavehill and had an early dinner in Belfast Castle, part of which had been converted into a restaurant complex.

Gus knew the route better this time but continued to feel nervous as he entered the club. There were fewer customers than before and he felt that they were watching him. He bought pints of Smithwicks. McLean cleared half of his first pint in a gulp and smiled. 'How are you getting on with our friend Mitchel?' he asked.

'I finished *Jail Journal* last week and had a look at some of your file. My wife and family came over on Wednesday and so I haven't got much further.'

'You know that he founded a second American newspaper called the *Southern Citizen*? From 1857 to 1859. Very controversial and a part of his life which mystifies me.'

'Why was that?' asked Gus.

'Well...given his previous staunch efforts for Irish freedom from the Brits, it never squared with me. He became opposed to the abolition of slavery and his second newspaper defended the interests of the slaveholders. Before moving to Washington, he initially published it in Knoxville, Tennessee.'

'I find that strange myself.'

'Yes. You often find it with a certain type of Irishman who has moved to England or America. A talent for racism. I digress. Mitchel went to Paris for a year but returned to America before the Civil War. He wanted to fight for the Confederates but was disqualified due to his poor eyesight. After the war, he went to New York and became editor of the *Daily News*. He continued to publish articles in defence of the Southern cause. In fact, at one point, he was arrested by the military and confined for five months in a place called Fortress Monroe.'

'I've heard of it.'

'I'll stop there. I always get carried away when I talk about Mitchel. You wanted to talk about something else?'

'It's not entirely unconnected. I told you that I was in Rostrevor purely for tourist reasons. That wasn't quite true.'

He told McLean enough of what he needed to know. His speculations on cloning were left out. McLean stroked his chin and then finished his drink. 'You'll have another pint?'

'One more. One of these days the cops are going to stop me.' McLean left to fetch the drinks.

'So. You think Patrick Tohill is your cousin and you want a kidney? A tall order.' McLean grinned.

'Do you know him?'

'I might,' answered McLean. He looked around the bar and lowered his voice. 'I'll need to think about it. We can't talk here.' He nodded at a passing acquaintance.

'I understand,' said Gus. 'Perhaps you could get back to me.' He changed the subject. 'What did Mitchel do when he was released from Fortress Monroe?'

'He went back to Paris as a financial agent for the Fenian Brotherhood which was based there at the time but he returned to the US at the end of 1866. Shortly afterwards, he was offered the post of Chief Executive Officer for the Brotherhood in America but refused it. By this time, he was at loggerheads with all his political friends at home and abroad. He then edited another newspaper in New York called the *Irish Citizen* but stopped when his health gave way in 1872.'

'And after that?'

'He returned to Ireland the same year. You should already have all that in the file I gave you.'

Gus saw that McLean had become preoccupied with Tohill – or so he hoped. They finished their drinks. Gus said that he would have to be getting back or the family would be getting worried.

'It might be wise to leave now. The Troubles may have ended but you don't want to be wandering around too late at this time of year. I'll give you a call. Nice to meet you again.'

CHAPTER 17

ED had risen early and worked on the computer as Gus made breakfast. They had been asleep when he returned from his visit to McLean. Gus looked over his son's shoulder and saw that he was working on a spreadsheet. He had always encouraged an interest in mathematics. A polite enquiry solicited no response for some minutes.

'At the end of the school year,' he replied, 'our maths teacher was telling us about prime numbers...those which are only divisible by themselves or one. Some of the guys weren't too interested until he started to talk about the applications. He mentioned a film called *Enigma* based on a book by a Brit called Harris.'

'I've read it. It's all about code-breaking during the Second World War. At a place called Bletchley Park in England.'

'A group of mathematicians was employed to break the German codes which gave away the movements of their U-boats. Cryptography I believe it's called. Our maths teacher said that it was based on a real life team from that era.'

'I believe it was,' said Gus. 'What exactly are you doing?'

'You probably know that cryptography involves scrambling secret messages so they can only be unscrambled by a receiver and not by anybody else who might intercept them.'

'Yes,' replied Gus. 'The process needs a secret key. Unscrambling the message requires the receiver to apply the key in reverse. Keep going.'

'So the key is the weakest link in the chain of security. The sender and the receiver have to agree on the details of the key. The exchange of the information is risky. If an enemy can intercept the key being exchanged, then they can unscramble all the new messages. Also, the keys have to be regularly changed in order to maintain security. Each time this happens, there is always the risk of the new key being intercepted.'

'Yes. It's coming back to me. The problem of the key revolves around the fact that the application of it one way will scramble the message – unscrambling a message is almost as easy as scrambling it. However, there are many situations when unscrambling is harder than scrambling. It's easy to scramble an egg but unscrambling it is far harder.'

Lucia came up behind them. 'Come on you guys,' she said. 'I've made breakfast. Bacon and eggs, as it happens.' She smiled.

Kay did not appear and the three ate breakfast together. Ed ate quickly and returned to the computer.

'He's eating well,' said Lucia. 'The fresh air over here must be doing him some good.'

'Maybe what we told him has made a difference,' said Gus.

'How did you get on with Mr McLean?'

'I told him most of the story. He seemed to know Patrick Tohill. He's going to get back to me. Wants to think it over.'

'I don't blame him. I don't know whether to feel good or bad about this whole business.'

Kay came into the kitchen and Lucia prepared her breakfast. Gus returned to the computer. 'I don't want to interrupt you but perhaps we could finish our conversation.'

Ed paused. 'Some guys in the 1970's came up with the idea of looking for a mathematical process which was easy to perform in one direction but extremely difficult to perform in the opposite direction. A process like that gives you an almost perfect key. I wouldn't mind anyone knowing the scrambling half of my key. However, only I would know the unscrambling half.'

'I remember some guys at MIT made some breakthrough on this,' said Gus. 'Over twenty years ago I think.'

'Correct. That's what I've been looking at on the computer. They realised that prime numbers are the ideal basis for the whole process. Take two enormous primes and multiply them together to achieve an even higher number which, of course, is not prime. Knowledge of the latter gives you the ability to scramble messages.'

'But to unscramble them,' Gus burst in, 'you would need to know the two original primes.'

'Exactly. Anyone may know the new big number, but only I know the two primes which made it. For someone to work them out is not easy, especially if you have a really large number.'

'I see. Even with a fairly small number I know it's not easy. Let me think. If I gave someone the number 221, it's not obvious that the two relevant primes are 17 and 13 i.e. $17 \times 13 = 221$.'

'Yes, but for that example, I could quickly work it out on this computer. That's in fact what I've been doing this morning. But for really big numbers this computer can't do it. It's not powerful enough. I think that you would need a giant computer to work out the right primes if you had a number with a hundred digits. So not everyone could unscramble your message. Then you make matters even more difficult by changing the number on a regular basis.'

Gus returned to the kitchen. 'Ed's really getting into mathematics. Looks like he'll be there for the rest of the day.'

'What time are we due for dinner tonight at Tony's?' asked Lucia.

'We're not expected until seven-thirty. Is there anything you'd like to do today?'

'Kay and I thought we'd do some more shopping. I doubt if you or Ed will be attracted to that idea.'

'Sounds good. There's some things I'd like to work on before this evening. Also, McLean just might ring.'

The discussion about keys had struck a chord in Gus's mind. He thought again about Burgess who had, according to Arna Breen, been interested in the key transformations involved in the cloning process.

Cloning involved the creation of a twin or copy of an individual by replacing the nucleus of an unfertilised ovum with the nucleus of a cell from that individual. The ovum is then stimulated to create an embryo. No sperm is involved. The person created has no genetic father. Nor does it have a genetic mother in the normal sense of the term: the only genetic material supplied by the woman whose ovum was used (unless she cloned herself) are the genes outside the nucleus.

Gus circled the room. In view of the latter genes – which don't come from the nucleus – the clone will not be a perfect genetic copy of the nucleus provider. He knew that cloning itself can cause genetic changes, in addition to those changes which occur naturally as the embryo matures. Differences in environment between the clone and the original will lead to differences in the clone's structure and behaviour.

Maybe his Bushmills driven thoughts of last week were not so crazy after all. Diogenes came into his mind again. The man would have to be at least ten years younger than Thomson, probably more...say fifteen. Let's say 1840 is his date of birth. He is at the peak of his powers between 1870 – 1890. Even Thomson's abilities had decreased significantly in the later part of his life. If Diogenes had discovered how to clone, he might have persuaded Mitchel to co-operate. Mitchel had believed in racial superiority. If he had lived in the twentieth century, his

119

racial views and his anti-Britishness could have made him sympathetic to the Germans.

The great felon had returned to Ireland in 1872 and died in 1875. Supposing the scientist had met him before his death and put the plan to him. Got him to agree. The clone would be in his late thirties in 1914 and would most probably be living in the right region.

His mind was clearer. Of course. Burgess had been interested in the transformations which occurred during the cloning process and so had *Diogenes*. You would need to have replication in such an experiment in order to make this possible.

Diogenes would have been fortunate to attract one woman in those days to co-operate with him – never mind two. Replication on that front would have been extremely difficult. It was indeed more likely that, if the first experiment was a success, the same woman would be approached a second time.

Mitchel could have been cloned in 1875 and Ross as late as ten years later, although this timing was only because of the date of the Baltimore Lectures given by Thomson in 1884. *Diogenes* could have obtained the necessary Ross samples in the late 1860's, performed his first experiment with the General and followed up a few years later with Mitchel.

Gus thought again of that morning's conversation with Ed about the keys. The two primes were the surrogate father and mother. The clone was the unique outcome. Burgess needed to know what differences there might be in the two unique outcomes. *Diogenes*, ahead of his time, had grasped the essence of the problem. Furthermore, he had the money, the ability and the lack of a conscience to perform the experiment. He must talk to Burgess again. He heard Lucia and Kay return.

Gus made the introductions as they entered Tony's. His son, Paul, fetched drinks. Ed had a Coke and everyone else tried Tony's finest white burgundy. Emma and Lucia warned them to keep off scientific subjects and everyone relaxed. Gus had brought two bottles of Fleurie and he insisted that Tony open them when he heard they were having rib-eye steaks.

'I'm trying to cut down on the whiskey,' said Gus. 'And so I haven't tried your Midleton yet.'

Tony laughed. Lucia looked at Gus. 'I found several empty bottles of Bushmills in a box outside the house. I warned him before he came over that he must cut down. Did he ever tell you how his mother died?'

Everyone tensed. 'I don't believe he did,' said Tony. 'He's told me all about the Connor side of the family. Any progress on all that?'

'We're going to see Dr Canavan on Monday afternoon,' said Gus, relieved that the subject had changed. He hated discussing his mother's death. 'He has no clearance to tell us anything but he's going to help us appeal the decision. I also have a firmer lead on George Connor's son.' He told them what he could. Tony had been tipped off not to mention the warnings.

After dinner, Emma showed Lucia around the house. Paul, Ed and Kay had beers while the two men finished their wine. 'You still haven't told them about the warnings?' said Tony.

'No. I don't want to spoil things. I'll wait and see what happens when the two students return.'

'Townsend was right. I don't know what can of worms you've opened. Let's change the subject. Young Ed seems keen on mathematics. That's nice to see. He's a good lad. It must be a tremendous source of worry to you two.'

'Lucia hides it but I know it's a permanent strain. I know everyone is advising me to watch my step but I've got to go on. I must find out who was responsible for the death of Eugene Connor and I'm determined to meet Patrick Tohill.'

'What about this Ross business?'

'I've been turning it around in my mind,' answered Gus. 'Lucia got hold of some material on his time in America. I haven't finished reading it yet. I've reached as far as August 1814. By that time, he is in command of a force which has attacked America, and wins a major victory in Bladensburg – the one that made his name. When I stopped reading, he had taken control of the White House and demolished many of Washington's finest buildings. President Madison had fled.'

'Hard to imagine that happening these days,' said Tony. 'The army would not have been able to reach dry ground in the first place.'

'He was a fantastically motivated character. If you wanted him on your side in a battle, he was a good man to clone.'

'You're still running with that?'

'That and Mitchel.' Gus told him about his latest speculations. 'I really need to talk to Burgess again.'

'You can only do that through Arna Breen. Does Lucia know about her?'

'I haven't mentioned it. Might give her the wrong idea. I guess I'll just have to leave it until the end of the month.'

Lucia yawned as she returned with Emma. 'I think it's time we were getting back. What are you two conspiring about?' She let it pass.

Paul said that he had made some arrangements for Ed and Kay in the following week. 'I'd like to show them a bit of nightlife. It's not as dead in this country as you might think.' Tony rang for a cab and they returned to the place Gus called home.

He checked the answering machine. A message to ring McLean. Nothing else. It was too late to ring back. When he tried the following morning, his wife said that he had gone down South for two days. He was not expected back until Monday evening.

Gus had hired a black Ford Mondeo for the week. The appointment with Canavan was not until mid-afternoon. Gus decided to repeat some of his previous itinerary. They left early for the North Coast. The sky was blue with no clouds. The Lough sparkled as the sea made its way along the North Channel to Scotland. It was Monday morning in high summer and the road was deserted.

They stopped in Carnlough and had salmon sandwiches in the Londonderry Arms. They read that it had once been owned by Winston Churchill. After lunch, they turned back. Gus had decided that there was one important place they had to see before their appointment with Dr Canavan.

He drove along the road from Larne looking for the correct left fork. The Ballygowan Road twisted at an acute angle to the main route. He parked on a grass verge beside the narrow road.

They entered by a little black gate at the side of the cemetery. The chapel doors were locked. He took them to headless gravestones behind the church. The poplars dwarfed the stone walls beside Eugene Connor's grave.

'I don't understand fully our relationship with him. Tell me again,' said Kay. 'It all came as a shock to me on Thursday evening.'

Gus explained it all to them once more. The background to Eugene's mysterious death and the reason for their visit to Dr Canavan who had under his care the brother of the boy who lay in the grave in front of them.

Lucia glanced at Ed. His face showed no expression. The boy in the grave was not much younger than him when he had died. A wasted life, Gus thought again. Tears brimmed in Kay's eyes. It was time to go. He noticed the adjacent farm. In the distance, cows grazed the lush late summer pasture. On the other side of the cemetery wall, he saw the vibrant garden, the leafy potato stems and the apple trees coming to full blossom. He did not mention the fat juicy earthworms and their subterranean journey to nourish the land. Father Campbell had never contacted him again. Gus reversed the Mondeo with difficulty and drove them to their appointment at the hospital.

As they entered, he saw them look with anxiety at the man with no shoes who stood smoking in front of Reception. Gus hurried them up to the ward and Canavan's office. The doctor introduced himself and explained that he was available to help them in any way possible.

'You appreciate that the matter is out of my hands,' he said. 'Men have been struck off for less.'

'We appreciate that,' answered Gus. 'And we're very grateful that you're taking the time to see us. My family return to the States next week and this is their only chance.'

'You know that my speciality is mental health although I'm qualified in general medicine and have the contacts to do whatever is required if I have the go-ahead.'

'Can you advise us on a constructive way forward?' asked Lucia. 'It is driving me out of my mind. Sorry, you know what I mean. We need to know.'

'I don't want to be negative. On the contrary. But the only way to break the logjam is for you to establish contact with George's son. I realise that this may be risky. If he's a reformed character…and we don't know for certain that he's ever done anything evil…it might be productive.'

'As a matter of fact,' said Gus, 'I think I've learnt his name although I'm not certain. Don't tell me to be careful. I've made up my mind.'

Canavan raised his eyebrows and sighed. 'I understand. I understand. I speak as a friend. If we had proof of the identity, he might be able to obtain access to the necessary records. You never know. He might be prepared to help you out.'

'How is George by the way?' asked Gus. 'We'd like to see him if that's possible.'

'I'll get the nurse to take you to him. But don't build up your hopes. In my opinion, he's going rapidly downhill. That's not to say he can't be jolted out of it. We can but try. Let's go.' The old man had fallen asleep in his chair. The egg-like head was slumped in his chest. There was nothing to do but leave.

They shook hands with Canavan who said that he hoped he would hear from them soon. He looked at Gus and asked him back to his office where he retrieved the small package.

Gus always checked the voicemail personally. McLean had rung from the South. He had left a message on the answering machine: 'The Eagle has landed in Dublin. The bird will sing for you at a price. You will receive a letter from me telling you what to do. When you've heard this message, erase it. Happy hunting.'

CHAPTER 18

MITCHEL returned to Ireland in 1872, initially for a short visit. The government did not interfere with him. He established new relationships and renewed old ones – not always to his benefit.

He went back to America and maintained his contacts in Britain and Ireland. In the General Election of February 1874, he was nominated as a Home Rule candidate to represent Tipperary at Westminster. He agreed, no doubt remembering the Rising at Ballingarry and Killenaule. Mitchel was not successful on this occasion.

However, in the following February, another General Election was held. Although in America, Mitchel stood unopposed and was elected to Westminster. He landed shortly afterwards at Queenstown, Cork with the intention of fully representing his constituents.

Disraeli himself prevented it. He proposed a motion in Parliament declaring Mitchel 'incapable of being elected or returned as a member' on the ground of his being a convicted felon. The motion was carried and a new writ ordered.

Mitchel was again returned by 2368 votes over a Conservative opponent, Stephen Moore. In his address of thanks to the electors, he once more declared his intention of 'discrediting and exploding the fraudulent pretence of Irish representation by declining to attend the sittings of parliament.'

It was Tuesday afternoon. Lucia and Kay had left on a shopping expedition. Ed was surfing the Internet. Gus studied the Mitchel file. He knew what was coming up next.

It had been difficult to concentrate throughout the day. The message from McLean refused to shift from the back of his brain. He turned the possibilities around in his head. When the letter arrived, how should he handle its contents? What was the point of speculating until he saw what was in it? Butterflies floated in his stomach. How soon would it be before he could meet Tohill? He opened a beer and gulped it down.

He decided to tell Ed. Lucia knew but had asked him to wait. He pulled up a chair alongside the computer. 'Son...there's something I'd like to talk to you about. Can you break off for a few minutes? It's important.'

'Sure Dad.' Ed logged off the PC. 'The prime numbers can wait.'

'They go on for ever as you know.' Gus smiled. 'Mom and I told you on Thursday about relatives that we have over here. Well, there's been a development despite the lack of progress on Monday with Dr Canavan.'

'What's happened?'

'The guy who I went to see on Friday night appears to have established a link with Patrick Tohill. You remember – the old man's son.'

'Difficult to forget. What exactly do you hope to get out of all this? I'm not too sure.'

'There are no easy solutions to life's difficulties, Ed. I don't know myself where it's all going to lead. I'm hoping that I can buy my way out of all this. If your health deteriorated, I like to think that there might be some option open to us. I have to try.'

Gus returned to the Mitchel files. Even if Ed never had a recurrence of serious kidney trouble, he knew that he would have to find out what had happened to the Connors.

The authorities had planned a petition against Mitchel being returned to parliament. Before it could be presented, Mitchel had become ill and died suddenly at Dromalane outside Newry on March 20th 1875. He was fifty-nine years of age.

Mitchel was buried three days later in the Unitarian cemetery in High Street, Newry. His widow had subsequently erected a monument to his memory. Two months later, in May 1875, the Irish court of common pleas decided that Mitchel, being both an alien and a convicted felon, had not been duly elected to parliament. Stephen Moore was returned in his place.

Gus drank a second beer. He had forgotten about Mitchel's wife and children. He found *Jail Journal* again and the relevant passages about their arrival in Australia after landing at Adelaide. Also the subsequent flight from Australia to San Francisco on the *Julia Ann*. It was not clear how many of them there had been.

He rang Carl Baker. There existed a variety of rarer books on the life of Mitchel. Many of these, Baker said, had not been consulted for over ten years. 'Don't go to any great trouble,' said Gus. 'I wanted some basic family details.' He guessed that the window of opportunity for *Diogenes* would have been a narrow one. They could have met socially on Mitchel's first return visit to Ireland and become reacquainted after Mitchel's election.

Baker rang back in the late afternoon. 'Mitchel had six children, three sons and three daughters. There is a paucity of information about the daughters. As regards the sons, the story is tragic. They all fought on the Confederate side during the American Civil War. The eldest was killed at Fort Sumter and the youngest at Gettysburg. The second son lost his right arm at one of the battles around Richmond, Virginia.'

'Have we any evidence of how Mitchel reacted to these tragedies? Life certainly dealt him some terrible blows.'

'I might be able to track something down. The only other family detail I have is that he had a sister, Henrietta, who married his old friend John Martin.'

There was a massive incentive for a man like Mitchel, in his late fifties, to agree to the cloning project. Whatever his faults, he had never lacked daring and courage. He would have been acutely aware of his own mortality and here was a unique opportunity to leave an Irish heir just like himself. Someone who could be relied upon to maintain the fight against the Brits in the crucial years ahead.

The letter from McLean arrived in the following morning's post. Basil apologised for the melodrama. He had gone to visit his brother in Dublin and decided to stay for a week. He stressed that there could be no possibility of revealing how contact with Tohill had been made.

The letter went on to say that the Eagle would be in a certain hotel on Friday afternoon and was prepared to meet him. Gus was to ring the enclosed number at a certain time on Thursday evening if he wished to proceed with the arrangement.

He showed the letter to Lucia and they discussed it over lunch. There was no alternative. He had to go. They discussed it with Kay and Ed. It was agreed that Gus would ring the number. They could all travel to Dublin on Friday.

They set off early. At nine o'clock, they got out of the Mondeo and he brought them to the giant obelisk. The grass around it was heavy. There was a chill in the air from Carlingford Lough. They saw white horses rising faintly in the seawater. The insects from early summer had gone. A solitary bluebottle buzzed around its target.

'What does PIRA mean?' asked Kay. 'It's eerie how silent it is round here. I can imagine how it would appear on a cold dark night to a young boy.' Gus told her what the initials stood for. They stopped for coffee in Rostrevor and he showed them around Kilbroney Parish Church.

'Amazing to find that a US battle from long ago is commemorated in this small church,' said Lucia. 'Who could have guessed it?'

Gus brought them to see St Bronach's Bell and told them the story of its background. 'Apparently it could foretell doom but chose to keep quiet when it suited.' Gus smiled ruefully.

'Maybe it attempted to warn the boys that night,' said Kay. 'This whole place is spooky. Let's go.'

He persuaded them to visit the Mission Convent. 'You can see why they called it TopsyTurvy House,' he said. 'Ross's descendants used to live here. I think it must have been his son – Sir John Ross – who planted all these shrubs and evergreens.'

Time was pressing and they drove around Kilbroney House. Lucia pointed out the entrance to a Fairy Glen. Gus said that it would have to wait for another day. One which he knew might never come for her.

The black Mondeo crossed the border and they reached the main route for Dublin. The traffic was heavy as he negotiated his way around a complex series of roundabouts near Dundalk. Roadworks were everywhere. The route then improved and they reached the outskirts of Dublin before one o'clock.

The city was gridlocked. At least in Columbus, the morning traffic moved. They inched towards the centre of Dublin and reached O'Connell Street. After a succession of wrong turns, they found St Stephen's Green and a parking slot. Gus fed the machine with coins engraved with a horse. They had a light lunch.

'What did the person say again?' asked Lucia.

'Not much. The Shelbourne Hotel at three o'clock. Introduce yourself at Reception. It's nearly time.' They agreed to meet at the car at five o'clock. They left to shop and see the sights.

Gus entered a lavish room festooned with antique chairs and tables. He ordered a pot of coffee and waited. Two couples sat back with drinks. He could have used one himself but decided to keep his head clear. A man's voice drifted softly across to him as he told the others of his recent trip to Galway.

Fifteen minutes later, he felt a tap on his shoulder. He turned to see a man who appeared to be about fifteen years older than himself. The man was several inches shorter than Gus and was well-dressed. He noted the dark blue suit and polished black shoes.

'Gus McWilliams I assume,' said Patrick Tohill in a harsh northern accent. 'I hear we may be related and you'd like to talk to me.' He sat in the chair opposite Gus and poured coffee.

Gus had decided to be as cagey as possible until he was surer of his ground. Tohill had grown jowlier since the time of the Warrenpoint photograph. Gus looked at the thinning black hair and was reminded of George Connor.

Gus finished his coffee and began the story of how he had come to be here.

'I was in hospital many years ago and met a boy who turned out to be my cousin. His name was Bill Connor. I've never met him since.' He paused and rubbed the sweat at the top of his forehead. 'His father was called Mike Connor. My own father was called John McWilliams and his father was Thomas McWilliams. My grandfather's sister was named Jane and she married Mike's father – a man called William Connor.' Patrick Tohill stroked his chin. Gus could see the gears changing in his mind. He extracted his passport as proof of identity.

'It's OK,' said Tohill. 'You don't need to show me that. You've been checked out carefully. Otherwise, do you think I'd to turn up to meet you? I just want to hear you tell it all.' He smiled. 'Go on.'

Gus ordered more coffee. 'Let's go back to Bill Connor. Before he left the hospital, we became friendly. He told me the story of George and Eugene Connor. How Eugene met his death and George ended up in a mental institution outside Belfast. I thought of it as a ghost story until earlier this year.'

'There's no shortage of ghosts in this country,' said Tohill.

'My mother and father – who died many years ago – were born in Ireland and emigrated after they married. I've explained my father's side of the family. My mother had a younger sister called Celia. She died this year and I came home – what I now call home – to sort out the estate. I work as a research scientist and I was able to get a sabbatical for a year.'

'I understand you have other family over with you,' commented Tohill. 'A wife, a son and a daughter.'

'We'll come to that. Without going into all the detail – which isn't important – I found out that George Connor was still alive and under confinement. We tracked him down and I visited. That's how I found out about you. Again it doesn't matter how I made the final contact but

I was keen to meet you. There's something I need to know. Before pursuing it, I'd appreciate it if you could tell me something about yourself.'

'I'd like a glass of Powers. Will you join me?' He snapped his fingers at a passing waitress and ordered their drinks.

'Everything you say squares up. I've done some research myself over the years.' He drank his whiskey, ordered two more and began. 'Yes. George Connor is my father. I don't remember much about my early life and it was only later that I found out where I'd come from. Times were hard in the late 1930's and 40's in Ireland. My real mother died some months after my father was committed for the second time. No, I wasn't adopted by strangers as you might have been informed. I was handed over to her older sisters who were spinsters. They lived together up in the Ballypalady area. My father was given a job as a farm hand in the area after he left the mental home. He met my mother Mary Tohill – they were both simple people – and they rapidly conceived me.

'He obviously had no mental ability to handle the stress of a marriage and a baby. He was only paid a pittance according to my aunts. They were good to me but very poor themselves. I remember being fed on pots of stew which had to last a week. We had no knives or forks and ate with our hands. It was like something out of Victorian times.

'At certain times of the year, like July and this time of year, there was a lot of trouble. That didn't make life any easier either. Although intelligent enough, I had to leave school at fourteen. In those days, you stayed on in primary school to that age and then were thrown out to look after yourself. I've always regretted that.

'I was accepted into an apprenticeship scheme and trained as a mechanic on the railways. When the basic training finished, there were no jobs. I went to London for a while and married a girl from Tipperary – born not too far away from Michelstown in Cork. It was very hard for Irish people to get lodgings in London then and we were often treated like dogs. Black people were treated in much the same way.

'I found work and I saved my money. We lived on Kilburn High Road and socialized in our own Irish circles. I became politically committed and joined the Movement. I returned home in the mid 1960's and renewed my Republican contacts. I'm saying no more than that. I had money put by me and my new mates fixed me up with a job in a scrapyard – no questions asked and no pack drill.

'We lived in West Belfast. After 1969, the Troubles led to increased involvement in the Movement. I was interned in 1971 and all that experience hardened me. After I got out, I became fully committed and rose in the Movement.

'I kept in touch with my mother's sisters and made sure that they were well looked after. Aunt Margaret died in 1975 and Aunt Kathleen followed two years later. It was only after the funeral that I found out about my father.

'They'd told me that he'd left my mother. Mental illness in those days was something to be ashamed of. Country people did not like it known that someone had been put away like that.' He paused to drink.

'I searched their house to see if anything valuable remained. They had some old trinkets which I kept for sentimental reasons. I came across a tin box under a bed. It contained a lot of old documents.

'I gradually pieced together my true history – who my father was and what had happened to him. I went to see him and I gather you already know about that. He was obviously just a vegetable – hadn't a clue who I was. I never returned. There was no point.' He stared at Gus.

'Yes, I know that I was a suspect for the Warrenpoint business. I can't tell you anymore than that. I was eventually arrested shortly afterwards for something else and jailed for life. I was only let out after the Good Friday Agreement in 1998.

'My wife had moved south to live and I joined her. Money is tight. It takes a lot to live down here. I'm not interested in politics anymore. That's all I've got to say. I've told you plenty. Give me something back.'

The room had filled up as Tohill had talked. Gus doubted whether he had ever told this story to anyone. He felt that some kind of trust had been established. Additionally, they were blood relatives. He knew he had to build on it. Tohill had revealed that money was tight. How tight, wondered Gus.

'I told you that I was fascinated with the tragedy involving your father and his brother. And I still am. However, I have another reason for wanting to meet you. You know about my own family. Well, I'll not beat about the bush. I was in hospital that time because of a kidney problem. My son Ed inherited a similar problem and last year it became serious. He lost one kidney. It's possible the problem won't stop there. If the second one fails, there are very few – if any – options open to me.'

Tohill stared at him but said nothing. He swirled the remaining whiskey in his glass.

'Your father was my first line of attack. He has been well looked after and has never smoked nor drank. But he's a very old man. On top of that, his mind has gone and he seldom speaks. An organ donation of any kind may be out of the question. Apart from that, the authorities won't release anything to me.'

'Nothing new there,' said Tohill. 'So…you're depending on me.'

'I've inherited money. I'm prepared to pay a substantial sum for you to sign a contract but all the checks will have to be made.'

'I might not match up you mean?'

'Exactly. If an operation ever became necessary, the blood type and tissue type have to be the same. Also, the greatest chance of success lies with a blood relative.'

Tohill finished his whiskey. 'I get the picture. You want permission to access all our records. Then you'll try and work on me after that.'

'I don't think – from what you've told me about yourself – that I could work on you without your consent.'

'Correct. However I'm prepared to play ball with you. It'll cost you even to look at our records. I could use a grand for starters.'

'No problem. I'm not going to haggle. Then we'll take it from there.'

'It's not going to be straightforward. My original records are with a doctor in London. The Brits will have copies but they'll not give them to you. I've never re-registered you understand.' He looked at his watch. 'I'll be in touch.' He offered his hand and they shook.

Gus had forgotten the time. It was six o'clock when he arrived back at the car.

'I was going to come for you,' said Lucia. 'But you warned me not to. I was getting frantic.'

'Don't worry. Everything's cool. You will have to drive. I've had one too many for a long ride.'

As Gus dozed in the front seat, Tohill's parting remarks at Reception came to him again. 'I was sent to Washington in the 1970's to raise money for the Movement and once met some powerful people at a St Patrick's Day Reception. I became friendly with one guy from the State Department. He had known Uncle Mike.

'After the election of President Kennedy, he became a made man and caught the eye of the Secretary of State for Defence. Mike was smart but

132

headstrong. He made enemies. Someone persuaded the Secretary to send him to Vietnam to boost his career. I guess that guy knew what was coming.'

'Who was the Defence Secretary at that time?'

'A man whose grandfather had emigrated from Ireland after the famine. You must remember Robert McNamara.'

CHAPTER 19

GUS poured two glasses of cold Semillon for himself and Lucia. They ate smoked salmon as she prepared steaks. Paul Hamilton had collected Kay for a Saturday night on the town. Ed was working on the computer.

They had an early start for the flight to London on Monday morning and so tonight was his last opportunity to discuss everything in a relaxed mood. Gus put on the Goldberg Variations – an old version by Shnabel - and lit the peat fire.

'I know you want to hear again how it was left with Tohill. I don't know how much more I can tell you. Arrangements will be made next week through an intermediary to give him five hundred pounds in cash. In return, Tohill will obtain a copy of his medical records. He has also agreed to write to Dr Canavan to support my access to George's complete records. When the process is finished, I'll give him the rest of the cash.'

'He might just walk off with the money. You'd never see it again,' said Lucia.

'That's a small risk. I feel sure that he'll come through. I'll give him the rest of the money no matter what they contain. If we have a direct correlation, I can think about how much I could offer him to enter into a contract.'

'How would all that work?' she asked. 'I didn't meet Tohill and, even if I had, I doubt very much whether I would have liked him.'

'Say there is a direct tie-up. I could offer him a substantial sum – say fifty thousand pounds – to be prepared to donate a kidney if Ed fell ill in the next five years. We couldn't keep the contract going indefinitely. I have a feeling that if Ed lasts that length of time, everything should be fine in the long run.'

'How would it operate in practice?' she butted in. 'Tohill lives in Dublin. Ed will be back home.'

'I'll find ways round all that. Ed loves it here. When I brought him to the University on Wednesday afternoon, he enjoyed it. He's not into College football and all that stuff so he won't miss it. He could study here.'

Lucia stared into the fire. 'What about me? I'd be left alone. Kay is building her own life in Boston. She wants to pursue a publishing career. You're suggesting Ed and you would live here?'

'If it was a matter of life or death, what would you do?'

'It doesn't leave me much choice. This is too gloomy. Let's have dinner.'

Gus poured a 1978 Gevrey-Chambertin which floated like velvet with the fillet steaks. Lucia picked at the Greek salad and the baked potato. She pushed it aside and left with a glass of wine to sit by the peat fire.

'You haven't been seeing anyone else over here?' she asked. 'A woman rang this afternoon when you were out.'

'Honey, we've been through this kind of thing before. Who did she say she was?'

'Ed answered the phone. He told me before dinner. She asked for Dr McWilliams. When he said that you'd gone for a walk, she thanked him and put the phone down. There was no message.' She studied his glazed eyes.

'It might have been a girl who works for Burgess. She's been helping me and Tony with some of our work. She would call me by my title.' His stomach tightened. There was nothing to hide. Apart from the threatening messages.

Lucia relaxed. 'You never said anything about a girl. Did she help you get into contact with Burgess?'

'As a matter of fact…yes. She did. She lives in his home.'

'You said Burgess didn't go for females.' Lucia glanced up at him.

'Not quite. I said that he didn't appear interested in sex. The relationship, as far as I know, was not sexual. She ran short of funding. His mother had died. It's as simple as that.'

'Why would she ring you?'

'She said something to us about a job interview. In return for helping us find Burgess, she asked for advice on preparing for it.'

'You better ring her back then.'

'It's getting late. I'll maybe do it tomorrow or Monday. It can wait. Relax. Enjoy the rest of our wine. It's our last full night together for some time. You'll be busy getting packed tomorrow evening and everyone will need an early night.'

The subject was dropped. The wine took a grip. Ed joined them and Gus explained again to him the proposition with Tohill. 'We love you, son. I'd raise any amount of money if necessary.'

Lucia said that she felt drained. When he finally called it a night, she was asleep. Her mouth hung open. She had forgotten to close the

135

curtains. He looked at the orange half-moon rising faintly above the Lough.

He could not sleep and made tea. He rummaged through his files. Shortly afterwards, he heard the key turn in the front door. Kay came into the living room.

'I saw the lamp on,' she said. 'Didn't think anyone would be up at this time. We had difficulty getting a cab. They have quite a nightlife here!'

'I couldn't get over,' said Gus. 'Sometimes I can't and so I read for a while. Would you like some tea?'

'That would be great. I had more beers than I'm used to.' As he poured tea, she asked about Ed. 'We talked about it tonight. Paul knew all about it from talking to his father. I hope you don't mind.'

'Not at all. They're great friends to have. Your mother and I have been discussing future plans. She says you're very settled in Boston.'

'Yes. I guess I'd like to live there when I've finished College. Columbus is a little dead for me right now.'

Gus outlined the possibilities. 'I've explained that it may be the only choice.'

'Doesn't that put Mom in a corner?'

'What can I do? But let's not get too excited. It might never happen.'

'It must be scary having to deal with these people. How can you trust this Tohill?'

'Don't forget. He's a blood relative. If he's suitable, I'll offer so much for him to sign up and keep everything on hold. Who can tell how far it will all go?'

'I'd donate myself if I matched up.' She sighed.

'You know you don't so it's only a hypothetical....thank God. I think it's time we got some sleep.'

They left on Monday morning to catch an early flight to London Heathrow. 'When you arrive, get the Paddington Express and then grab a cab to take you to Bayswater. You could have stayed in UCL but the accommodation is cramped. I've booked you into a good hotel near Kensington Palace. You won't be too far away from all the sights. Call me when you get there.'

He saw them onto the plane, they hugged and he left. Gus went into the bar where he had drank in July with the red-veined man. It seemed like a long time ago.

There was a small parcel for him in the post when he returned. It was from McLean. It contained a brief letter and a book called *The Guinea Pigs* by John McGuffin. Thought you might like to read this, wrote McLean. Don't think too hard of men like your cousin. They never found him guilty of anything. That's not to say that he's not a tough character. The letter had a C.C – to UFB file. What could that mean?

He scrambled three eggs with the remains of the smoked salmon from Glenarm. The book dealt with men who had been interned at the same time as Tohill. Apparently, many of them had been experimented upon to see how they would cope with the extremes of psychological pressure. They might, for example, be blindfolded and taken to a helicopter. They were told that they would be pushed out over Belfast Lough. Gus added the book to his collection.

At six o'clock, he rang Arna Breen. 'Did you call on Saturday by any chance?'

'Yes. You said you could help me with the interview. It's on Wednesday.'

'Sorry I didn't get back to you. Everything was a bit hectic. The family had to leave this morning. They're staying in London for two days before going back to the States on Wednesday.'

'How is your son? He answered the phone on Saturday.'

'He's surviving. That's all I can say. Do you want to meet me?'

'I've taken tomorrow off to prepare for the interview. Perhaps I could see you for lunch.'

'That's fine. You suggest somewhere.'

On the following morning, Gus called at the Linenhall to thank Baker for his assistance.

'I was happy to help. Was the information on Mitchel of any value to you?'

'It was.' Gus paused. 'Yes. A complex man. It's strange how things move. The files were of great benefit to me. Apart from anything else, it led me to my cousin.' Without revealing the name, Gus sketched out the details of his meeting with Patrick Tohill.

He could see that Baker did not want to pry. 'What about Ross?' he asked. 'Any joy on that front?'

'My wife was over last week and she brought some information with her. All about the time when he invaded the States just before he died – or was killed rather.'

'I could probably have got you all that myself,' said Baker. 'But I've been on vacation. Has it given you any kind of lead?'

'In a way. I'm a long way from being out of the woods on it. I still want to know what happened to George and Eugene Connor…no matter how it goes with Tohill. But I accept that I may never find out.' He glanced at his watch. 'I have a lunch appointment. Before I go, someone sent me this book in the post. Have you heard of this McGuffin?'

'Yes. He used to be very active when the Troubles began. Was wrongly interned at one time in 1971. Belfast's last anarchist. I attended a meeting once where he spoke with extreme eloquence against the futility of all violence. He was really an old pacifist.'

'Is he alive?'

'I believe he is. Someone told me that he lives in San Francisco. He would be popular there with certain people.'

'Any idea what UFB means?'

'I could hazard a guess. Better that you find out for sure.'

They ordered chicken pasta with basil and tomato sauce. She had Ballgowan still water and he drank a glass of House Red which tasted of rust. 'You want to talk about tomorrow?' Gus asked.

'You were at the major Conference in Holland. You have probably extensive experience of interviewing people.'

'Some. You're experienced enough to be aware of the general questions they'll ask. Ability to work in a team etc.'

'Yes. I know all that crap. However, for a research post like this, you need to be able to go the extra mile. Tell them what needs to be done. Show them you're ahead of the game.' She sipped her water and dabbled with the pasta.

Arna was less confident than she at first appeared, thought Gus. 'Let me think back. The Conference. Your post deals with applications of molecular biology to animal production science. I gave you the paper from Professor Dietz.'

'I read it but you know as well as I do that it's not the same thing as being there. Hearing the questions and his replies. The discussions afterwards. The hot debates.'

'I accept that. OK. It's coming to me. I gather that the poultry industry is very important to the Northern Ireland economy.'

'That's developed over the last twenty years. I don't mean the egg market which was always there. I'm talking about the broiler industry.'

'Dietz gave a very good example. He cited the poultry influenza outbreak in Hong Kong about four or five years ago. The virus involved was H5N1 and it spread from the birds to humans…apparently via pigs. If a disease like that appeared here, it would wipe out the poultry industry and those dependent on it if not controlled rapidly. One human death and that would be it.'

'Just like BSE and vCJD.'

'Yes. He quoted the Spanish flu epidemic of 1918 when millions died. So, you could say that the government should be prepared for those emergencies.'

'I think I can run with this approach. There was a major foot and mouth outbreak earlier this year. It cost billions and that was for a disease which is not transmissible to humans.'

'Exactly. So, if you had a mystery outbreak, it would be ideal if research scientists were able to isolate its genetic material and determine the DNA sequence. They would then be able to characterize the virus and develop therapies to eradicate it.'

'I think I will have a glass of wine after all,' she said. She ordered a glass of Beaujolais Villages. 'You've given me what I need. I can talk round all that.'

'I'm happy to assist. No contact with Burgess I take it or anything else?'

'No. He hasn't been in touch. I've left messages but with no reply. There's been no more trouble. No sign of the Rover car. Unfortunately, the police haven't got anywhere with their enquires about the break-in.'

'Townsend seems to think that the Serbian girl was behind it. I doubt if they'll do anything until she returns. The other possibility is the guy in Australia.'

'Let's not talk about it anymore. Tell me about your family.'

'There's a lot to talk about since we last met. The meeting with Basil McLean was very productive. I met my cousin in the Shelbourne Hotel last Friday. There was progress.' Gus gave her all the details although he could see that her mind was elsewhere. 'When your interview is over, give me a call. There's some other science I'd like to run past you.'

He wished her well and watched her walk away. The sky had darkened and a sharp wind blew across Great Victoria Street. Papers swirled around everywhere. When he reached the MX-5 in the carpark, he noticed a small rip in the side of the black canvas. He complained to the attendant at the exit. He shrugged and grunted that it happened all the time. He hadn't seen anything.

Gus stopped at the bank and withdrew five hundred pounds. The big house was silent when he returned. The voicemail had one message. He was told to park outside a small supermarket at five o'clock on Thursday afternoon. Someone would establish contact and expect the cash to be handed over immediately. In return, he would be given a white envelope.

Gus opened a Budweiser. The fire had not been lit since Saturday. The house felt chilly and he switched on the central heating. From the main bay window on the bottom floor, he looked up and down the Avenue. The leaves on the elms were beginning to turn and some had dropped.

He prepared a fire and heated up chicken tikka masala in the microwave. All he could do was wait. He flicked through the collection of opera recordings and found *Aida* which he had not listened to for many years.

Later, he was tempted towards a Bushmills but remembered that it had all gone. He thought of the Midleton whiskey from County Cork. No, that could wait until he had something to celebrate. Gus opened the files again. Mitchel was dead and General Ross was about to depart from Washington to Baltimore.

Then he thought of Patrick Tohill. His time in The Maze. He read through McGuffin's testimonies and went to bed at midnight.

The helicopter flew high across the Cavehill and halted above the Lough. Sleeping lightly, he heard the propellers whirl and whirl. His eyes were closed. He was blindfolded and pushed out. There was no parachute. The water was black. Gus struggled to breathe. He woke at two in a cold sweat.

CHAPTER 20

THE NIGHTMARE made further sleep impossible. He brewed strong Assam tea and then opened his files on the final movements of General Ross that had been provided for him by Baker.

It was decided by the General and the Admiral that the next stroke should be at Baltimore. The troops, now reduced to less than four thousand, were landed at North Point on 12th September, and had to march through twelve miles of thickly wooded country to reach the city. About six thousand militia were drawn up to protect it, and skirmishing soon began in the woods. Ross, riding to the front as usual, was mortally wounded, a bullet passing through his right arm into his breast. He died as he was being carried back to the boats. The advance was continued, and the militia were routed; but the attack on Baltimore was eventually abandoned, as (apart from the irretrievable loss of their commander) the navy found it impossible to co-operate, and the troops re-embarked on 15th September.

The British reprisals excited great indignation in America. Monroe, the Secretary of State (afterwards President), wrote to the British admiral: 'In the course of ten years past the capitals of the principal powers of Europe have been conquered and occupied alternately by the victorious armies of each other; and no instance of such wanton and unjustifiable destruction has been seen.' The same feeling found voice in the House of Commons, but Mr Whitbread, while giving expression to it in the strongest terms, acquitted Ross of all blame, and said that 'it was happy for humanity and the credit of the empire that the extraordinary order upon that occasion had been entrusted to an officer of so much moderation and justice' (Hansard, xxix. 181).

The ministers showed their satisfaction with his work both in public and private. The Chancellor of the Exchequer said in the House of Commons (14th November): 'While he inflicted chastisement in a manner to convey, in the fullest sense, the terror of the British arms, the Americans themselves could not withhold from him the meed of praise for the temper and moderation with which he executed the task assigned to him.' Lord Bathurst wrote to Wellington (27th September): 'The conduct of Major-General Ross does credit to your grace's school.' Goulburn, one of the commissioners who were treating for peace at

Ghent, wrote (21st October): 'We owed the acceptance of our article respecting the Indians to the capture of Washington; and if we had either burnt Baltimore or held Plattsburg, I believe we should have had peace on the terms you have sent to us in a month at latest.' Lord Liverpool (on the same date) wrote to Castlereagh regretting that more troops had not been placed under Ross, instead of being sent to Canada, adding: 'The capture and destruction of Washington has not united the Americans; quite the contrary. We have gained more credit with them by saving private property than we have lost by the destruction of their public works and buildings.' The actual damage done, as assessed by a committee of congress, was less than a million dollars.

Combined operations have too often failed from friction between the naval and military commanders; but in Ross, the admiral (Sir A. Cochrane) said, 'are blended those qualities so essential to promote success where co-operation between the two services becomes necessary.' Rear-admiral (afterwards Sir George) Cockburn, who was with him when he fell, wrote: 'Our country has lost in him one of its best and bravest soldiers, and those who knew him, as I did, a friend most honoured and beloved.'

The body of the general, Gus read, had been preserved in a barrel of rum and carried to a ship in order to transport him home to Ireland. However, HMS Tonnant had been diverted due to an impending battle in New Orleans. And so the corpse was landed and buried in the cemetery of St Paul's Church in Halifax, Nova Scotia. An obelisk had subsequently been erected to his memory.

The phone rang. It was Lucia. 'We're at Heathrow and about to board. The hotel was cool and we've had a chance to see most of Central London. St Paul's Cathedral was stunning. We're staying overnight in New York and going home tomorrow. I'll hand you over to the kids.'

After lunch, he visited Belfast Central Library and consulted *Energy and Empire*. In August 1858, Thomson had sailed on the ship *Agamemnon* as part of the project to lay the first Atlantic submarine cable. Gus found the important passages:

'After an extremely violent storm, during which the *Agamemnon* came close to foundering and taking William Thomson with her, ships rendezvoused in mid-ocean during June, 1858. Some 500 miles or more of cable was then lost as a result of three partings, and the ships returned to Queenstown (now Cobh) in Ireland for supplies. But then, in only one week, between 29th July and 5th August, the two vessels finally laid the first transatlantic cable, even though the unfortunate *Agamemnon* encountered head winds throughout most of her eastbound passage. With the initial communications between the Old World and the New, the celebrations were spontaneous and brilliant, not least the setting on fire of New York's Town Hall during a torchlight procession. At the age of twenty-six, Charles Bright received his knighthood, and *The Times* observed that 'since the discovery of Colombus, nothing has been done in any degree comparable to the vast enlargement which has thus been given to the sphere of human activity'. The President of the United States, James Buchanan, in his reply by telegraph to Queen Victoria's congratulatory message (which had taken sixteen hours to transmit) also captured the emotional appeal of the technical achievement by two nations whose relations since the War of Independence had not always been so warm:

The President cordially reciprocates the congratulations of Her Majesty the Queen on the success of the great international enterprise accomplished by the science, skill, and indomitable energy of the two countries. It is a triumph more glorious because far more useful to Mankind than was ever won by conqueror on the field of battle. May the Atlantic Telegraph under the blessing of Heaven prove to be a bond of perpetual peace and friendship between the kindred nations and an instrument destined by Divine Providence to diffuse religion, civilization, liberty, and laws throughout the world.

New York's mayor, in spite of the accident to his Town Hall, regarded the success of the cable as a triumph of science over time and space which would unite 'more closely the bonds of peace and commercial prosperity, introducing an era in the world's history pregnant with results beyond the conception of a finite mind'. And the humble folk of Sackville, New Brunswick, no longer felt 'as distant colonists, but that we actually form a part of the glorious British Empire – God save the Queen!'

Charles Bright had been the chief engineer to the recently founded Atlantic Telegraph Company. Gus noted the early age at which he had received his knighthood for the project. Sir Charles was to side with Thomson against Whitehouse, the other electrician on the team, when the major dispute subsequently broke out over the use of the instrumentation designed by Sir William.

For the initial triumph in laying the cable had proven to be short-lived. It ceased to function in October, 1858. As Captain Moriarty of the *Agamemnon* expressed the sad news in a letter to William Thomson on October 4th: 'I am really very sorry for the poor Atlantic Cable but fear it will never speak again.'

It was to be seven years before the cable project would be successful, largely due to the success of Thomson's theoretical approach over the 'suck it and see' attempts of Whitehouse.

'With the ship *Leviathan* refitted in time for a cable laying attempt in the summer of 1865, and with 500 people aboard, including William Thomson as a consulting expert, the *Great Eastern* steamed west from Valencia with the new design of cable paying out. Snapping around the half-way point, the cable sank two miles to the ocean bed. In vain the epic ship grappled for the thread. But the following year a cable was successfully laid in a period of two weeks, and the 1865 cable was picked up and completed also. The major step in the unification of the British speaking world had at last been achieved, and in recognition of his contribution to the prestige of the British Empire, Queen Victoria knighted Thomson at Windsor Castle on 10th November, 1866.'

Gus noted the number of passengers on board the *Leviathan* on its way to Trinity Bay, Newfoundland. He felt sure that *Diogenes* had been one of them. The insertion of a fresh nucleus within an egg was as nothing compared with the laying and connection of the giant cable stretching for thousands of miles from Valentia Island to Newfoundland – a short distance from Nova Scotia.

The project had reached its triumphant conclusion as the Civil War had raged in America. There would have been no opportunity at this time to meet Mitchel or his dead and wounded sons. Nothing was known of the daughters.

On the following afternoon, Gus arrived early at the arranged place of appointment. Fifteen minutes later, a woman with a white pinched face approached him confidently and asked him his name. Gus gave her the brown envelope. She scanned the contents quickly and then produced a white envelope. As the woman rapidly walked away, a car pulled up behind her. She jumped into the passenger seat and the car accelerated.

Gus extracted the letter from the envelope. It had been dated that same day and was addressed to Dr Canavan as requested. A copy of proof of identity was included. He had no doubt that it would be sent. It could be easily checked. That would have to wait until after the weekend.

The following day was spent with Tony Hamilton. He needed to maximise his time with him in September before the new term began. 'I gather Kay and Paul got on very well the other evening,' he said. 'My thanks to him for looking after her.'

'I can't remember what time he got in. I was fast asleep. No other developments before we begin?'

'There was a message on my voicemail that they'd arrived home safely in Ohio yesterday. Ed will be going back to school next week and Kay will be leaving soon for College in Boston.'

'So your wife will be almost alone?'

'Ed will be there most evenings.'

'There's something else you want to tell me?' Tony looked at him with concern.

'We saw Dr Canavan again last week. He had still no clearance but was helpful. As it happens, there's been swift movement on the other angle. I've met my cousin. He's called Patrick Tohill.'

Tony listened attentively as Gus told him about the contract. 'I'll not say the obvious thing,' he said. 'Life is full of risks. I agree that you have no option but to proceed as you are doing. If I had the money, I'd probably do the same myself in your situation. You're going to ring Canavan on Monday?'

'Early next week. Give him a chance. OK let's go. I need to focus on something else.'

As Gus turned the key in the lock, he heard the phone ringing. It was Arna Breen. 'How did your interview go?'

'Very well indeed. Your tips were valuable. The Chairperson was excited by my ideas and I got a chance to talk. It will be some weeks before I hear anything.' She paused. 'I'm going to my parents for the weekend. Thank you again for all your help. Keep in touch.'

She had seemed in a hurry so he had not pushed. The day had gone well and he opened a Budweiser. Then he boiled potatoes, mashed them with garlic and fried calf's liver with bacon. The Puglian wine had matured and, as he relaxed with a glass, he heard the rain beating savagely on the roof. It did not stop until Sunday night.

The first Monday in September was cool and bright. He waited until the afternoon before trying to contact Dr Canavan.

'Yes. I received his letter in the second post. I see that he has no difficulty in allowing you to gain access to George's records. That's positive. I can work with it when we send off our appeal. They will wish to check everything out.'

Gus hesitated and then continued. 'He has agreed to co-operate with me on the relevant aspects of his own records.' There was silence at the other end. The doctor was better not knowing anything about the agreement with Tohill.

'I can't comment on that aspect of the matter. He's not my patient. I wish you the very best of luck.'

Gus put down the phone. Everything was moving well. He had not arranged a further meeting with Tony until later in the week and was at a loose end. However, he decided to wait for a while longer and then work on Arna Breen to contact Burgess. It was the only way that he could see of tracking down the true name of *Diogenes*. He had to know.

He spent Tuesday working on the laptop. After the conversation about primes, he had not taken any interest in what Ed was doing on the computer. As long as it was useful, he did not mind what he did. He now wondered what sites he had been accessing.

He trawled through the files but everything appeared kosher. Ed had copied parts of files downloaded from the Internet. They all appeared related to his 'prime' project. There was a proof that the primes went on forever and associated quotations. It proved that God existed said a Christian commentator. The largest one discovered had hundreds of digits but it was known for certain that there were infinitely more after. There was a program to work out factors for smaller primes.

Then came a file entitled *Cicadas*. Gus opened it up. Why would Ed be interested in these insects? He studied it closely.

As well as finding a role in espionage, prime numbers also appear in the natural world. The periodical cicadas, most notably *Magicicada septendecim*, have the longest life-cycle of any insect. Their unique life-cycle begins underground, where the nymphs patiently suck the juice from the roots of trees. Then, after 17 years of waiting, the adult cicadas emerge from the ground, swarm in vast numbers and temporarily swamp the landscape. Within a few weeks they mate, lay their eggs and die.

The question which puzzled biologists was, why is the cicada's life-cycle so long? And is there any significance to the life-cycle being a prime number of years? Another species, *Magicicada tredecim*, swarms every 13 years, implying that life-cycles lasting a prime number of years offer some evolutionary advantage.

One theory suggests that the cicada has a parasite which also goes through a lengthy life-cycle and which the cicada is trying to avoid. If the parasite has a life-cycle of, say, 2 years then the cicada wants to avoid a life-cycle which is divisible by 2, otherwise the parasite and the cicada will regularly coincide. Similarly, if the parasite has a life-cycle of 3 years then the cicada wants to avoid a life-cycle which is divisible by 3, otherwise the parasite and the cicada will once again regularly coincide. Ultimately, to avoid meeting its parasite the cicadas' best strategy is to have a long life-cycle lasting a prime number of years. Because nothing will divide into 17, Magicicada septendecim will rarely meet its parasite. If the parasite has a 2-year life-cycle they will only meet every 34 years, and if it has a longer life-cycle, say 16 years, then they will only meet every 272 (16 x 17) years.

In order to fight back, the parasite only has two life-cycles which will increase the frequency of coincidences – the annual cycle and the same 17-year cycle as the cicada. However, the parasite is unlikely to survive reappearing 17 years in a row, because for the first 16 appearances there will be no cicadas for it to parasitise. On the other hand, in order to reach the 17-year life-cycle, the generations of parasites would first have to evolve through the 16-year life-cycle. This would mean at some stage of evolution the parasite and cicada would not coincide for 272 years! In either case the cicadas long prime life-cycle protects it.

This might explain why the alleged parasite has never been found! In the race to keep up with the cicada, the parasite probably kept extending its life-cycle until it hit the 16-year hurdle. Then it failed to coincide for

272 years, by which time the lack of coinciding with cicadas had driven it to extinction. The result is a cicada with a 17-year life cycle, which it no longer needs because its parasite no longer exists.

Gus closed the file and opened a Budweiser. An idea swirled in his mind. The concept appealed to him. He thought of the clones battling each other until one was defeated. Perhaps one had died. The other was unaware of it and kept trying to defend his patch.

As he watched the local news that evening, it came back to him again. A politician spouted threats about the dangers of a United Ireland. When Gus had been in the South, he had never detected any interest in the subject. Tohill himself – a Northern Republican – had abandoned politics. And here the politicians fought on with no endgame in sight.

At the end of the week, he met Tony again and they finished their research paper. They agreed to meet again on Tuesday afternoon to tidy up the details. He met no one else and spent the weekend working in the garden.

Before meeting Tony, he decided to have lunch in the University staff room. He finished a hamburger with difficulty and noticed a crowd forming around the television in a corner of the bar. 'What's the big attraction?' he asked someone at the back of the pack.

'Hardly the correct word,' he replied. 'There's been a major terrorist attack in New York.'

Gus stood and watched with horror as a Boeing 767 hit the second tower.

CHAPTER 21

LIFE ceased as students and staff watched the Twin Towers fall. They saw emergency workers scramble to rescue survivors from the rubble of the World Trade Centre. Reports flashed through of attacks on the Pentagon and of a hijacked plane crashing south of Pittsburgh. It was estimated that thousands of people had lost their lives.

Gus had rang Tony and he came into the bar with eyes bulging. He described to him what had happened.

'Have you tried phoning home?' asked Tony.

'All the lines to the States are jammed. There's no reports of anything near Columbus.'

Tony was looking at him closely. Clearly something had occurred to him but he did not want to speak. Then it hit him. Kay had intended to go back to Boston in early September. Gus had not contacted home recently. One of the hijacked planes had taken off *from* Boston but they did not yet know what had been its intended destination.

He returned home in the late afternoon. The phone lines were blocked. He poured a Budweiser and tuned into the latest updates. The plane that had been hijacked in Boston had been bound for Los Angeles but had been diverted to New York. He checked e-mails. There was one from Ed asking him to ring home urgently. Maybe one of his friends or someone he knew had been on one of the hijacked planes or had been visiting the World Trade Centre. Gus did not know anyone who worked there.

He opened a second beer. Speculation mounted as to the origin of the attack. It seemed increasingly likely that the hijackers were of Arab origin. Reports speculated that the operation had been coordinated by Osama bin Laden in Afghanistan. Gus, like many of the people interviewed, had never heard of him.

At eleven o'clock, Ed came through on the phone. Gus heard the panic in his voice. 'Dad. I have some very bad news although we can't know for certain.'

'I've been following the news all day. Did you know someone?'

'I've been talking to Kay. We fear the worst.'

'What are you talking about? Let me speak to your mother.'

'That's the problem. Mom flew to see Kay at the weekend. Stocked up the fridge and asked me to look after myself for the next few days.'

'She never said anything to me about that,' said Gus.

'Mom has been behaving strangely. I think it was something to do with a letter she received last Thursday afternoon. When I got back, she was staring at it. I asked her was anything the matter and she shook her head. There was a faraway look in her eyes as if she wasn't listening. Later that night she said she had to go to Boston but would be back on Tuesday. She'd arranged cover at work. Told them it was an emergency. I only found that out later.'

'Have you spoken to Kay?'

'Briefly. There's big problems contacting anyone.'

'What did she say?'

'She'd been surprised when Mom said she was coming to spend some days in Boston. There was someone she had to meet there. She stayed in the spare bed. One of Kay's friends is not coming back to the end of the month.'

'Get to the point, Ed.'

'Mom caught a cab this morning for the airport. When Kay awoke, there was a message to say that Mom would be in touch. She had to catch an early flight.'

'You don't mean to say that Mom for some reason decided to go to LA?'

'Kay was tidying the bedroom after Mom left and found a scrap of paper with details of flights to the West Coast. She thought nothing of it at first but then panicked when the news broke. She finally got through to me. But Mom hasn't returned.'

'Perhaps she couldn't reach you.'

'I don't know, Dad. Kay has a spooky feeling about all of this.'

'I'll ring now and get back to you.' Gus put down the phone in a cold sweat. These things didn't happen to ordinary people, he thought. But of course they did. Thousands of ordinary people had died today after a terrorist attack that was totally unexpected.

He finally reached Kay at 2.00am. 'I've been speaking to Ed about Mom and he's filled me in on all the background.'

'I can't tell you how I feel,' said Kay. 'She hasn't contacted me. I've tried the airport but it's impossible to pin anyone down. There's total panic over here.'

'What did Mom do when she was in Boston?'

'She was on the phone quite a bit but was secretive about it. We can check the numbers. It's out of the question tonight. She said when she arrived that an old friend had contacted her and suggested a meeting. I know that she went to meet someone for lunch on Sunday and didn't return until late. She was out most of Monday. Said she had a lot of shopping to do. That's about all I can tell you. We're going to have to wait.'

Gus was mystified. Surely not an old flame. He recalled their conversations before she had gone back to the States. She had been worried about the family breaking up. Suspicious of him. Still, it didn't all make sense. Someone from the past. Why would she get so excited and go to such trouble?

All that was secondary. He feared the worst. Perhaps she had caught that plane. Fear gripped him. He tried to get some sleep but it was impossible. Finally, he rose at five and made tea.

Gus spent the morning in fruitless attempts to make phone calls and send e-mails. He watched the news bulletins constantly. The previous speculations about Arabs were proving correct. His brain tormented him.

Someone from the past. Lucia had spent many years trying to find out who her real parents were. Many private agencies had investigated without success. The first agency had indicated a firm lead but it had petered out. The latest one had not been in contact for some time. He had remembered asking her about it when she was in Ireland.

Maybe it had met with success and one of her real parents, or someone close to them, had written. That could explain her actions. Someone with a Boston connection gets in touch through the agency.

On an impulse, she makes the arrangements...grabbing at any straw she can. Not only for herself but for Ed. It would make sense that she wouldn't inform anyone until she was absolutely sure.

The Sunday contact reveals that she has living relatives on the West Coast. Maybe one of her parents, half-brothers or sisters. She goes for it and catches the fatal plane. A nightmare come true. He was paralysed. There were no flights to the States. All cancelled until further notice.

Work was impossible. He phoned Tony to tell him what had happened. 'I'll have to get a flight back home as soon as possible. I don't know when I'll be back.'

'We're devastated. If there's anything we can do, you know you only have to ask.'

'Thanks. Perhaps you could keep an eye on the house for me. I'll leave a set of keys with you.'

He phoned Townsend and told him also that he would be away for some time. 'We'll watch your home and check with neighbours for anything suspicious,' he said. 'I hope that your wife was not on that plane but I admit it sounds bad.'

Gus hesitated. 'It's not the time to talk about it but when my wife was here we went to Dublin and met Patrick Tohill.' He did not tell Townsend the full story.

'What can I say? It hardly matters now…with all your other problems. There have been no developments with the students. The Serbian was due back soon. We'll check with Dr Jones when she does. I wish you well.'

Gus had forgotten about the second five hundred pounds. On Thursday evening, he rang McLean. 'I know that it's not up to you to help in any way. But you've been very helpful. I need to forward a package to Patrick Tohill when I'm away. He has to give me something in return but I'll have to trust him.'

'I know what you mean. I will be happy to help you.'

'It's doubtful whether I'll get away just yet and maybe I could meet you tomorrow evening.'

'No problem.'

Gus called at the social club at the same time as before. He drank a pint of Guinness in record time, spoke briefly to McLean and handed over the package. 'I appreciate this. If there's any development, you could call me in Ohio at this number.' He gave McLean all his contact details.

The journey did not bother him now. He drove along the Shore Road by the Lough and noted again the sardonic terrorist slogan on a giant gable wall:

PREPARED FOR PEACE
READY FOR WAR

The first time he had seen it he had grimaced. Then he had smiled at the irony of the slogan with its masked backdrop of a hooded figure clutching a machine gun. He did not laugh now. Going crazy, he drove home.

There was an e-mail response from Ed to say that friends were looking after everything in Ohio. Kay had remained in Boston to await any further news. A Lucia McWilliams had purchased a ticket for the flight but there was no record of her checking-in. Also, Kay said that Mom had arrived in Boston with hand luggage and presumably had left in the same way.

Gus could only wait for flights to resume. He reckoned that his best option would be with Aer Lingus from Dublin or Shannon to New York. Given the background to the terrorist attack, he assumed that British Airways would be a non-starter.

After more phone checks on Saturday morning, he decided to lock up the house, pack his bags and drive to Shannon Airport. He had told the old neighbour what had happened and she promised to keep an eye on the house. They exchanged numbers.

At midday, the MX-5 was on the motorway for Dublin. He could worry later as to where he would leave it. On the long journey South, his mind dwelt on his time in Ireland and the unexpected outcome.

The traffic was light in Newry and he thought of his visits to Rostrevor. George Connor. Eugene Connor. What was the other boy's name? John McManus. All but forgotten about. He wondered whether he had missed something. Then John Mitchel and his friend from Kilbroney House. Burgess. Kelvin. Diogenes. Patrick Tohill.

The car navigated the busy M50 toll road directing traffic around Dublin and he saw the sign for Limerick. New dual carriageways and sections of motorway cut across the thick green fields. Everywhere you could see the plump black and white Friesians grazing the grass and chewing the cud.

He found a hotel near the airport. A large carpark was almost deserted. Gus explained his plan to the receptionist and showed her his passport. 'I hope to get a flight by Monday. I don't know how long I'll be away.'

'That's terrible, Sir. I'll have a word with the manager. I'm sure there won't be a problem. Many of our bookings over the next few weeks have been cancelled. Business has dropped right off since the tragedy. And that includes enquires for next summer.'

He checked into his room and then went to the bar. A range of exotic malt whiskies sat like soldiers behind the bartender. 'I'll try a glass of Midleton,' he said, making himself comfortable on the red plastic barstool. The whiskey calmed his nerves and he had two more before eating a solitary dinner in the hotel restaurant.

The drinks had given him an appetite and he ordered a sirloin steak. He tried to walk it off but the country road was dark and broken occasionally only by white one storey houses. He turned after twenty minutes and went back to the bar. 'I'll try one more glass of that Midleton and then I'll hit the sack,' he said to the young bartender. He noticed his tight waistcoat with its green and white stripes. Although it was late evening, the bar began to fill up with local customers and a band began to set up their drums in a far corner. A local businessman invited him to have a drink and he did not feel like refusing. At four o'clock, he went to bed.

He woke about nine. His head throbbed and his mouth tasted like bird droppings. He showered and managed to eat a buffet breakfast. The air outside was clear and cool. In the distance, he saw an aeroplane.

The immigration checks were rigorous and the queues long. It was Tuesday September 18th and he had obtained a business class booking on a flight to New York. An old man from Atlanta sat beside him. The Georgian was tense and closed his eyes immediately. As a result, there was little attempt to strike up a conversation. His large jowls folded like a bullfrog's over his check shirt.

Gus restricted himself to a Heineken and two glasses of Chardonnay with a salad. He was feeling liverish from the last two days and the second half of the flight was spent sleeping.

There was a more than usual panic at JFK airport as he struggled to grab his bags. After the peace of Shannon, this was like bedlam. New Yorkers were screaming in the battle to get out of the airport with their luggage.

He found a trolley and squeezed on his suitcase. Security seemed to be everywhere. Passengers watched bags intently. Repeated warnings came over the tannoy not to leave anything unattended. There was a flight to Cleveland in the early evening and he had managed to book a seat. The monitor told him that the plane would be delayed by at least an hour. He pulled out the laptop and read his e-mail. The first one was from Ed saying that he and Kay would meet him at the airport. The second was from a source that he did not recognise. It said: DON'T COME BACK

CHAPTER 22

ICEBERGS drifted into the harbour of the capital of Prince Edward Island as the light aircraft landed at midnight. Gus McWilliams had flown in from Toronto to pay a brief visit to his old friend Bob Picking. He had left Ohio at lunchtime and caught a connecting plane to PEI. Weather conditions had deteriorated and there had also been a delay at takeoff due to a security scare. Following the recent atrocity in New York, the atmosphere in the airports was tense. Picking's wife met him at the airport.

'Bob's been drinking again. Not too much,' she said. 'But too many to drive.' Her plump face was weary and resigned. As she drove the old Chevrolet she updated him on his friend's condition. 'The tumour was discovered about three months ago. He'd been having a lot of severe headaches,' she went on. 'I know what you're thinking, but these belonged in a different category. He's been getting the full treatment, but he hasn't really changed his ways.'

Snow drifted lightly and a faint residue covered the cold empty streets of Charlettown. The car pulled up in front of an apartment block. Gus pulled his luggage from the car and they entered the house. Picking sat slumped in front of a large television screen with a glass of whiskey at his side. He looked up, grinned and roared: 'Well! McWilliams!' They hugged. His wife, Thelma, fetched fresh drinks.

'I'll leave you too it,' she said and went to bed. They sat quietly for a few minutes. Gus did not know what to say but that had never mattered. Picking turned off the football game and drank.

'She's filled you in, I suppose,' he said quietly.

'Yes, I'm sorry.' Picking had one of those faces that had never been pretty. Heavy and pockmarked still, the ageing process had not been as unkind as expected. 'You look well,' he said. 'Tell me everything.'

'What about yourself?' Gus said. 'How did you end up here?' Picking told him about his post at the University. He'd been in Toronto for a while but the usual hectic lifestyle had taken its toll. The problems had begun again and he had been lucky, after a short break, to be offered the post in Charlettown.

'There's a lot of people like me out here,' he said, looking vacant now.

'A lot of guys who've been about and now settled for the quiet life. The only disadvantage is the winter. It gets bloody cold here.' Heavy flakes pinged off the windows from the blackness outside. Gus felt the burn of the whiskies as Picking's eyes dropped. 'Time for bed!' he suddenly shouted.

Gus unpacked his bags in the sparse but comfortable bedroom. A huge radiator grumbled along one wall. Sleep came easily and he woke at six. The house was silent and the snow shone in the early light. Finding the kitchen, he made tea and returned to bed. He thought back over the last few weeks.

Ed and Kay had met him in Cleveland. Kay had driven the 4x4 through the night to their home outside Columbus. Gus sat in the front seat with Ed crouched behind him.

'There's been no progress,' she sobbed. 'It's been nothing but a nightmare. They are certain about the ticket purchase but have no record of check-in by someone under that name.'

Gus tried to stay calm as he heard the details of the frantic searches for information. Identifications would take weeks or months. Maybe never.

The five bedroom detached house had been built ten years before. They had stretched their finances for a new home in a rural neighbourhood after Gus had obtained his last promotion. He unpacked. They were talked-out after the drive and they went to bed. Gus was exhausted but could not sleep.

The neighbours, Fred and Jean Olsen, called early. Gus thanked them for looking after Ed and they said they would catch him later. He repeated the calls that Kay had made and hit only blanks. There was nothing to do but endure the wait.

Kay went back to Boston and stayed with Ed. They agreed on a visit to her later in the month. He called in at the Research Unit and talked everything over with the Chief. As he was on a sabbatical, there was nothing to negotiate. He was told to rest.

It was almost impossible to relax. He could not read or take an interest in anything. The days were passed feeling numb. When Ed had gone to High School, he made coffee and read a newspaper. Afterwards, he often did nothing except stare out of the reception room window for hours.

On some days, he drove the 4x4 to a place he liked in a forest near a bend of the Ohio river. He walked through a trail to an observation point high above the water. Outside the vacation season, the area was nearly always deserted. He found a spot where he might jump.

He visited his doctor and a course of anti-depressants was recommended. 'They'll take the edge of things,' said Doctor Hill. 'Don't worry. You won't get addicted.'

Gus was tempted but he hid them away where Ed could not find them. In the evenings, he drank beer and made dinner. When Ed went to bed, he found the Wild Turkey and tried to limit himself, without success, to two glasses.

The afternoons were long and he began to get the bottle out at lunchtime when he came back from the river. He knew that Ed was concerned but his son said nothing. There was no talk of prime numbers.

It was nine o'clock one morning when he found himself sitting with a full glass of Austin Nichols. It was empty in ten minutes. Ed found him slumped on the floor in the early evening and put him to bed. He decided next morning that he had had enough of that.

He checked with the neighbours. 'I'm going to Boston for a few days and I appreciate that you're going to look after Ed. I'll call you when I get there.'

The trip was not a success for there had been no developments. Kay had her own life and he felt in the way despite their situation.

He flew back to Ohio and took stock. The neighbours could see to Ed. They were good people. His son was holding up well but you could see the fright in his eyes. The bad spells from earlier in the year occasionally returned. There was always the possibility of failure of the remaining kidney. He could not forget it.

Gus stirred and thought about the future. Kay was independent. She had told him about her new relationship. He felt sure that Lucia was dead. His life here was finished. The only purpose for him lay in Ireland where he could do some good. He found Dr Canavan's package and made arrangements to visit Canada before returning home.

Picking rose mid-morning. They had coffee and went over the background for the third time. Gus gave him the package.

'I'm only there part-time, especially now,' said Picking. 'I'll need to clear it with some people and get the lab boys on my side.'

'If they do it,' said Gus, 'I'll pay good money.'

'I know that but it will take time. Our boys don't like to make mistakes. Everything will be triple-checked.'

Thelma worked nearby in a hospital and had walked there earlier. The Chevrolet sat coated in snow. He helped Picking wipe it off and they attached the chains onto the wheels. They drove through town and out along a wide Avenue which led to the University. Cars lay abandoned from the previous evening.

Gus waited in the car while Picking entered a large two storey building with the package. He looked out over the campus which was sparse and bleak. It was early winter and he imagined what it must be like in January and February. And yet Picking had said that the staff liked it and preferred its isolation.

Gus shivered as Picking opened the door of the car. 'Sorry. Didn't mean to take so long. I've cleared everything and it has been logged for analysis. They've got the history as well.'

'That's one half of the problem addressed,' said Gus. 'What can we do about the second part?'

'If the weather hadn't turned, I might have been able to arrange a trip to Halifax by boat. In the summer, it would be straightforward. As you know, I'm prevented from flying...especially in light aircraft. You could go over yourself but I don't think you'd get very far.'

'Was your friend from St John's difficult?'

'Not really. He's working in Halifax until Christmas and he owes me a few favours from way back. I'd have to handle it face to face. Leave it with me.'

'I appreciate all this, Bob. I know it's a long shot but it can do no harm to try.'

'No problem. You can't stay on after tomorrow? I'd have enjoyed your company for a while longer.'

'Unfortunately not. I have to get back and make all my arrangements. Tidy everything up.'

'Sure. I know how it is. If the weather wasn't so bad, I could have shown you the island. It's a lot like Ireland. Big potato industry.' Picking grinned. 'About all you guys are good for.'

Gus smiled too at his friend's resilience. There wasn't too much to look forward to for either of them. He thought of his times above the Ohio river. It would have been easy.

They returned to the apartment. Picking opened two ice-cold Molsens. 'Nothing like the first beer of the day,' he yelled. 'Thelma's working this evening. We'll microwave something later.'

They kept away from difficult subjects and exchanged stories from Picking's time in Ohio. Gus told him about his visit to see Primo and it reminded his friend of a night on the town which all three had enjoyed, as he said, in their pomp.

The curries were washed down with tannic plonk. They walked around town afterwards as the snow fell again. Picking's favourite bar was small and dimly-lit. Country music played in the background as they enjoyed two final whiskies.

They went back to the apartment, slipping and sliding on the pavement. 'I'll not see you in the morning,' said Gus. 'I'll grab a cab to the airport. The weather will hardly be bad enough to prevent a flight. I can see they're used to it here.'

Picking dozed off. Gus shook him and they called it a night. He left early next morning and they did not meet again.

The journey to Ohio was again delayed by snow and he did not arrive in Columbus until midnight. Ed was asleep. He thought of going through his mail but decided to leave it until morning. Gus stared into the darkness. Lucia was dead. His old friend would follow soon. If Ed deteriorated, it could be the final straw.

In the morning, he steeled himself to make the final arrangements. He called Kay and confirmed what he had decided. She did not object. In the evening, he talked it over with Ed again. 'Fred and Jean will be delighted to have you stay with them. They have plenty of space since Jim left. I may be gone until just before Christmas. We'll keep in regular touch. You know to phone or e-mail me if there are any problems.'

'I'll be fine. Don't worry. There's a busy schedule ahead at school.'

He had one more trip to make before the long haul to Ireland and he had arranged to do it at the weekend.

It was the Friday evening of the last week in October. The air was crisp with the fading of Autumn. Gus walked along Pennsylvania Avenue, turned right at the White House and entered the restaurant one hundred yards along. His contact who had worked in the State Department was seated at the bar with a dry martini. Gus had described himself to him.

'Hi. I'm Ron Greene...spelt with three e's,' he smiled. 'Will you have a drink?'

'Thanks. A draft Bud would be swell.'

They talked about the weather for a while, then about 9/11 and the potential reaction of the Bush administration. Gus told him about his wife.

'How did you get my name again? I'm curious.'

'It's a long story which you won't want to hear. When I was back in Ireland, I traced two long-lost relatives. A father and son, as it happens. The son, my cousin, is called Patrick Tohill. He said that you were a sympathiser and would not mind talking to me.'

'I can't remember anyone by that name but, over the years, I met many people at the Irish Embassy.'

'It's not these relatives that I wanted to talk to you about directly. In fact, it's another old relative of mine. A direct cousin of my father. A man called Mike Connor.'

Ron Greene smoothed his fingers across the grey moustache and stared into his martini. 'Ah. Poor Mike. I see.'

'You knew him well…according to Tohill. His father is Mike's older brother – George Connor.' Gus explained again.

'And the old guy's still alive. Well, well. It's a small world.'

'I'd appreciate it if you could tell me about Mike Connor. It could be important.'

'I'll tell you what I know. I was quite a few years younger than Mike but we became friends. Mike was divorced…as you probably know…and I was single. We drank after work. He was very bitter about the break-up of his marriage and threw himself into his work. With his background, he had no difficulty running with the Kennedy crowd. I had come up from the South with Johnson. Mike didn't have quite the same influence after the assassinations…particularly the second one. We shared all the political gossip but lost touch after I got married. Then Mike got shafted.'

'What happened?'

'Mike got on the wrong side of a guy called Alex Cochrane. An apparatchik of Lyndon Johnson who had come into the Administration after being wounded in the Marines. Cochrane was contemptuous of bureaucrats although he became an effective one himself. Mike said that he had Masonic links and detested Irish-Americans of a certain ilk.'

'Meaning?'

'Irish-Catholics. The Kennedy pack as he called them. When Johnson went, he had no trouble obtaining a post with Nixon in 69. However, even before that, he managed to set Mike up. I have this from the very best sources.'

He paused to look at the menu again and ordered a second martini. Gus had salmon and Greene selected a large sirloin. They agreed on a Pinot Noir from Oregon.

'This is on me,' said Gus. 'You know that none of this will go any further.'

'You remind me of Mike,' said Greene. 'I like a man who likes a drink, he used to say. No, I know when to trust a man. It's a pity we never met before.'

They were shown to their table. Pausing to sip his wine, Greene took up the story again as the restaurant filled with diners.

'Cochrane was a slippery customer. Slippery, tough and smart. He waited for his opportunity and chose his battleground well. It came in 1968.'

'The year of rebellion,' said Gus.

'Funnily enough, his downfall originated with the Irish Troubles starting up again. Certain Irish Republicans with a very radical streak got a hearing from Mike who apparently went the extra mile to help them. At that time, he did something which was inappropriate for someone in his position.'

'Money?'

'Indirectly or so I was informed much later. Cochrane was tipped off about this through the British Embassy. Some of Mike's friends had big mouths and spouted too much when they got back home.'

'And then,' said Gus. 'I think I can guess.'

'Yes. Cochrane went right to the top with it. Mike was subjected to an investigation. McNamara, apparently, had sympathy with Mike's position and tried to protect him. He suggested a posting to Vietnam to allow things to cool down and maybe help his later career.'

'How did Mike react to that?'

'Don't forget. We'd lost close touch. I know that Mike was very much in favour of the war and maybe kidded himself that administrative experience out there could help him. I don't know for sure. In any case, he left before Johnson lost the election to Nixon. As you know, he never came back.'

They had coffee in the bar and Gus offered brandy. 'Did you ever find out who tipped off the British Embassy? That's not a fair question, I suppose.'

'As a matter of fact, I did get some information on that one through a mutual friend and Embassy gossip. I don't know whether the name was for real or just a name used by the Brits. The tip came through an Ulster politician at Westminster who had been informed by a man called Ross.'

CHAPTER 23

HALLOWEEN passed and, on the following evening, Gus caught his flight from JFK to Shannon. Security was as intensive as he had expected. There were long queues and random searches. He had forgotten about his razor which he had always carried in hand luggage and it had to be transferred to his main bag.

Gus buckled his seat belt and prepared himself for the schedule ahead. He intended to return for Christmas unless there was a development with regard to identification. If it weren't for his problems, he would have been able to relax in the business class cabin which was almost deserted. He drank a Bud and promised himself that he would cut down when he got back. There was too much to resolve.

He had parted with Ron Greene on the friendliest of terms and they had agreed to link up after Christmas. An elderly blond woman had collected him and taken him to their home in Silver Springs.

Gus could not fathom the connection between Mike Connor and a man called Ross. And yet Ron Greene had been sure of his facts. The man, despite his age, had instant recall of the key events of the 1960's. They had discussed Vietnam and the new war with Islamic terrorists. Greene with his experience felt pessimistic about a short-term outcome.

'McNamara...who must be in his mid-eighties...has changed most of his views on war. I understand that he's writing a book or preparing a television documentary on the subject. According to an insider I know, he believes the Vietnam War to have been a waste of time. He's denounced our possession of nuclear weapons which he thinks will be used eventually.'

'Strange views...coming from him,' Gus had said. 'The leopard has changed his spots.'

'Quite. His new opinions are relevant to what we're seeing at present. My belief is that Bush will attack Iraq as retribution for 9/11 but it will backfire just like Vietnam. McNamara is warning that regime change in some of these Arab countries will not solve the problem. Someone else has made the point that bin Laden's men have in the past tried to assassinate Saddam Hussein and the latter has responded in kind.'

'The politics of the Middle East are a mystery to most Americans.'
'And now good guys like you are paying the price.'

After a bland meal of rubber chicken ameliorated by a fine Zinfandel, Gus sipped coffee and then slept through most of the flight. He dreamt of Picking and his colleagues pouring over the Canavan package. Then of Mike Connor struggling through a jungle in Cambodia and waking up in Hanoi.

Early morning mist shrouded Shannon Airport and the green winter fields. Gus picked up his luggage and caught a cab to the hotel. He saw the red MX-5 with its black canvas hood. At least it hadn't been stolen. He had decided to risk an overnight stay in the hotel and then drive to Belfast via Galway.

In the evening, the restaurant was deserted as he ate in magnificent splendour. Afterwards, he restricted himself to one glass of Midleton and rang home. He checked his e-mail. There had been no more threats.

He left after the full breakfast eaten in a dining room inhabited by one other guest wolfing down fried eggs with bacon. Fog hugged the Shannon as he drove along empty roads which were punctuated by towns with Saturday shoppers. A sequence of huge roundabouts took him past Galway.

Despite the two hours that it would add to his journey, he made his first diversion and drove the sixty miles out to Clifden. The pale winter sun spread its iridescence across the lakes beside the road and split through the clouds which obscured the Twelve Pins.

In a lonely place outside the town, he found the commemoration to the life of Guglielmo Marconi. In 1907, his research work had led to the establishment of the first transatlantic wireless service between the Old World and the New. Commercial telegraphy had first operated between Clifden and Glace Bay, Nova Scotia.

He drove back along the deserted road to Oughterard where Michael Furey lay buried in a lonely churchyard. The rain fell without cease as he reached Galway again and pointed the car to the North-West.

There was a second diversion to be made in Sligo. He had always wanted to see the grave of Yeats and this was his only opportunity. The visitors' book was crusted with names that were heavy in the summer and sparse as the year had progressed. There had been none from the States for some time.

He crossed the border at Belleek and found the fast route from Enniskillen to Belfast. It was late evening when he entered the Avenue. The big elms outside Celia's house were bare and the pavements were cluttered with brown leaves.

The house was freezing. He switched on the central heating and lit the fire prepared by his neighbour. The peat flared and the room filled with smoke. The fridge had been stocked. He fried potatoes and ate them with cooked breasts of chicken and the wine from Puglia.

With the time difference, he knew that he would find it difficult to sleep. The files were extracted as he drank a glass of Midleton. He had promised himself only one and he kept his promise. Gus thought of those who might know about his return. He hoped that they would wait until Monday November 5th.

On the following morning, he was apprehensive as he went to fetch the catalogue of mail from his neighbour. She offered tea which he declined. He told her that there were no developments and thanked her for all her help.

Gus sifted out the obvious junk mail and bills. He opened the two significant letters. Dr Canavan acknowledged receipt of the letter from Patrick Tohill and asked him to make an appointment at his convenience. The letter was dated late September. At around the same time, a letter had been sent by McLean asking him to make contact if and when he returned. He waited until the afternoon before ringing. 'Thank you for the risks you're taking,' he said. 'I gather you might have something for me.'

'I can't say too much on the phone. All I needed to know is that you've returned and suitable arrangements can be made for the collection of the data you ordered. I'll be in touch.'

Gus phoned Tony Hamilton and updated him on the lack of progress. They arranged to meet later in the week.

He had decided to leave Townsend until the following day. The voicemail had been on his mind. He grasped the nettle and rang Arna Breen. 'I'm sorry I didn't tell you before I left for the States. You can imagine my state of mind.'

'I ran into Tony Hamilton one day and he told me what had happened. I'm sorry.' He voice sounded flat and tired. 'I had some other news for you but it can wait.'

'Would you like to get together?'

'Fine. Wednesday evening.' She suggested a time and place.

On Monday morning, he made an appointment to see Dr Canavan. The laptop was checked again and he drove to the police station.

'You may be in luck,' said the young cop at reception. 'He's just come back this morning and I happen to know that his diary is free...for a change.'

The Inspector asked him to sit down and sent out for coffee. 'No news I take it. Sometimes the uncertainty is worse than anything. Many people here disappeared years ago and their relatives have been left permanently in limbo. It's not much consolation to you.'

'That's one sure thing,' said Gus. 'Anyway, I've come to report something else. On my way back home, I checked my e-mail on this laptop and there was a warning not to return. It appears to have been sent around September 17th. I cannot decipher the sender name...SAUL@HAS.AC.TIM. It's from a different country and I suspect some pains have been taken to hide the originator. Any news on the two students?'

Townsend sighed. 'Whitley is expected back later this month. But there is something I should tell you. I said to you before that we couldn't interview his relatives...not without good reason. However, we have made some enquiries. His mother's dead. His father is called James Whitley and we have the address. One of my men recognised the name from somewhere and we're checking that out. I can't say any more than that.' The Inspector paused to finish his coffee. 'I needed that. The other piece of news I have is that the Serbian girl has not returned and there have been no messages to Jones. He has suggested that, with all the anti-Islamic feeling, she decided not to return to the UK.'

'She wasn't involved by any chance?'

'Your guess is as good as mine. Allow me to change the subject. You've had no more contact with Tohill?'

Gus looked at him directly. 'No.' He guessed that Townsend knew more than he was admitting. 'I can't promise you that I won't meet him again.'

'I've advised you. I'll say no more. There's one thing I must warn you about before you leave.' He paused. 'When you were away...it must have been late October...one of our Landrover patrols spotted a blue Rover car near your home.'

'Did they get a number?'

'Unfortunately not. As soon as they drove into the Avenue, it made off at great speed and they lost it. So watch out.'

It was Wednesday evening. Gus entered the Crown Bar and ordered a pint of Guinness. As it settled, she came in by a side entrance and smiled in welcome. 'I heard today that my application had succeeded. I'll have a large glass of cold Chardonnay.'

'Congratulations. Why did they take so long to make up their minds?'

'Security checks take time.' She gulped her wine and apologised. 'I'm sorry to be in such good form. You must be feeling dreadful.' She looked into his eyes.

'It's OK.'

'I'm starting my new job in the New Year so I've something to look forward to. Shall we go and eat?'

Gus finished his Guinness and wiped the creamy froth from his mouth. She had suggested a nearby bistro. He guessed that she had something to tell him about Burgess. They both ordered roast duck with rice and salad. Gus ordered a bottle of Fleurie to celebrate her good news.

'He rang one night a few weeks after you'd left,' she opened. 'Asked for you almost immediately and I told him why and where you'd gone. There was silence and then he complained that the weather had turned and indicated that he might come home.'

'What kind of mood was he in?'

'Apart from the complaint, he seemed fine. He questioned me closely about what you'd been doing before the tragedy. We discussed the cloning business.'

Gus interrupted. 'Sorry to be rude about it, Arna. There's something else...isn't there?'

She looked at him closely and then turned away as the waiter arrived with their wine. 'I told him about your interest in Mitchel. Also about McLean and your cousin in Dublin.'

'I'll tell you all about the developments there when you've finished. Go on.' Gus dabbled at the food.

'He began to quiz me closely about Mitchel...which I thought was unusual. I did not understand how he could possibly have any curiosity about that subject.'

Gus paused to drink his wine and looked around the busy restaurant. 'You remember that I told him all about Ross. And the possibility of a hostile force preventing him from succeeding. That might explain it.'

'Possibly. I thought that it was more than that. He seemed to know all about him. There was no surprise in his voice that you'd gone in such a direction.'

Gus stopped and rubbed his chin where he could feel the orange sauce. 'What about Diogenes? Did he mention him?'

'Not directly. It was as if he wasn't listening to me but talking to himself.'

'Can you remember exactly what he said?'

'Yes. He said…let me be sure…John, John, John…Diogenes man.'

'It could make sense,' said Gus. 'I don't know. I need to talk to him. Make sure you tell him that I'm back.'

'Of course I will. In fact, I'll ring the contact number and give him your details.' She yawned. 'Sorry, it's been a long day at the lab. If you don't mind, we'll skip coffee and get back.'

He drove her to Burgess's house and dropped her off in the empty Avenue. She thanked him and left. A strange woman, he thought. The bubble had burst quickly when all he wanted to talk about was Burgess. He hadn't even asked her about the new job.

He had arranged to see Dr Canavan at 11.30am. The morning was dark and the sky studded with thunderclouds. The MX-5 was not suitable for this kind of weather. However, he liked it despite the faulty heater and the draught.

As he drove along the country road to the mental hospital, he thought about Townsend and the students. The Serbian had given an address outside Belgrade and it niggled at his brain. Whitley's home address was given as near Larne and he had remembered driving through it earlier in the year.

If the weather had been better, he might have repeated the earlier two trips but he was not in the mood on such a black day. Rain poured from the heavens and the wipers struggled to cope. Nobody stood outside the hospital today. The water pelted off the flat roof and the blocked drains were flooded. Even in the short walk from the carpark, he was drenched in heavy rain. Dr Canavan extended his right hand and commiserated with Gus about the weather. 'It looks like it's on for the day,' he said. 'Some of our fellows get very morose on days like these.'

Gus explained what had happened and why he had not been in contact. He recapped on the visit to see Tohill in Dublin. 'I knew that he had written to you. I've paid him for his co-operation. I'd just like to make that clear.'

'It doesn't matter. He provided me with what I needed. I did hear about your wife from our friend in the Department. I'm very sorry.'

'I'll just have to wait and see. Have you any good news for me?' Gus scanned the doctor's cautious eyes as he removed his gold-rimmed spectacles and placed them on his desk.

Canavan smiled and looked back at Gus. 'I have to be very careful. Let's double check.' He took a key from his pocket and pulled out a large white envelope from the desk drawer. 'You have your son's records with you?'

'I have them here.' Gus retrieved them from his overcoat pocket and gave them to Dr Canavan. The doctor replaced his spectacles and studied the two sets of records.

After a long pause, he took the glasses off again and beamed. 'Yes indeed. As I thought. An exact match.'

CHAPTER 24

THE RAIN pelted down in sheets as Gus sprinted to the car. He sat behind the wheel and closed his eyes. The quest had been worthwhile. However, a major problem remained. He recalled the conversation with Doctor Canavan.

'The blood type is the same,' the doctor had said, peering at the records. 'The blood tissue matches. He is a relative. I've talked it over before with a nephrologist. The chances of success would be reasonable.'

'George is an old man,' said Gus. 'I had been concentrating on the son.'

'George has led a clean life. He's been well fed and watered as they say round here. Occasionally, he will puff at a cigarette and sometimes a nip is given to him in order to help him sleep. It doesn't do any harm. The main point is that, for his age, his renal function is quite good. It is of course preferable that a younger kidney is used. You mentioned George's son?'

'Very complicated and maybe you don't want to know. But I expect to find out soon whether he matches up as well.'

'Throwbacks like these are not uncommon. I'd advise you to keep up your pursuit and I'll help you if I can. We still don't have any permission to do anything with George. Don't forget that.'

'I know. When I was back in the States, I travelled up to Canada to visit a former research colleague. I gave him the package. It shouldn't compromise you in any way.'

'Don't worry. I'll be interested in what they come up with.' Canavan glanced at his watch. 'I have someone else to see before lunch. Call me if there are any developments.'

Gus turned on the ignition. The water cascaded across the windscreen as he drove towards Belfast. On an impulse, he decided to visit Father Campbell. The housekeeper recognised him and invited him in. 'Such awful weather. Dry yourself out. I'm sure he'll be glad to see you.' She showed Gus into the room where he had been before.

The priest dabbed at his mouth with a napkin as he came in. He grasped the side of a chair. 'I was just finishing lunch. Would you like something to eat? Margaret made some sandwiches and there's plenty over.'

'You're very kind. I'm sorry to intrude like this. I was at the hospital visiting Dr Canavan and called on the off-chance.' Gus noticed the old man's watery eyes and hunched step.

'Not at all. I don't see many people and I'm happy that you called again. I remember you in my prayers. Unfortunately, my memory is not good on other matters and I lost your telephone number.' He broke off and smiled. 'Ah. Here's Margaret with coffee and your sandwiches.'

She stoked the coal fire and it roared up the chimney. They sipped their coffee and the priest warmed his hands. 'These old bones aren't getting any better,' he said. 'Now. Tell me what you've been up to. A wee nip to warm you up perhaps?' He smiled.

Gus told him about his wife. Father Campbell raised his eyes and sighed. 'Holy Mother of God. What a world we're living in. I'll be glad to be out of it soon.'

'You've a few years left in you yet,' said Gus. 'You asked me what I'd been doing. Well, I have some news for you. I don't know where to begin.'

'Take your time. I remember all about your son. It would be lovely to hear something positive today. Margaret always reminds me that things happen for a reason.'

'Sometimes. Although it's not good news, I have managed to find out something about your friend Mike Connor.'

'How did that come about?' Father Campbell added a second nip of Powers to their coffees and sat forward in his seat grasping his invalid cane.

Gus hesitated. He remembered the old man's reticence when the subject had been raised at their first meeting. Maybe he would be more open this time. 'Before the 9/11 atrocity, I managed to track down George Connor's son.' Gus drank his coffee and paused.

Father Campbell shifted in his chair. The pale blue eyes did not look at Gus directly as he spoke. 'I know I should have told you more when you were here in the summer. My conscience pricked me and then I lost your number. I admit I was in two minds and didn't make any great effort to find you. May God forgive me.'

'I understand. I assume that you are aware of his background and I'll proceed on that basis. As you probably know, his name is Patrick Tohill.'

'I do. His mother was Mary Tohill. A simple girl who had been plagued with illness from childhood. She was excited by the attention and the marriage was a quick one. I checked the records after you left. Mary died of tuberculosis before the Second World War. I don't know the exact date.'

'It doesn't matter. I found her son through a contact in West Belfast. I met him in Dublin. We had a drink together in the Shelbourne Hotel.'

'It's a long time since I was there. A lovely place. I can guess why he's down South. I heard something about Patrick Tohill's later life. Just by chance you understand. When he came back from England, I was surprised at the path he took. I supported the Civil Rights campaign and then matters got out of hand. Who could have predicted all the bombings and murders? None of it was worth a single life.'

'I don't believe my cousin was ever actually convicted of anything,' said Gus.

'It's not a surprise that he got involved. Foreigners think of Belfast but the conflict runs like a thread through a great deal of rural society.'

'Before I tell you about Mike,' said Gus. 'Is there more that you can tell me about the Tohills? How would they have reacted to Patrick Tohill's political activities?'

'They would have sympathised…up to a point. I understand that he helped them out when he could.' Father Campbell shifted his cane and stared into the fire.

'They would have been your parishioners?' asked Gus casually.

'Yes. They were very religious and only missed mass if extremely ill. I cared for them both at the end.'

'Did they talk about Patrick Tohill?'

The old man looked startled and did not reply for some minutes. Gus sensed that he had gone too far. 'That's not a fair question to put to me Mr McWilliams.'

'I'm sorry. I didn't mean…'

'Let's leave it at that. You haven't told me yet about Mike Connor.'

Gus recovered himself. 'My cousin told me that he had visited Washington on political business…back in the 1970's…and had made the acquaintance of a man called Ron Greene. He turned out to have been an old friend of Mike Connor. When I was back home, I met Greene and he told me what had happened.'

Father Campbell listened to Gus's story and sighed. 'Mike was a good man. He wouldn't have supported violence.'

'He went to Vietnam. Thought the war was just.'

'That's different.'

Gus did not want to argue the point. 'It's interesting how he was betrayed.'

'But not surprising. Let's leave it. What about your son?'

Gus told him some of his plans. 'You were looking earlier for good news. I don't know if it is good news but I can tell you...in total confidence...that my son's blood and tissue type match exactly with George Connor's.'

'So if George died, his kidney could be used if necessary?'

'I have no permission. He would have to come round sufficiently to sign a consent form.'

The old man sat up again. 'Maybe I could help you there. I'll speak to Father Murphy if you like.'

'I hadn't thought of that. I'd be grateful if you could. Look, I've kept you long enough. I must go. Please, don't get up.' They shook hands.

It was late afternoon. The rain had stopped. Darkness fell as Gus drove back to Belfast. He knew that Father Campbell had again kept something back from him. Perhaps a secret which he could not break or he would pay the price in the next world.

The house was cold. He lit the peat fire. The nips of Powers had soothed and warmed him earlier. One more could do no harm. Gus added logs to the fire and fetched a glass of Midleton.

The final years of Mitchel came back to him. Despite his success, he is crippled by his health. Two of his sons are dead and the third has lost an arm. At an important point in Ireland's history, his destiny is thwarted. Along comes a proposal to change that destiny.

Gus added more whiskey and cast his mind back to Greene's story. A man called Ross betrays Mike Connor and has him sent to Vietnam...from where he never returns. It was time to eat.

He heated a clove of garlic and pushed it to one side of the pan. The fillet steak was cooked quickly with fried potatoes. He ate it with green peas and drank a glass of Primitivo.

Afterwards, he put on the thick navy Crombie which he had purchased in London. The night air was freezing. He looked up at the black Cavehill and the orange moon irradiating the dark blue of the Lough.

On his return, he watched the News. The atrocity did not fill the main slots or even the secondary ones. A reporter in Regent Street talked about asylum seekers and the problems of beggars in the streets as the season of Christmas approached. The time of good cheer and good will to all men.

It wasn't even Thanksgiving yet, thought Gus. There would be little to give thanks for. He switched off the television set and went to bed. New theories swirled in the back of his mind. How could he have missed the connections? Father Campbell, by saying nothing, had revealed a lot. And so had Townsend.

Monday morning's post contained a letter from McLean informing him that the previous arrangement would operate on the following Friday. The girl would meet him at the same time and place as before. Gus noted the appointment in his diary and made coffee.

He would have liked to have talked his problems over with Tony Hamilton. However, there was little opportunity to do this during the academic year. Their session on the previous Thursday had been interrupted sporadically by students and colleagues.

Gus mulled over his strategy. If Tohill did not match, it was the end of the dilemma. A tie-up with Ed's records would pose a problem of a different level of difficulty. Tohill was short of cash. He lived a precarious existence as an ex-prisoner and could disappear at any time. Gus weighed the possibilities.

A substantial sum would have to be offered to stay in contact. Then, if Ed's second kidney failed, a period of dialysis would follow until a suitable hospital, North or South, could perform the private operation on Tohill. On completion, his cousin would receive the balance of fifty thousand pounds. Gus knew that everything would not prove so straightforward.

The afternoon was cold and clear. He found his boots and walked to Belfast Castle. A pint of Guinness settled his thoughts and he decided on his first winter stroll to the top of Cavehill. The elms and chestnuts had lost their leaves and they cluttered the clearings in the forest. At its edges, the evergreens endured.

He reached the summit and looked at the remains of the fort where Mitchel's predecessors had gathered. In the distance, he saw a solitary walker struggling in the wind which bent the purple heather.

The giant gantries sat rooted beside the Lough. The Titanic had set out from there in 1912 as had other massive liners in the nineteenth and twentieth centuries. Only the largest one had sank. Its captain had underestimated the danger of an iceberg floating near the coast of Newfoundland. The great ship had carried several Thomson compasses on board and, like all White Star liners of the era, had been constructed in Thomson's own birthplace. Nothing in Belfast was beyond the wit of man.

He descended through the gorse some of which had been burnt in the summer. The single roamer had disappeared. The wind increased in ferocity as Gus reached the first set of evergreens. The downward path led past the Castle. It was beginning to rain and he jogged to the house. The chill had entered his bones. He had a hot shower and poured a glass of Midleton. As he did so, the phone rang to shatter his peace. It was Burgess.

'I hope that you don't mind my contacting you,' he said in his precise voice. 'Have you time available to speak with me?'

'David. I am delighted to hear from you. I had dinner with Arna Breen last week and hoped that she would link up with you. How are you?' Gus pressed his ear to the phone as Burgess spoke softly.

'Not so good. I hope to return in the next few weeks. I have lectures to give in the New Year.'

'Don't they miss you at the University?'

'A colleague of mine once went hiking in the Mourne Mountains. It was January and he became trapped in a snowstorm near the summit. He was found dead about a year later. Nobody noticed that he had been away.' Gus heard Burgess laugh. 'Arna told me about your wife. And I haven't forgotten those kidneys. Excuse my warped sense of humour. I've been feeling guilty since we met.'

'That's OK. I understand. What have you to tell me?'

'Had I known that you were interested in Mr Mitchel, our previous conversation might have been more fruitful.'

'I didn't get into that until I returned and stumbled on it by chance. If nothing else, it led me to my cousin.'

'Arna told me. I've decided to give you some information about Diogenes. His real name was Bartholomew Perry. I believe that he was a distant relative of a scientist called John Perry.'

'I know the name from my researches on Thomson. He was friendly with Thomson at the beginning of his career but, like many others, fell into a major dispute with him. How did you find this out?'

'From the Trinity diaries. They required considerable deciphering as it all was written in complicated code. Let me continue. Bart Perry came from a neighbourhood called Loughorne...about seven miles from Banbridge. His father was a wealthy farmer and he married into wealth but his wife died in first childbirth. As a child, the father dispatched him to relatives and, as soon as it was pragmatic, put him in a boarding school. Rather hellish I would imagine.' He paused to gather his thoughts and continued. 'Perry grew up to be a cold and calculating man but one with great ability. His father sent him to Glasgow in order to study the new veterinary sciences. He made the acquaintance of a man called Knox.'

'The name rings a bell,' said Gus as he tried to write down what Burgess was telling him. He found it hard to control his excitement. 'Sorry. I'm interrupting. Go on.'

'Thank you. When he was at College, his father...whom Perry had grown up to detest...was killed by a tenant connected with the Fenian movement. I hope you don't mind my using that term.'

'Of course not. You know me better than that.'

'Perry graduated *summa cum laude* and came home to Loughorne. He maintained a minimum of staff. A new farm manager and farmhands with their wives as domestic servants. He established a modern laboratory. All staff were sworn to secrecy on pain of immediate dismissal. Apart from that, he paid them well.'

'I get the picture,' said Gus. All that he was hearing corresponded with his recent theories. 'Go on.'

'He maintained good relationships with many politicians. His views were the opposite of his father's. He travelled widely and maintained his scientific contacts. There is no doubt that he attended William Thomson's classes in Glasgow and made his acquaintance. Perry continued to visit the great Universities. All the Trinities, Edinburgh, Glasgow and also on the Continent, America and Canada.'

'When did he visit the States?'

'Almost certainly around the early 1860's. In fact, this is when he begins to mention John.'

'John Mitchel?'

'I didn't know that for certain at first. When Arna mentioned your interest, I meant to contact you but the tragedy happened and you returned to the US. But...yes...he met Mitchel and made his acquaintance again when Mitchel returned on his political campaigns. By that time, Perry had mastered the technique of animal cloning and was ready for bigger experiments.'

'Did you realise most of this from your initial discovery in Dublin?'

'Some of it.'

'What did you think you could achieve when you fled to Italy?'

'Perry was a genius. He made very highly significant advances. He was not restricted by any code of ethics and, like the Nazis, did as he wished in the name of science. In the name of the future. I decided to build on those in order to publish new work on the transformations involved in cloning.'

'That's when you became jealous of others discovering your work and usurping it? And so you fled.'

'A subterfuge. That's not the reason why I ran to Italy.' He paused.

'Are you going to tell me or not?' said Gus with exasperation.

'Yes. I didn't go to Italy because of our local bores.' Gus heard the tremble in his voice. 'It was one day in the early summer of this year. I had left some agonising departmental meeting and decided to walk home. As I passed the entrance to the Botanic Gardens, I looked to the left and saw a bald youth staring up at Kelvin's statue. A person whom I recognised.'

'Who was it?'

'Diogenes.'

CHAPTER 25

GUNFIRE raked the front of the store as Gus strode to meet the girl. The Rover accelerated and turned down a road to its right. A silver Mondeo, passenger door swinging open, raced up to the screaming girl. She jumped in clutching the white envelope. The Ford disappeared in the opposite direction.

Gus picked himself up from the pavement and brushed the dirt from his Crombie. Staff and shoppers gathered around. The manager called the police on a mobile. Minutes later, a Landrover pulled up and two cops jumped out carrying machine guns. They questioned Gus about the shooting and listened with suspicion to his accent.

'So you'd just come out of the store when a car drove past and shot into it,' said the older cop. He turned to the manager. 'Have you had any trouble before like this? Threats or anything?'

'We had a bit of trouble last week with a young thug. One of my girls caught him stealing. I grabbed him but he escaped. He ran off yelling abuse. It happens every now and then.' He eyed Gus.

The cop turned to Gus. 'Are you on holiday over here?'

'No. My parents were Irish. I'm over here sorting out an estate matter.' Gus asked him if they could speak privately. He told him that he'd been having some trouble and Inspector Townsend was dealing with it. That's all he could say.

The cop raised his eyebrows and pulled out a mobile phone. He turned his back and made a call. A few minutes later, he put it back and spoke sharply to Gus. 'OK. The Inspector will contact you.' A small crowd had gathered and the younger cop asked them to disperse. The older man looked at the bullet holes in the walls of the store. 'We'll be back later for a full report.' He turned and spoke to Gus. 'Mr McWilliams...it would be best if we drove you home. Let's go.' They dropped him off and exchanged curt farewells.

Gus poured a glass of Midleton and clutched his stomach. Shortly afterwards, the Inspector and two cops arrived at the front door. Gus asked them to come in and they positioned themselves as before.

Townsend did not remove his cap. The lines in his cheeks looked deeper. 'I warned you about this place. You could have got yourself killed. I'd be obliged if you'd tell me everything before you do.'

Gus's glass was empty and he placed it beside his chair. His stomach had settled. One of the cops took notes and he saw him grimace. He did not speak but Gus could sense that he thought he was a fool. Maybe he was right. 'I should have told you before. However, I've always felt that you haven't been telling *me* everything.'

'We'll ask the questions if you don't mind,' said Townsend with a first hint of humour. 'I'm sorry. In my position I can't.' He changed the subject. 'So you lost your money?'

'Yes. It all happened in a flash. There was no exchange.'

'Don't follow this up. I know you have good motives but you must forget it. There's nothing more we can do tonight. I should have been off-duty an hour ago.'

Gus noticed the black shadows beneath Townsend's eyes as he showed him to the door. He had always distrusted him. Maybe he had been unfair. These guys had to keep the balance. He retrieved his glass, filled it and heated up Bolognese sauce as he drank. At the height of all his troubles, he had still been able to eat and drink. It was one good thing that he'd learnt from his father.

Afterwards, he sat back with a glass of Primitivo. He suspected that he had lost Tohill. There was only George left and a dependence on an old priest. He thought of ringing home but the idea depressed him.

He still could not believe that anyone would want to kill him. Maybe someone was after the girl with her Republican connections. But why do it as she went to meet him? The gunfire had razed the wall at a point two feet above their heads. He had been warned and the level of threat was increasing. Maybe it had been a final warning. It had to be connected with his search. He thought again of the conversation with Burgess.

'I find it difficult to credit,' Gus had said. 'Diogenes or Perry lived over a hundred years ago.'

'You're not thinking straight. Anyone who had discovered the secret of cloning could do it to himself. The second possibility which I had to consider was that the boy was a normal descendent of Perry. Hence the close resemblance. If so, it must have been via an illegitimate line since there is no record of Perry marrying anyone.'

'What became of him?'

'We don't know for sure. He kept detailed journals up to the turn of the last century. At some point after that, they were deposited in the library at Trinity College, Dublin and catalogued. You could make some checks at your end. I will be home soon in any case and do it myself.'

179

'What frightened you so much about seeing the boy? There was no sign that he would do you any harm.' Gus had been puzzled by the extreme reaction.

'Knowing what I did about Perry, I felt sure that he had cloned himself and passed the secret on. The knowledge sent shivers up my spine. The journals demonstrated a streak of absolute ruthlessness in the man. They record a sinister incident when he is crossed by a drunken farmhand. The man was found soon afterwards hanging from the rafters of his home in Loughorne. When I unscrambled the notes in the journals by my usual method, it was clear that Perry had been responsible. The man was a psychopath. If you study the early life of any serial killer, you will always find an emotionally deprived childhood.'

'Does he ever mention Ross in his journals? You remember our conversation in the summer?'

'I scoured the diaries. I've told you about the reference to John. After you told me your story, I surfed the Internet. At first, I thought that it might have been a reference to John Ross – the son of the General and a contemporary of Perry. However, the man's character did not correlate with an alliance with Bartholomew Perry. It was not credible to me. I could be wrong.'

'If you were so frightened, why are you coming back?'

'I was going through a bad time mentally. Arna will have told you. It was the final straw. A few months out here in the sunshine have revitalised me. I accept that I can't stay here for ever. I will see you soon. Goodnight.' He put down the phone.

Gus had forgotten to ask him the reason for the name Diogenes. He found his files. The philosopher had spent most of his life in Athens. Its citizens had thought of him as mad. The first Diogenes referred to himself as the 'Dog'. Perry had been trained in veterinary science and had flouted all the scientific conventions of his age. In the nineteenth century, scientists were often referred to as natural philosophers. Reasons enough for the code name allocated to Perry.

Arna Breen must be warned. He had forgotten about her. Her phone was engaged. Gus rang the police station. Townsend had gone home. A cop logged his call. He said that there had been a lot of incidents in the city that evening but they would do their best. The Inspector would be informed. Gus finished the Midleton.

On Monday morning, he visited the Public Records Office in Belfast.

'If you can provide us with the name, approximate year of birth and the townland,' said the assistant, 'then within a few days we should be able to get you a copy of the death certificate.' Gus made his other requests and left.

He called with Tony Hamilton. 'I didn't want to ruin your weekend thinking about my problems. You did warn me but I'm not going to be intimidated.'

'You're out of your depth. Our Troubles may be over but there's plenty of killers on the loose. Forget this mission of yours.' Tony's eyes bulged. A student entered the room after a polite knock on his door. Tony waved him away.

'Tohill has the money and I have no records. However, he showed good faith by trying to get them delivered to me.'

'He had a clear incentive. If there was a match, he stood to make a substantial sum of money even if the operation didn't go ahead. There was ample opportunity for a double-cross.'

'I may have to forget that line of approach. Tohill will go underground for a while. It looks as if it's all going to come down to George Connor. I told you that he matches but we still have the problem of consent. I'm getting help from Dr Canavan and Father Campbell. I don't know if that will work either. My hunch is that a major trauma will be required to jolt George out of his current state of mind.'

'I suppose Tohill could have helped you there.'

'It's possible. We'll just have to wait and see. Anyway, I have other news for you which is connected. Burgess rang me last week. I could tell you it all if you're free for lunch.'

Afterwards, they walked to the Botanic Gardens and looked at the statue of Kelvin. 'Burgess was electrified by the guy whom he was convinced was Diogenes. He admitted that he was in a bad mental state at the time but he's not stupid. The resemblance must have been startling.'

Tony looked sceptical. 'I have classes this afternoon so I'll have to leave you. Keep in touch...and for God's sake...watch yourself!'

Arna Breen rang him back that evening. 'The police called with me on Friday. They told me what had happened. I rang you later on but there was no answer. It was late.'

'I needed a few glasses to settle me down and then I really hit the sack. Went out cold. Foolish I know but my nerves weren't too good.'

'I decided to spend the weekend with my parents.'

'I have some other news for you but it can wait. Perhaps we could meet up again.' They agreed on Friday evening.

Gus triple-checked his security. The attack and the dark nights prevented his evening walk. There was no news from the US. He felt that Ed was hiding his feelings. Gus had been the same at his age. He remembered again the long slow death of his mother from cancer of the liver. Since the Midleton had gone, there had been no whiskey. He stretched out the wine as far as his nerves could stand it.

On Thursday morning, the certificate arrived in the post. It confirmed that Bartholomew Perry had been born in August 1840 in the area of Loughorne. The death detail was more gripping. It recorded the date of death as August 15th 1913. Perry had been burnt to death near where he had been born. Nobody else was recorded as being present at his demise. The news shook Gus from his gloom. The rain pelted down from a black sky as the MX-5 headed for the city.

'We haven't seen you for a long time,' smiled Carl Baker. 'How can I help you?'

'You remember you dug out those old newspapers from 1914. When I was trying to find out something about the deaths of the boys. I'd like to have a look through them again.'

'No problem.'

In the middle of the afternoon, Gus found what he was looking for.

MYSTERIOUS FIRE NEAR LOUGHORNE

The report was short but provided what he required. A farmer who had risen early to milk his cows had seen a huge blaze in a distant field. Alarmed, he had awakened a son to do the milking and he had gone to investigate. Other farmers were there when he arrived. They had found the burning shell of a house that had belonged to a woman called Cross.

Gus found other reports on succeeding days. Her husband had committed suicide some years previously. They had both been employed by a rich landowner called Bartholomew Perry – a recluse who had not been seen for a considerable time. The two bodies in the burnt-out house had been identified as Rose Cross and Perry. The woman was believed to be in her fifties and Perry was understood to be in his seventies.

Gus scanned through the papers for the months ahead. The cause of the fire had never been found. Nobody knew what Perry had been doing in the house. She had left his employment many years before.

He had copies made and returned home. The day's findings had drained him. He opened a Budweiser. The death certificate had proven the existence of Perry. It had to be the same man. He looked through the reports again. Cross had lived alone after the death of her husband and the subsequent departure of her only son. The latter could not be traced.

CHAPTER 26

'WHITLEY froze when he saw me,' said Arna. 'And so did I.' She had explained to Gus in the Crown Bar that she had made an appointment with the Research Unit to be shown around her new workplace.

'You don't begin until January.'

'It's always a good idea to prepare for a post like that. I wanted to hit the ground running.'

'What happened exactly?'

'I had arranged to meet my new manager first thing this morning. A man in his late fifties called Dr Ellis. A big plump bald guy…gruff at first but actually very nice. After he had showed me around the laboratories and introduced me to my staff, we went for coffee in a small staff room. It was late morning and the place was deserted. He had begun to sketch out the direction in which he wanted my research work to go when two other men entered the room. Dr Ellis introduced the older man as Ken Jones. It was obvious that he couldn't recall the name of Jones's companion. Jones introduced Frederick Whitley whom he said had finished his Ph.d in the summer and was coming back if post-doctoral funding was available.'

'How did Whitley react after the introductions were over?'

'Difficult to say. Let me describe him. He was in his late twenties. Middle height and already running to fat. A liverish cast behind each iris. He mumbled in a strong rural accent and then they carried their coffees outside.'

'You didn't say anything to Ellis?'

'No. I think he sensed that there was something wrong but was too polite to ask. We finished our conversation. I rang the police. They said that they would follow it up. I had taken the day off so I returned home and waited until I was due to meet you.'

They finished their drinks and walked to the bistro where they had eaten before. The night was cold with a hint of fog. Gus thought over the possibilities. He would have to leave it to Townsend and assumed that he would be contacted.

He ordered a rib-eye steak with garlic mash. Arna ordered pasta with chicken. The waiter brought their Beaujolais. 'We don't know that Whitley's ever done anything,' said Gus. 'Although I assume we'll know next week. I don't think Townsend will drag his feet on it…especially after last week.'

'I took an instant dislike to Whitley and he sensed it. He recognised me. I know it.'

'You might be imagining it. Perhaps he's just some tongue-tied hick. You're a very attractive woman.' He lifted his glass and looked into her eyes. She turned aside as the waiter arrived with their food.

Gus cut into his steak. She dabbed at the pasta and gulped the wine. 'I'm positive he knew me. I've been thinking about it all afternoon.'

'How do you feel about working in the place?'

'I'm not going to let a creep like that block my career. Let's change the subject. You had something else to tell me?'

'Yes. About Burgess. He rang me last week and revealed the name of the mysterious Irish scientist. You've maybe forgotten all that.'

'How could I? I remember David's behaviour in the summer only too well.'

'The real name of Diogenes was Bartholomew Perry who lived between 1840 and 1913. I've checked it all out.' He finished his steak, paused to drink a glass of wine and told her the whole story.

'So he fled because he thought he'd seen this man,' she said. 'It's difficult to take this in. And the fire at the house. Do you think it was the same one?'

'We may never know. I told you that David was returning before Christmas. How do you feel about his coming back?'

She sighed. 'I've got used to living by myself. This other business has frightened me. Perhaps I should make plans to move out.'

'Perhaps David's mind was so deranged in the summer that he made a mistake.'

'Maybe. It sends a shiver up my spine to think that someone like this Perry is alive.'

They finished their coffee and he drove her home. She invited him in. He sensed her state of mind and agreed. She offered cognac. 'He has cases of it in his cellar. Some of it is extremely rare. He won't mind.'

'I'd love some but it'll put me well over the limit.'

'You could stay. There's plenty of room.'

When he returned home on Saturday afternoon, there was a voicemail message to contact Townsend.

'We'll be going to see Mr Whitley on Monday morning. I've warned Jones not to tip him off but I'm not relying on it. The good doctor isn't

185

taking this very seriously. He's been spouting quite a bit about human rights and solicitors. I'll ignore it. We'll inform you about the outcome.'

'No trace of the Serbian girl?'

'Not a peep. Disappeared as far as we know.' He advised him again to take care and rang off.

Gus looked over his mail. There was nothing of significance. A third reminder from the library that a book *Village in Seven Hills* was overdue and was incurring a fine. When they had written before, he could not find it and had forgotten about the reminder.

He suddenly remembered where it might be. The book had caught Kay's attention one evening and she had taken it to bed. Gus found it in a bedroom locker. He sat on the bed and flicked through it again. There were only two references to Sir John Ross. The first referred to his fine collection of non-indigenous shrubs and trees. The second was more interesting. It occurred in the middle of a section on the Crag Graveyard in Rostrevor. It read:

'Craggy it was then and craggy it still remains; and it is still known as the Crag Graveyard. Being in the centre of the village this old church of Saint Paul could not be missed by the interested sightseer. Let him not imagine, however, that the Celtic-looking cross, visible from the main road, is a symbol of ancient Irish Christianity. Though it is a pleasing-looking cross in the Irish idiom, it is a nineteenth-century monumental piece of sculpture, designed and executed by the widow of David Ross of Bladensburg. The cross was erected in memory of her husband, son of Major-General Sir John Ross of Bladensburg; the widow, Elizabeth Catherine, also sleeps in this rocky unkempt place. Here too is the grave of the Rev. Thomas Ross, brother of the General, and Vicar of the parish, 1800-1818.

Oh, that one could record the lives and stories of all who are buried in this old half-buried place of graves! Such an account would make interesting reading for many; valuable, however, as it might be, such a task would probably be beyond my powers. There is one inscription – on flat granite in a railed enclosure – that did excite me very much. It reads as follows:

'Robert Martin son of Samuel Martin and Jane Harshaw his wife born at Lough-horne May XV A.D. MDCCCXIV died at Kilbroney October IX A.D. MDCCCLVIII Millicent Martha Martin daughter of Thomas Millar and Millicent Dalway his wife born at Carrickfergus OCT VII A.D. MDCCCXXIV married to Robert Martin October II A.D. MDCCCXLVII died at Kilbroney October III A.D. MDCCCLVIII.'

All a little difficult to disentangle no doubt; but, reading this I was especially interested for two reasons: the Robert Martin referred to must surely have been the brother of 'Honest' John Martin of the Young Irishmen; and Robert's father, Samuel, appears to have married one Jane Harshaw of Lough-horne (or orne). Now Lough-horne was a lake – no longer in existence – where Patrick Bronte used to take his Glascar pupils for nature study rambles, and for skating in suitable weather. Patrick's sponsor, friend, and tutor was the 'stickit minister,' the Rev. Andrew Harshaw, a relative of the Loughorne Harshaws. Indeed, had it not been for Andrew Harshaw's inspiration, Patrick would probably never have reached Cambridge; and the world might never have known of 'Jane Eyre' and 'Wuthering Heights.'

In those days Catholics and Protestants were put into their final resting places side by side; this was true of both Kilbroney and the Crag. In these progressive times we no longer do this; we are literally separated from the cradle to the grave; it is surprising to find that in some ways in 'the ould days' they evidently took a broader view.'

Burgess had surely been correct about John Ross. The character and chronology did not match. However, he could not dismiss the paragraph on Lough-horne – as Crowe had spelt it. A lake which no longer existed.

He felt exhausted after the heavy evening and he put the book aside. It could be renewed on Monday. Nobody had requested it. Feeling guilty, he rang the Columbus number of the Olsens.

'I'm fine, Dad,' answered Ed. 'They've gone out. I'm working on the computer. There's no news. Kay keeps trying but we are getting no response. I told you I'd ring if there was.'

Gus told him about the proposed school arrangements. He put down the phone and groaned. He would liked to have taken a walk to clear his head but the late afternoon was already black and he sensed a thunderstorm. Instead, he took a long shower and opened a beer.

The weekend passed and Monday morning came. One that would never be the same again. He made coffee and thought of Whitley. Could the explanation be so simple? Gus thought of the forthcoming confrontation.

In the evening, Townsend rang to say that the interview had not taken place. Whitley had been expected at the Unit earlier in the day. Jones was to contact them after he arrived. Rights or no rights. 'We'll try again tomorrow. Jones says he promised to turn up. These fellows don't keep regular hours.'

'What if he doesn't appear this week?' asked Gus.

'I believe we have enough to go on to take it further. We'll give him some more time and then my men will be paying a surprise call to his father's address outside Larne. That's all I can tell you.'

Gus found it impossible to concentrate on the paper which Tony had mailed him. It had come back from the editor of the Journal with the assessments of the referees. He studied it for an hour and then placed it in a drawer. It could wait.

He secured the hood on the MX-5. The Mazda headed for Newry and his final visit to Rostrevor. A solitary tricolour fluttered in the wind as he passed through Warrenpoint. The giant obelisk dominated the field outside the village but he did not stop until he reached the Crag Graveyard.

The wind howled around the tombstones in the empty cemetery. All that Crowe had recorded was true. Gus was reminded of Pip and the appearance of Magwitch. He thought of the other churchyard where Eugene Connor lay buried. Lonely John McManus had been forgotten. A young boy who had been born at the beginning of the last century. The most murderous in human history. Perry's diaries had ceased at approximately the same time as John's birth.

Gus left the graveyard. He recalled Lucia's desire to visit the Fairy Glen on their last visit. A premonition had struck him that day before they had continued on their journey to see Tohill.

The path was wide and flat at its beginning and narrowed towards the end where the walls of an old linen mill stood. A project which had never got off the ground. It had been started, Crowe had stated, during the American Civil War. The world cotton trade had been ruined and, as a result, the Ulster linen industry had boomed.

The owner of the half-finished mill had thought that it would be a good idea to bring his drays and horses up the Fairy Glen rather than have them make the long drag up Chapel Hill. And so he had begun to widen the path. Unfortunately for the prospective linen baron, the Civil War had ended. The path and factory had never been completed.

He left the Glen and drove out to the spot where George Connor had crossed the barbed wire fence. It had puzzled Gus why the assailant had held back. If he had been recognised, why stop at that point?

Gus fetched the binoculars from the car and focused on the distant white bungalow and adjacent barn. Had they been constructed on the same ground as the burnt-out house? The spare green fields were damp and deserted with the cows housed for the winter. His imagination traced again the events of that night. Two pieces of the jigsaw were missing but he felt sure that he knew what had happened.

He drove the car back into Rostrevor, made some more checks and drove home in torrential rain. After a hot shower on his return, he opened a beer and watched the early evening news. An initial report on a political development was followed by a news item concerning a shooting incident.

'This afternoon, police visited a farm outside Larne,' said the commentator, 'on what was believed to be a minor enquiry. Reports are coming in that, as they approached the driveway, they were fired upon by a man with a shotgun. The man is understood to have leapt into a Rover driven by a younger man and it accelerated away from the scene. That's all we have at the moment. If we hear any more, we will come back to it.' At the end of the news, there was an additional flash that the police were hunting two men in connection with the attack.

Shortly afterwards, Gus received a phone call from Townsend. 'If you watched the news this evening, you will have seen policemen visiting a farmhouse. It belonged to James Whitley – the father of Frederick Whitley. We were working in co-operation with the local police.'

'Yes, I saw it,' said Gus, 'but didn't connect. No names were mentioned.'

'For confidential reasons, I couldn't tell you before that the older Whitley has had strong links in the past with loyalist paramilitaries.'

'I'd have appreciated knowing.'

'It's only recently that we linked the two men. Earlier in the year, informants fed us some gossip – you can never be sure of what they tell you – that an American in Belfast was attracting the attention of men with terrorist links on the loyalist side. If true, I suspected that they had somehow stumbled on your links with ex-Provisionals such as Tohill. I knew that such a link could get you in big trouble and I warned you.'

'To be fair…you did.' Gus waited. He sensed that there was more.

'We will catch the two Whitleys unless they've already crossed the Border. The South won't be the safest place for them either. Especially with the other news I have for you.'

'Yes?'

'One night during last week, our men in the West of the city were called to a house where there had been a shooting. The family said that they had been fired upon from a car. The front of the house was covered in blood but no body was found.'

'What's this got to do with Whitley?'

'We've been searching Whitley's house and found some key information. Take extra care with your security in the coming weeks.'

'There's something else…isn't there?'

'We are almost certain that the man shot in West Belfast last week was Patrick Tohill.'

'Why so sure?'

'We've found his body in the Lough. Near Larne.'

As Gus put down the phone, he heard the back door crash open and then felt the hammer thud into his kidneys.

CHAPTER 27

'KATRINA KIMINSKI is in Guantanamo Bay,' said Townsend to Dr Jones. 'We've been contacted at the highest level by the CIA.' He noticed the man's weak chin now that the beard had disappeared.

Jones pulled at the missing hair and then at the moustache which straggled his lips. 'She had radical views on life but I can't believe that she would be involved in anything like that. She was a conscientious and bright student.'

'The Muslims in there haven't been convicted of anything. Most of them are being held on suspicion. She appears to have had odd contacts all over the world – by e-mail and mobile phone.'

'Where was she picked up?'

Townsend did not blink as he replied. 'New York – shortly afterwards. She hasn't given a convincing explanation of why she was there although we don't know what she's said to them yet. They've asked us to check out her background over here. We can do that with some assistance from you.'

'I'll do anything to help my students,' said Jones. He shifted in his chair. 'Any news of Whitley?'

Townsend stared directly at him again. 'Were the two of them friendly?' He motioned to his colleague to take notes.

'Not as far as I know. They knew each other but worked independently. He wouldn't have been her type of person.'

'It's ironic that we've located her and he's gone missing. You'll have seen the news?'

'I read it in the newspaper on the following morning. Despite his manner, he was clever, hard-working and very ambitious. I've seen students like him do well for themselves.'

'We have evidence to link him with a number of crimes. I'll say no more than that. If you can give us what we require, we'll pass it back to the authorities in America.'

'You will have it this afternoon,' said Jones. 'This has given me much to think about over the weekend. Two of my projects are down the tube.'

Townsend curled his lip. 'That's the least of our problems.' He noticed that Jones had not asked about McWilliams. The man lived in a world of his own. The Inspector looked at his watch. Four o'clock on a Friday afternoon with no relief to come. The police car attracted the attention of

191

staff and students as it left the Unit. There would be plenty to chew upon for the remainder of the week.

On his return to the office, he asked his junior officer for the Whitley file and the material which had been taken from the farmhouse. He asked not to be interrupted except on a matter of life or death. The fluorescent lighting was switched off and he pushed the button on his reading lamp. Many of the papers had yellowed with age.

Afterwards he phoned his wife and asked her not to wait up for him. He called for his car and told them that he was going to the Royal Victoria Hospital.

As the car slowed for the exit, a constable came running from the station with a fax in his hand. Townsend grabbed it and then ordered the driver to reverse. Their hospital trip would have to wait.

'We found the younger Whitley dumped in Denmark Street. He's been badly beaten,' said his colleague in West Belfast. 'I take it you want him over there for questioning.'

The Inspector waited for Whitley to be delivered. He guessed what had happened to James Whitley. It looked like he was in for a long weekend. He inhaled and looked into the darkness. A great weariness came over him.

At approximately the same time, Tony Hamilton turned the key in the lock of Celia's house. He had waited for over two days before obeying the instructions which Gus had given him. The back door had been patched up and he saw the blood stains on the kitchen floor.

He found the key which unlocked the desk and found the folder. Gus had also told him that, in such an emergency, he must open his mail unless he had some reason to believe that it posed a threat. Tony thought of the press reports about letters contaminated with anthrax.

He abandoned the junk mail and placed two letters with foreign postmarks into the back of the folder. Shivering as he toured the house, he thought with bitterness of what had been done to his friend. He regretted that he had not seen him more often in recent weeks.

Tony drove home across the side of Cavehill and updated Emma. He gulped a Bushmills without water and picked at his Irish stew. Then he apologised and went to his study. He turned up the lamp and opened the folder.

The slip of paper at the top was handwritten. Tony put on his gold spectacles and squinted at the scrawl of Gus's writing. He noticed the whiskey stain at the bottom. He found his fountain pen and made a careful summary. At dawn he went to bed.

The trembling wreck that was Frederick Whitley sat in front of the Inspector. Townsend's junior sat to his right in order to take notes of the confession which they intended to obtain quickly. The student had not asked for a solicitor.

'Where's your father?' asked Townsend. 'There's no point your holding anything back.'

'He's dead. They pumped him in the head.' He paused and asked for tea. When it was brought to him, he gulped it and continued. 'We drove across the Border to a place in Monaghan. My father said he knew a guy who was working there. Somebody from old times who would help us. That didn't last long. It only took them a couple of days to track us down. They found us last night. They blindfolded us and drove away. I don't know where. Kept us overnight.'

'What happened today?'

'They tortured him from early morning while I watched. Cold water treatment. The works. When he confessed, they shot him in the head. They tortured me but I think they'd got what they wanted. Blindfolded me again and whacked me across the head. I must have passed out. I woke up in West Belfast...lying on the street.'

Townsend waited. He knew that James Whitley was beyond salvation. He whispered to the younger policeman who then went out to make the phone calls.

When he returned, Townsend began again. 'How did you...a student with a good life ahead of you...get mixed up in all this?'

They heard the tremor in his voice as he answered. 'The firewall on the computer system at the Research Unit was undergoing maintenance...for the umpteenth time. The computers were out of action but we had permission to use the computers on the main University site. I had to get my Ph.d finished. It was late one afternoon in June. I picked up on the Yank's accent as he asked the librarian for help. As I passed behind him on my way from the toilet, I picked up on what he was doing.'

'Tell us. We need to know everything. It's for your own good.'

Whitley looked at them with a mixture of hatred and terror. 'He was surfing the Internet for information on old Anglo – American wars. I thought that he was an historian.'

'Did anyone else seem to take an interest in him?' asked Townsend.

'I remember when he left that day, there was only me and the girl...apart from the librarian. As a matter of fact, I noticed her taking quite an interest as well.'

'You knew her?'

'Of course. She'd come to work there for the same reason as me. The Arab bitch I mean.'

'Be more precise.'

'She said she was from Serbia. Always grafting. I'll give her that. But I'd heard she hung out with Fenians.'

'We'll maybe come back to that,' said Townsend. 'Go on with what you were telling us about the American.'

'The computers in the Unit were still out of operation the next day so I came down to work on the main site. I met a friend and we went for lunch in the Great Hall. I noticed the Yank talking to his friend. We were behind them and I could hear their voices. I can't remember it all. I wish I hadn't heard any of it.'

'Tell us what you remember.' Townsend's weariness had disappeared. His antennae knew that they were approaching the heart of the matter.

Whitley shivered in the hot room. His sweaty eyes glared at the two policemen. 'The name Rostrevor hit me again. He told his friend the story of two boys who had been killed near there in 1914. He talked about a third boy who was still alive and who knew the killer was called Ross. The killer had never been found. Then he said something about the boys being connected with the IRA. I couldn't follow it all but I'd heard enough to want to know more.'

'And did you?'

'Not really. On the Thursday evening, I stayed with my father. He made a fry for us, then he got cleaned up and we went to his social club for a drink. We had pints of Guinness and I chatted with old mates for a time. I went back to my father who had now moved on to dark rum with his pint. He asked me about my plans. He was well-pleased. Then I told him about the Yank. I remembered he had contacts down near the Border. Thought he might be interested.'

'And was he?' asked Townsend.

'He went berserk. Totally unexpected. The club was packed by this stage and a band had started to play but everyone looked around when he exploded. He caught himself on and didn't say much afterwards.'

'Did he tell you later why he had reacted that way to the story?'

'On the following morning, he was badly hungover. After his breakfast, he made a lot of phone calls. Then he said he had urgent business in Belfast. It was better if I stayed at home. I could tell when he returned that he was in better form and I could smell the dark rum off him. Then he told me.'

Whitley grew faint as he ended his story. The policemen smelt the urine as he went blue and fell from the chair. Townsend rang to have him removed to a cell. The potential charge would be murder.

Tony sat with a mug of tea and read his summary again. Eugene Connor had been born in 1902. He had been killed before he could reach full maturity. Mike Connor had been born in 1919 and had survived until 1970. Patrick (born Connor) Tohill had been born in 1936 and was still alive according to the notes. Gus McWilliams had been born in 1953. Mike Connor had died in Cambodia in 1970. In 1987, it was recorded that Gus had made a visit to stay with Aunt Celia after being plagued at home. Tony noted the seventeen year intervals.

Then he worked backwards. In 1885, Diogenes had returned from his last trip to America and Canada. In 1868, he had established his initial contact with John Mitchel. Seventeen years earlier, the latter had a reunion in Tasmania with his wife and family. Shortly after his spell in Launceston jail. And his meetings with other 'Young Irelanders'.

In 1834, Mitchel is recorded as having taken his degree at Trinity College, Dublin but there is no trace of his name in the 'Catalogue of Graduates'. The notes fizzled out in 1817. ???? was followed by the word CICADAS! And then the date 2004 followed by another question mark.

Tony tore open the first envelope with the Italian postmark. It was from Gus's friend Primo in Naples. He recalled his friend's trip to see him in July after the Conference in Holland. His old colleague made some routine remarks before detailing the main reason for his letter.

It appeared that one of his students – called Adnan Shoukri – had been interrogated by the Italian police about terrorist links. Primo reminded Gus that he had met Shoukri in July and that the Moroccan Arab had performed some useful work for him on the Internet.

The Italians were under pressure from the Americans. Shoukri had been e-mailing Islamic contacts throughout the world. The e-mails suggested links between Palestinian groups and the IRA. Could Gus do anything to help him?

Tony put the letter to one side. He could not make any sense of it. He slit open the second letter with the postmark from Prince Edward Island in Canada. This one had been sent by a man called Bob Picking who appeared to be in very bad health. Again, it opened with routine remarks and then provided a summary of the DNA tests that had been performed on the material provided by Gus in October.

On Saturday morning, they woke Whitley up at six and gave him a mug of tea. After he had rinsed his face, they restarted the interview. The bruises from the South were coming up well, thought Townsend.

'I feel like shit,' said Whitley. 'Can't it wait?'

'Let's get it over with,' replied Townsend. 'What you say has ramifications in the highest places. The US Embassy has been harassing us. Tell me the truth. Begin where you left off last night.'

Whitley groaned, coughed and clutched his head. 'Tohill first came to my father's attention in 1968. A group of men beat up my Uncle Jack...my father's brother. My grandfather blamed the beating on Uncle Jack's death. He discovered that Tohill had been involved. There was nothing he could do about it directly. It must have been around that time that he told my father about Tohill and his history.'

'Let's get back to McWilliams,' said Townsend. He rubbed the side of his cheek and glared at Whitley.

'My father put the wind up me. We had my life mapped out and didn't want any problems. My old man had connections all over Belfast, especially the North and West. He had the Yank watched. Johnny did most of the work for him. My father would come to Belfast to drink with friends. He lent Johnny the car.'

'Johnny who?' asked the Inspector.

'I never found out his second name. Johnny was tough and smart. That's all I know.'

'Who made the first threatening phone call?'

'I heard my father do it – one Saturday night when he was drunk.'

'What about the e-mails?'

'I admit that I sent those. Initially as a friendly warning. My father was getting obsessed and angry with McWilliams poking his nose in. He was afraid it would all come out and the publicity damage my future opportunities.'

'Dr McWilliams received a threat around about the time when he returned to America. Do you know anything about it?'

'I kept in touch with my father when I was in Australia. I visited a relative up in Darwin and we sent it one night after a few beers. He stole an e-mail address from a tourist.'

Townsend switched his attack. 'Do you know anything about a burglary and attempted rape of a friend of Dr McWilliams – a Miss Arna Breen? You're facing a very serious charge. Who did it?'

'Johnny had been keeping an eye on McWilliams. He followed him one evening to her home. Saw the Yank come out late. Put two and two together.'

'Who attacked her at the beginning of August?'

'I had finished my studies and was at a loose end before going to Australia. Johnny insisted that I got involved. Otherwise, he believed if things got awkward...I would squawk. I picked up Johnny in the Rover that Friday night. We were parked well away from the house. We expected McWilliams but he didn't turn up. Johnny decided to give Breen a fright. Went in by the back. He came out running, jumped into the car and we drove back to my father's place.'

Townsend looked towards the ceiling. 'I don't believe that you're telling us the truth. We'll soon find out. What happened next?'

'When McWilliams started going to Andersonstown, my father went ballistic. Johnny had been cool about it up until then. After that, he got very excited as well. But he said that they would have to be patient. He suspected this was far bigger than anyone had thought. When they went to Dublin, we had them followed. Johnny had big support for this. They saw a big coup. When it was reported back that the Yank had met with Tohill in Dublin, they went crazy. Many of the boys had old scores to settle with Tohill. Johnny guessed correctly from what he had learnt that Tohill might be flushed out.'

Townsend halted the interview and he went out for a smoke. He returned and walked around the room. Whitley twisted around as Townsend circled him. The Inspector cast his mind over the sequence of events. 'Your father kept you informed about all this when you were in Australia?'

'I told you that we stayed in contact.'

'When did you return?'

'Mid-November – around the 11th or 12th.'

'What do you know of the events of Friday November 16th?'

'I wasn't involved. Johnny had an operation set up all over town. My father nearly screwed it up. He had his gun with him. When he saw the bitch approach McWilliams, he let loose. Johnny's friends followed her car and it led them to Tohill. Johnny shot him on the following Friday night. He thought he'd bungled it when they came after him but he managed to lose them.'

'We'll get this typed up and come back to it on Monday,' said Townsend. 'Let's go back to what you told us earlier. I have to be sure of your grandfather's name. What was it again?'

'Ross Whitley.'

CHAPTER 28

GUS tried in vain to get the trickle into the urinal. He pushed it aside and lay back. The winter sleet swirled in the darkness outside the hospital windows. A nurse came to check his pulse. The empty receptacle was inspected. She sighed and returned to her desk. The lamp was dimmed. He was alone.

He hoped that he would not have to stay here for long. The problems had begun again as the jet had approached JFK in a thunderstorm. It had circled for an hour as the lightening crackled outside. He heard someone scream as he held his side in silent pain.

The cabdriver brought him directly to the hospital. He produced his VISA GOLD and was admitted for tests after he had related his history. 'Our computerised records show that you've been here before,' said the young nurse. 'Earlier problems in the same area.'

Gus closed his eyes. He had been released from the hospital in Belfast after three weeks. Just before Christmas. The weather had been cold but not as freezing as in New York. It had been early in December when the visitors started to arrive.

'We were here before but you weren't compos mentis,' said Townsend. 'Are you OK to talk? The doctor has allowed us in for a while.' He smiled sympathetically.

'I'd like to know what happened.'

'We heard the crash over the phone...just before you put it down. The call probably saved your life. He gave you a bad beating before we arrived. It could have been worse.' The Inspector stared coldly at the yellowing bruises on Gus's face.

'Who did it?'

'He heard the Landrover and escaped through the back garden of your house to where the car was parked. We have a good idea who it was. At least, we think we know his first name. That might not seem like much but it will lead us to him eventually. Let me explain.'

Gus lay back and tried to take in what he was hearing. 'Slow down. This sounds complicated.'

Townsend began again. 'The person who threatened you by e-mail was called Frederick Whitley. The guy who disappeared to Australia in August. He returned in the middle of last month.'

'Why was he threatening me? What had he against me?' Gus tried to sit up and then fell back.

'Your lost boys. I apologise for being sceptical about all that although you will admit that I had good reason when you hear what I have to say. The person who was responsible for the deaths of young John McManus and Eugene Connor was Whitley's grandfather.' Townsend paused to check his notes. He told Gus the full name. 'What appears to have happened was this. In August 1914, he'd gone down to Rostrevor from Ballypalady to spend some time with relatives who lived there.'

'What age was he?' asked Gus.

'I guess late teens. He went to a party one night at a farm outside the village. He got into conversation with young people from the area. They told him about a conversation they'd had with three Belfast boys earlier in the day. When Whitley heard the names and ages of the two brothers, he immediately caught on to who they were.'

Gus thought back to what Father Campbell had told him. 'The Connor family had moved to Belfast shortly beforehand from the Ballypalady homestead. Of course.' He fell back again.

Townsend continued with the story. 'As he and his cousins returned home in the gloaming, they saw in the distance the three boys wandering along the road and Whitley guessed what had happened. They hid behind hedges with a plan to frighten the Connors and their cheeky friend McManus. However, it was at this point that the boys decided to cross the barbed wire fence and approach the deserted farmhouse. Whitley then cooked up a nastier plan in his head.' Townsend paused for breath. 'Would you like to take a break?'

'You can't stop now...not after all this time,' replied Gus. He motioned for him to go on.

'They returned to their own farmhouse and went to bed. Whitley could not sleep in his excitement. He went out to the barn where he discovered an old military greatcoat. People kept old coats like those for covers over bedsheets on cold nights and they came in handy for nocturnal calvings. Whitley also played some trick to give his eyes a yellow hue.'

'I think I can guess the rest,' interjected Gus, 'apart from the final part. Why did Whitley not kill George Connor?'

'From what we can piece together,' said the Inspector, 'at the crucial moment, he saw someone approach from the road on his left, then panicked and fled to where he was staying before anyone was awake.

The affair died a death...especially with the impending World War. Everyone forgot about it. It was ironic that the Connor family moved back up to the Ballypalady area and had a third son after the War. It must have been clear to Whitley by then that he was safe. He was confident enough to get married and later have two sons.'

'What about the time when George was released?'

'He proceeded carefully at first. Their first meeting must have been a strange one. However, George had his mental problems and Whitley was able to terrify him in order to shut him up.'

'Which he did very successfully,' said Gus, 'until this day.'

'Tohill and Jack Whitley were born around that time.'

Gus let the fact sink in. 'Come back to what happened recently.'

'When you returned to live here last summer, it was all stirred up again.' Townsend outlined what Frederick Whitley had told him.

'Everyone had their wires crossed. Patrick Tohill never mentioned the Whitleys to me. I suspect he knew nothing about it.'

'We may never know. He had major worries of his own. According to our informants there were serious financial problems...heavy gambling debts.'

'What became of Ross Whitley?'

'He always kept up political interests and links...especially when matters starting heating up again in the 1960's. Died about 1987. The death of his daughter-in-law may have finished him off.'

'What happened?'

'James Whitley's wife fell down the stairs one Saturday evening. She was a spinster whose farm he'd married into. There was evidence that he had pushed her. He admitted that there had been a violent row but she had tripped by accident. It was difficult to fathom the truth of the matter and he was released without charge. One of my men was stationed in the area at the time. I can see you're becoming tired. I should go.'

'What about Patrick Tohill?'

'We think he was killed by the man who attacked you with a hammer. My men have interviewed two young men from the house in which Tohill was shot. From what we can make out, Tohill made them jump into a car and follow the killer. However, your cousin was in bad shape and burst a blood vessel. They stopped outside Carrickfergus and washed him with sea water. It was too late. They dumped him in the sea, returned home and cleaned the car.' Townsend looked at his watch. 'I'll come to see you again.' He left the room and motioned to the man standing outside.

Gus closed his eyes and then tried again with no success apart from the stinging pain. At least he was alive. If he hadn't come over here, Patrick Tohill and James Whitley would not be dead. He guessed that Townsend wasn't too worried about that. There were positive angles. George Connor's torturer and the killer of the boys had been identified. John McManus had been terrified to death and the panicking Whitley hits Eugene Connor a killer blow on the head. There remained the puzzle of the man who had panicked Ross Whitley. The answer did not arrive until Christmas.

Arna had come to see him many times and she arrived after Townsend had departed. 'Are you sure you that you don't want your family to know? They'll have to be informed at some stage.'

'It'll have to keep until I'm much better. I don't want to upset them. Kay has exams and Ed...well, you know his condition. That's why I'm here.' He smiled ruefully.

'At least you've gained a better sense of humour since you came here. We'll drop it.' She put her hand under the bedclothes and felt him. 'How's it feeling?' She laughed.

'Pretty stiff.'

She removed her hand. 'Tony Hamilton wants to see you. He's going to try again tomorrow. I believe he has something for you. Do you need anything before I go?'

'A bottle of whiskey and a pack of Buds. That would get me going.'

'I think not. Maybe by Christmas.' She kissed him on the lips and said that she would call later in the week.

On Tuesday afternoon, Tony had arrived as promised. Gus assured him that he was going to be fine. He told him Townsend's news.

'I was seriously worried about you last week. As you instructed, I opened the file and your letters.'

'So you know my CICADAS theory. I had begun to dot the i's but hadn't crossed the t's. The Inspector's news supports the theory.'

'Quite. Nobody really knows why they wait 17 years. The adults die after mating. The eggs hatch tiny cicada nymphs in the branches of trees. They drop to the ground and burrow into the soil. There, they suck on tree roots and somehow know they have to wait to 17 years before emerging. It's been speculated that the cicadas hide underground to build up their sexual energy for the final fling.'

'I prefer the other theory. There's a constant battle between predator and host.'

'And even when the threat no longer exists, a species gets ready for a pre-emptive strike.'

Gus changed the subject. 'You said you had mail for me?' Gus scanned over the letter from Primo. There wasn't much he could do about it from his hospital bed.

He read the letter from Picking and raised his eyes at Tony. 'You've read it so you know what's in it already. With what we've heard from Townsend, we can put two and two together.'

'We can date the military greatcoat to 1817. You already knew that it belonged to a militia man from Ross's old regiment. Many of them joined up from the Rostrevor area. He may have returned in that year after the end of the Anglo-French wars.' They looked over the DNA report.

'I'll need to discuss this report with Arna when she comes back. I'm very grateful for everything that you've done.'

'Think nothing of it.'

When Arna had returned later in the week, she brought news of Burgess. 'I received a letter from him in this morning's mail,' she said. 'He's coming home before Christmas. The letter, after some personal details, refers to you. Tell Gus that I've tried to contact him about our previous conversation. The key fact that he highlights is that the big experiment commenced on March 28th 1875. I take it you know what he's talking about.'

'Up to a point. My concentration's not what it was. It'll come back to me. Leave it. I want you to have a look at this DNA report.'

Arna studied it for some minutes and looked puzzled. 'It's frightening if it's correct. The coat was contaminated with all kinds of substances. A mutation of H5N1 virus appears to have been identified. Through the mixing vessel of a farrowing pig. You remember Professor Dietz from your Conference in Holland. I'll need to contact him urgently. You have his number.'

Gus had been released from hospital before Christmas. He had phoned Boston to tell Kay that his old kidney infection had returned. 'I hope you've been looking after yourself. Mom warned me about your drinking. And before you ask, we've heard nothing at all. I can't even talk about it anymore. I'm completely numb.'

'Tell Ed that I'll e-mail him. But I guess I won't be home for Christmas after all. I have been advised not to travel until the New Year.' It was a partial truth.

The fridge had been stocked. He made his favourite omelette and opened a bottle of Puglian wine. Urination had not been a problem. He checked his security. Tony had mended the door at the back. His neighbour had scrubbed the floor. Townsend had warned him to think again about his future plans. Informants had told the Inspector that Johnny had gone abroad. Portugal, Spain, Italy. Somewhere like that.

Gus searched for the disturbed files on Mitchel and checked the final photographs and the date of his death. His memory had been correct. The hair and the baldness. March 25th.

Arna came to see him on most evenings. Just before Christmas, he noticed her worried eyes as she entered. 'When I returned from the lab,' she said, 'I checked my voicemail. There was a terrified message from Burgess. He sounded just as he had done in the early summer. Thinks someone is following him and won't tell me who. Said you would know.'

'Anything else?' Gus closed his eyes and groaned.

'I don't know whether it's connected or not. You will need to hear the message. He repeats the name…John Knox. The first experiment had almost succeeded. After the death of his friend, John had been persuaded. His time with Mitchel in 1851 had cemented their friendship forever. Unfortunately, the boy had been blind from birth. Perry had looked after him. For scientific reasons…if nothing else.'

The sleet from the Manhattan night beat against the windows. Gus thought it all over again. Kay would collect him at some stage and, for a year, he would try to rebuild family life. If they could live apart for a year, the relationship might survive. Burgess had willed his home to her.

Gus closed his eyes and Blind John appeared to him again. Rochester. By riding down that lonely road to search, he had prolonged the life of George Connor by almost ninety years. His thoughts turned to James Whitley washed up in Carlingford Bay. He fell asleep.

The sky was blue and the afternoons were lengthening when his new visitor arrived. 'A William Kiminski to see you, Gus,' said the nurse. 'He says that he's related to you. Has a foreign accent but seems to know his way around.'

Bill removed his fedora and Gus looked up at his fat shiny head. He reminded him of Khrushchev. His cousin introduced himself and told him about his life after his mother married Kiminski. 'I married a woman from Kosovo province. She had a mixed Islamic background. Katrina is our only daughter.'

'I gather she's still in there,' said Gus. 'I'm sorry.'

'Part of it's my fault. I encouraged her to go to Ireland and study. See if she could find anything out about relatives. Katrina began to suspect who you were but wasn't sure. She was a keen Internet user and hooked up during the summer with a guy called Shoukri in Italy. Amazingly, he knew all about you. She told me when she came back in the summer. I encouraged her to visit the States before she went back to Ireland. Big mistake.'

'If only I'd known,' said Gus. 'She should have introduced herself.'

'She's a good girl despite her politics. Completely innocent and now she could be locked up for years in that place. We'll do anything for her release.'

'Anything?'